BROKEN LULLABY

AMBER JOI SCOTT

DEDICATION

To my family and friends, who support my love of writing

CHAPTER ONE

The club's neon lights flickered against the dark Boston sky, creating a mesmerizing dance of colors. Noah was feeling overwhelmed and needed a release from his pent-up frustration. The workload from his professors was becoming unbearable. He was juggling studying for finals and writing several papers at the same time. With all the work, he hadn't had time to get his dick wet. However, he was going to take care of that problem tonight.

He pulled his Maserati into the parking lot and smiled at the prime parking spot available. He stepped out of the car, straightened his jacket, and ran his hand through his unruly hair. His eyes darted across the street, and he spotted the two SUVs with blacked-out windows where his guards were stationed.

It was time to become Tony Hayes. It was the concession he made to attend college in Boston. His father was a powerful man and his enemies wouldn't think twice about hurting him to get to his father. After nodding towards the SUVs in recognition, he made his way around the corner.

The line waiting at the entrance was so long that it almost wrapped around the corner. Noah Kelly never stood in line, not even once. He passed the long line of people waiting, hearing them grumble about who did he think it was. He approached the massive man standing in front of a velvet rope with a clipboard. He couldn't resist smirking when he thought about it. What people didn't know was there was nothing on it. The doorman, Jason, only used it as a prop to maintain control over the crowd.

"Tony, my man."

"Jason, good to see you. How are the pickings this evening?" Noah asked as the corner of his lips turned upward.

"Fucking perfect. There are several fresh beauties who haven't been here before. One, in particular, is sublime. I might try to pick her up if she is still available when I get off," Jason said, wagging his eyebrows.

"What does she look like?" Noah asked. His interest peaked at the prospect of a new pussy to conquer.

"Not telling you, man, because I wouldn't have a chance if you get a look at that beauty," Jason said with a chuckle. He unhooked the rope and motioned for Tony to come through. "Happy hunting."

Giving Jason a fist bump. "Oh, I am sure it will be."

He had come out tonight on the prowl to find one of his regular hookups, but the thought of fresh pussy made his cock twitch. She must have been truly exceptional to catch the eye of a man who saw beautiful women every day. He had to locate her and convince her to spend the night with him. He wasn't interested in long-term relationships. His future was already decided and until then, he would relish his freedom.

Noah's smile widened as he walked into the lively club. The lights strobed with the beat of the bass, creating a dizzying effect. Fuck, he loved this place. With a confident stride, he made his way over to the bar, catching the bartender's attention with a simple nod.

Luke knew Tony and his drink preference. He also knew the exceptional tips Tony was known to give out. He took one of the expensive tumblers, used only for the priority one guests, and carefully placed three ice-cold stones. Cold stones were used instead of ice because they didn't melt, which prevented the expensive top-shelf Jameson from diluting.

"Here you go, Tony," Luke said as he placed the glass in front of Noah.

"Thanks, Luke," Noah said. He took a sip, savoring the smoothness of the whiskey as it warmed his throat.

He slid his black credit card to Luke. "Open a tab."

"Sure thing," Luke answered.

Noah shifted his attention toward the club and began checking out the attractive women in the room. He noticed a few women he had fucked before and was about to signal to one of them to come over when he saw her. Based on Jason's limited details, Noah was confident that this was the woman he was referring to. She was dancing with a group of girls and looked like she was having a great time. He surveyed every curve of her body in the tight dress she was wearing, and he couldn't help but lick his lips. The sight of her shapely hips swaying and the bright smile had a hypnotic effect on him. Fuck, he had to have her. He downed the Jameson and strode towards her. When he was close, he lightly skimmed his hand down her arm. He leaned in and whispered in her ear, drinking in her flower scent.

"May I have this dance?" he asked. She turned, and he gasped. Damn, she was even more gorgeous closeup. She had the face of an angel, but her body was made for sin. She nodded her head and bit her bottom lip. So innocent, yet so fucking sexy. Fuck, he wanted to bite that lip, among other things.

He placed his large hands on her waist and pulled her close. Her eyes grew large when she felt his erection pressed against her stomach. She would just have to get used to it because there was no way it was going away anytime soon. Their bodies moved to the beat of the music in an erotic dance. With each song, they moved closer together, their bodies rubbing against each other. He couldn't stand it any longer. His cock was so hard that it was painful and he needed to sink deep into her hot, wet pussy. However, he didn't want to scare her away because he needed to know if she was as sweet as she looked.

S carlett couldn't believe she was enjoying dancing on the crowded dance floor. For the last four years, she has avoided visiting places like this. However, tonight, her roommates wouldn't take no for an answer. Hell, they even hid her books and laptop. Then they forced her into this tight, extremely short dress. They even took all her simple cotton underwear except for a tiny red lace thong. If she weren't careful, she would flash her bare ass cheeks to everyone.

When they arrived at the club and she saw the line, she couldn't help but get excited. Not with getting into the club, but the possibility they might not get in.

"Scarlett, I am so happy you are smiling," Brooke said.

"Yeah, we thought you weren't excited about coming out tonight," Eve said, bouncing up and down.

Scarlett was about to correct them when she heard Brooke squeal.

"Eve, they are waving us forward."

Scarlett turned and saw the man with the clipboard motioning for them to come forward. Just seconds before, she had been beaming with joy, but her expression quickly turned to disappointment. Eve and Brooke locked their arms through hers. They walked past the never-ending line and approached the velvet rope.

"Ladies, I would like to invite you into the "O"," he said, releasing the latch to the rope.

"Thank you," Brooke and Eve said with broad smiles.

Scarlett's attempt at enthusiasm was half-hearted as she forced a tight smile and gave the man a nod. As she passed him, she felt his gaze on her and heard him whisper "perfection" under his breath. He must be talking about Eve and Brooke, but she was far from perfection.

Unlike her roommates, she was of average height and a curvy figure. Eve told her many times that her body reminded her of Marilyn Moore, with her 38D bust, 23-inch waist, and 38-inch hips. She was confident in her body and her curves accentuated her figure. After she walked across the stage with her diploma, she planned on hitting the gym more. Her hard work was payoff, as she was graduating summa cum laude and valedictorian.

Scarlett's connection with Eve and Brooke went beyond the typical relationship of college roommates. They were her family. The two beautiful women pulled her into a hug the moment she entered the dorm room on the first day of freshmen year.

Eve was tall slender, with jet-black hair and steel-blue eyes. Her beauty could have easily landed her a job as a model, but her sights were set on design in the fashion industry.

Her other roommate, Brooke, was hard to miss with her red-hot body, platinum-blonde hair, and warm chocolate eyes. Whenever she would walk into a room, people would stop whatever they were doing just to look at her. Her goal was to one day take over her father's business.

Their backgrounds were vastly different. Eve and Brooke came from the bustling New York City, while Scarlett came from the sleepy town of Castle Rock, Washington. Unlike Scarlett's parents, who never showed one moment of love toward her, Brooke and Eve's parents were loving and supportive. They welcomed her into their home and showered her with love. Brooke's father, Robert Martin, even had a room decorated to her taste in their high-rise apartment.

It was the first time in her life Scarlett felt love. Her father, Weston Murphy, was the pastor at the Abundant Life Church, and her mother didn't work. It was a sin for a woman to work outside the home. Those were not Scarlett's words but her crazy father's.

Throughout her life, her father never showed her even a little bit of love. When she turned thirteen, he began actively pursuing a husband for her. She implored her mother to end this, but she refused.

"Your father knows what is right for this family to keep us doing God's work," she told her without an ounce of concern for her feelings.

She faced the prospect of marrying and bearing two or three children before the age of twenty. Her father and the church were against the concept of birth control.

He would invite prospective husbands one by one to their home to introduce them to Scarlett. Nobody was her age or even remotely near it. They were all at least fifty or older. While some were from her father's church, the majority came from other churches across the nation who held similar beliefs. The intensity of their gazes sent shivers down her spine. She didn't want to know what they were thinking.

She was relieved that her father allowed her to go to school, but it came with the condition of following strict rules. She was expected to dress conservatively, and having any male friends was considered a violation of the rules. The school she attended was where most of the congregation sent their sons and daughters. She didn't trust them enough to interact and feared they would tell her father anything she said or did.

Most of the teachers were also members, except her English teacher, Mrs. Gaines. As time passed, she found herself relying on her company more and more. Scarlett confided in Mrs. Gaines about the abuse she was facing at home, and Mrs. Gaines urged her to seek help from the police or social services. Scarlett revealed the police force were church members and shared the same views as her father.

So they knew the only way to get out of the town and away from her father's grasp was to get a scholarship to a school on the other side of the country. She would need a full-ride scholarship. With that, she could escape her father and never return. After looking at all the East Coast schools, she decided Northeastern in Boston was her best option.

She studied hard and applied for every scholarship Mrs. Gaines and her could find. She graduated valedictorian with a perfect weighted grade point average of 5.0. Not wanting her father to learn what she was doing, Mrs. Gaines offered to have all the correspondence sent to her home. Every few days, she would walk to Ms. Gaines's home to see if any news had come in.

The day her award letter arrived from Northwestern was the happiest day of her life. She received a four-year scholarship covering her tuition, room, food, and books. Her dreams were finally coming true.

She stuffed the letter in her backpack and headed home with a smile on her face. When she walked into the house, she was greeted by silence. It was very uncommon for both of the parents to be out at the same time. However, she remembered they both needed to attend today's church function.

She placed her backpack on the kitchen table, took the acceptance letter, and reread it. It was really happening. College was paid for, but she had to find a way to get to Boston. She had no money and wasn't allowed to work. But this would not stop her. She would find a way, even if it meant she would have to walk all the way to Boston.

Lost in her thoughts, she didn't hear her parents come in until it was too late. Her father ripped the letter from her hand. His black eyes narrowed as he scanned the paper in front of him. He looked up at her, crumbled the letter, and threw it on the floor. The sight of her father's eyes burning with anger was something she would never forget. Her head snapped to the side as the powerful blow of his fist landed. Blood flooded her mouth. The searing pain radiated until she saw spots in her eyes.

Although he had hit her before, this was the first time he had struck her in the face. In the past, he only hit or kicked her in places where the marks could be concealed by clothing. He didn't want someone who didn't have the same views to see the abuse and report him to the authorities.

Many times, the punishment he inflicted on her was so severe that she thought she would surely die from the pain. He dedicated a room in the basement where he used special tools to inflict pain. His instruments of choice were whips and canes, which he used with expert precision. The scars from those punishments would forever be etched on her skin, a reminder of her father.

He ruthlessly grabbed her long hair and threw her on the hard kitchen floor. Where he began an onslaught of kicks. When he tired, he crouched down and seized her jaw in a tight hold.

"I can't stand looking at you. However, I won't have too much longer," he said through gritted teeth. "I've chosen your husband and the wedding will be held the evening of your eighteenth birthday."

Her heart raced at his confession. Her eighteenth birthday was only two days away. Tears welled up in her eyes, blurring her vision. She had just found a way to escape, but it was too late.

He stood and landed one last kick. He spit at her and walked out of the house, dragging her mother with him. She picked up the crumbled letter, stuffed it in her backpack, and crawled to her room. It was a slow and painful journey, but after an hour, she finally reached the top of the stairs and into her tiny room.

She pulled herself up on her bed and looked at the damage. She winced in pain, clutching her wrist, which was most likely broken. As she took a breath, a stabbing pain ripped through her and she knew she had one or more broken ribs. Her lip was split open, and her left eye was swollen shut.

She had to get out of there but had nowhere to go. As she felt defeated, she recalled Mrs. Gaines had given her her phone number. Maybe she could help her. She slowly stuffed as many of her clothes into her backpack and slowly made it back down the stairs. Her parents had not returned, which she was thankful for. She picked up the phone and dialed Mrs. Gaines's number.

"Hello."

"Mrs. Gaines, this is Scarlett."

"Oh, Scarlett dear, are you okay?" she asked.

Scarlett swallowed back a sob. "Can I stay with you?"

"Scarlett, dear, what happened?"

"My father found the scholarship letter and he is really mad. I need a place to stay until I find a way to Boston."

"Can you make it to my house?" she asked.

"I don't think so, but I can't stay here. They will be back at any moment."

"Get out of the house and hide behind the big bushes at Mr. Owen's house. I'll be there in less than five minutes. Do you think you can get there?"

"I think so. Just please hurry."

As promised, Mrs. Gaines picked her up and brought her to her house. She supported her by getting a bus ticket to Boston and connecting her with a friend of hers who lived there. Scarlett stayed at Melissa's house until she could move into the dorms. She had a small bookstore and employed her to assist.

She received a call from her mom once. Her mother stated that she remembered the scholarship letter had Northeastern on it and tracked her down. She didn't ask how she was. Instead, she scolded her for her selfishness and demanded her return home.

"No daughter of the congregation ever leaves for good. They return either voluntarily or by force," her mother said.

The thought of being forced back sent a chill through Scarlett. She went to the admissions office and informed them never to tell her parents any information about her. She was eighteen and in the eyes of the law, was an adult. Thankfully, she never heard from them again.

B rooke and Eve dragged her across the club to the bar, where a round of top-shelf whiskey was ordered. Eve handed him her credit card and told him to start a tab.

The bartender took the card and gave her a wink. "Sure thing, beautiful."

Three glasses were placed on the table in front of the girls moments later. They each picked up a glass.

"To us finding the perfect penis," Brooke said, raising her glass.

Scarlett's eyes grew large. It should have shocked her that Brooke had spoken those words out loud but it didn't.

Eve bumped Scarlett's shoulder. "And to Scarlett punching her golden virgin card."

Brooke and Eve burst into laughter at the comment while Scarlett blushed. They had been teasing her about it for four years. She had no desire to wait until marriage to have sex. However, she hadn't found anyone she was attracted to.

After another round of whiskey, they pulled her onto the dance floor. One song led to another, and with each passing one, she began to enjoy dancing. The music changed to a slower song and when she looked up, she noticed Brooke and Eve wrapped in two guys' arms. Not wanting to dance alone, she decided to go back to the bar. As she turned to leave, she felt an electrical spark as someone ran their finger down her arm. Never had she felt anything like it before. Then she heard the velvet voice whispering into her ear, asking her to dance.

She licked her parched lips and turned. When she looked up and saw his face, she almost orgasmed. Damn, he was hot. He was over six feet tall, with reddish brown hair and pale green eyes. He was all man, unlike the college boys she was used to seeing. There was an air of confidence about him. She was so overwhelmed that she couldn't even form words. She bit her lower lip and nodded yes.

He wrapped his arms around her and pulled her close. Scarlett wouldn't call it dancing. It was more like sex with their clothes on.

He pulled back and asked. "Would you like something to drink?"

"I would love that," she said, smiling at him.

He placed his hand on her back and directed her to a small table in the corner. Once they were seated, he waved to the server to come over.

"Mr. Hayes, what can I get for you?" John asked.

"I'll have the usual. What would you like, beautiful?" Noah asked the goddess sitting beside him.

"I'll have Jameson and ginger on cold stones if you have them," she said.

"Fuck," Noah groaned softly and shifted himself to find some relief. Not only was she a goddess, but she also drank the same drink he did.

Noah took her hand in his once the server left for their drinks. "I enjoyed dancing with you. I'm Tony."

"I'm Scarlett."

"A beautiful name for a sexy woman," Noah said as his eyes looked deep into her emerald eyes. They were almost the same shade as his mother. He wondered if she had Irish blood running through her veins.

"Thank you. You must come here a lot."

"Yeah, however, I have never seen you here before."

"I don't go out much. I've been too busy with school."

"Oh, where do you go?" Noah asked.

"Northeastern."

"Well, that answers why I hadn't seen you on campus. I go to Boston College."

"What are you studying?" she asked.

"Business and you?"

"History. Yeah, I know. What kind of job will I find with that kind of degree?"

"There are many things you can do with it," Noah said.

John returned with their drinks and placed them on the table. He stared longer at the beautiful person next to Mr. Hayes. Fuck, she was hot and images of him fucking her against the wall bombarded his thoughts.

Scarlett looked up to say thank you, but the server's intense gaze made her uncomfortable. He looked as if he was undressing her with his eyes. Her fingers interlaced with Tony's hand, seeking reassurance.

Scarlett's sudden grasp of his hand startled him, and when he looked at her face, he saw she was ghostly white. He followed her gaze and quickly spotted the source of her fear. John was looking at her like she was a fucking juicy steak. In a flash, he was on his feet with his hand around John's neck, squeezing the life out of him.

"You will not look at her that way," Noah growled in a menacing tone. The fucker did not know what he was capable of. He could kill him with a flick of a wrist and his heart rate wouldn't even rise one beat. John's face was turning red, and he was fighting to get free.

"Tony, please," Scarlett said as she touched his arm.

The red haze clouding his vision faded at the sound of her pleading voice. Clamping his hand firmer around John's neck, he gave it one last squeeze, then threw him onto the floor. Noah then turned to find Scarlett beside him, tears flowing down her delicate face. She was afraid of him, and he couldn't allow that to happen. He wrapped his arm around her shoulder and pulled her close.

"I won't hurt you," he said.

For some reason, she believed him. Her voice shook. "I know."

"Can we get out of here?" Noah asked.

Scarlett looked up at him and saw a look of concern and compassion. "Let me tell my friends."

She looked around the club, but it was so packed it was impossible to find them. So she sent them a text telling them she was leaving with a friend. She knew they wouldn't see the message until they left the club or looked at their phone.

Not wanting to wait a moment longer she looked up at Tony. There was something about his eyes that made her think that he might be the one. "I'm ready to go," she said, stuffing her phone back in her purse.

CHAPTER TWO

They walked out of the club and were greeted with the crisp evening air of April. Scarlett's sleeveless dress provided no protection against the chill. She wrapped her arms around herself in an attempt to find some warmth. Noah noticed the movement and immediately took off his jacket, draping it around her shoulders and placing a kiss on her temple. Although his father may have educated him in the arts of becoming a powerful mafia Skipper, his mother had instilled in him the importance of treating women with respect and ensuring all their needs were taken care of.

Scarlett had been a little unsure about leaving the club with him, but her concern became somewhat subdued when he wrapped his coat around her. Without a word, he had put her needs and comfort above his own.

"Thank you," she said, smiling at him.

Noah leaned close to her ear. His warm breath sent shivers of pleasure through her. "I promise to take care of you like my momma taught me."

Knowing that he followed his momma's advice made her feel secure. This meant that family was important.

In her dreams, she would have a wonderful family of her

own someday. A husband who loved and adored her unconditionally, with children who were aware that they were the most important thing in their parent's lives. She would not allow her past with her horrible parents to ruin a happy future for herself.

They walked around the building and came up to a luxurious car. Even though Scarlett knew little about cars, she could tell this one was expensive. Noah opened the door for her and assisted her into the passenger seat. Just as he was about to close the door, he paused and caressed her cheek.

"You're so fucking beautiful," he whispered as his eyes locked onto her lips.

Her heart pounded, urging her to explore the sensation of his lips against hers. Licking hers, she leaned towards him and placed her lips on his. He froze like a statue, and she feared she had misread the situation. As she began to pull away, he grabbed her neck and kissed her fiercely. He demanded access, and their tongues collided in a passionate dance. The kiss was filled with an urgent, almost desperate need that left them longing for more.

Noah was captivated by the woman's kiss and couldn't get enough of it. She started a bit timidly but quickly matched his intensity. He thought she was perfect and couldn't wait to discover if her passion matched his own in bed. Just as his lungs were about to burst, he broke away. He leaned his forehead to hers, gasping for breath. "I would love to continue this when we get to my apartment."

"So would I," she said with a sexy smile.

Noah stood up, closed the door, and went to the driver's side. Before he opened his door, he took a quick look at the black SUVs parked a few vehicles back. He gave his guard a nod before getting into the car. He revved up the engine, feeling the power beneath him, and let out the clutch. The car jolted forward and Noah weaved in and out of traffic with ease. He loved the sensation of speed and the rush of adrenaline that came with driving this car. He never felt the need to slow down or drive cautiously. His father's rein reached even Boston. Police would never give his son a ticket.

Scarlett felt that she was going to die at any moment. The man was driving so fast that the street signs were all a blur. At one point, she glanced over to the speedometer which read ninety-six mph. Holy shit, they were going over ninety on a busy street. Saying a silent prayer, she grabbed hold of the leather seat with one hand and had a death grip on the oh-shit handle over the window with the other.

Noah glanced at Scarlett and saw that her complexion had lost all color. Placing his hand on her leg, he gave it a gentle squeeze. "I have never had an accident."

"Really?"

"Well, maybe once. Mom made me go the speed limit," he said with a chuckle.

Scarlett swatted his arm as her laughter filled the air. "Asshole."

God, this was refreshing. No one other than his parents and brothers ever talked to him this way. Yet this slip of a woman had more balls than most of the men he knew. A few minutes later, he pulled into the underground parking garage at his apartment building.

Well, not his building, but his father, Liam Kelly. For the last four years, Liam had been quietly buying properties under one of his many shell companies. The previous owners, the O'Sullivan family, led by Grady O'Sullivan, had a stranglehold on Boston, but their grip was slipping. Boston had always been on Liam's radar, and he was eager to establish a foothold by taking over the port.

Once Noah was parked in one of his assigned spaces, he reached over and brought her hand to his lips. He placed a sweet kiss on the back while looking deep into her eyes. "I'm sorry I scared you."

How could she be mad at him when he looked at her that

way? She narrowed her eyes and let out a low growl. "Don't do it again."

Noah chuckled at her growl. It sounded like a mother cat protecting her babies. "Stay right there." He got out of the car and went to the passenger side. Opening the door, he offered his hand and smiled when she placed her hand in his. Why did her hand fit so perfectly in his? Once she was out, he didn't release her hand. They walked over to the elevator and got in. He pushed the P on the pad and used his electronic key fob for all access.

"The penthouse?" Scarlett asked.

"Yeah. I'm not going to lie. My family has money," Noah answered. His family didn't have a little money. They had a shitload of money, more than they would ever spend in their lifetime.

"Oh," Scarlett said. "My family isn't rich."

Noah was about to respond, but they had arrived at his apartment. They stepped out into the foyer. He reached over and turned on the lights.

Scarlett gasped at the luxury of the apartment. She knew it was expensive. Not only was it the penthouse, but the furnishing inside. She had shopped with Brooke and Eve, and they taught her the difference between inexpensive and expensive. All furniture, artwork, and accessories were of the finest quality. The decor of the place was expertly crafted, with every detail carefully considered. Most college students lived in cramped, cluttered apartments, but this place was different. She couldn't see anything out of place. Hell, it looked as if no one lived here.

The apartment she, Eve, and Brooke shared was nice, but this place made it look subpar. Eve and Brooke's parents paid for the apartment and refused to let her get a part-time job to pay rent.

While Eve and Brooke had job prospects, Scarlett struggled to find employment after graduation. After graduation, Brooke's father bought them a high-rise apartment, and they planned to move in soon. Upon arriving in New York, Scarlett was optimistic about finding employment, even if it wasn't something in her field of study.

Noah could see she was overwhelmed and for some reason, he wanted her to feel comfortable. "Would you like something to drink?"

"Please."

He took his jacket from her shoulders and motioned for her to enter the living room, which overlooked the city. At the bar, he fixed two tumblers of Jameson with ginger. When he turned, he saw Scarlett standing at the window, the moon's soft glow illuminating her face. He came up beside her and handed her the drink. He saw her hand tremble as she reached out to take it from him. He sipped his drink before lightly tracing his finger along her bare arm. Her arm broke out into goosebumps once again. "Are you cold?" He asked softly.

"No," she answered. She wasn't cold, far from it. She felt a burning desire coursing through her veins, and her body responded with a growing wetness between her legs.

"Scarlett," Noah said in a husky voice. "I don't give a fuck if you come from money. When I saw you across the club tonight, your beauty mesmerized me. But there was something else that pulled me to you."

She smiled at him and placed her glass on the table beside the window. She reached up, wove her fingers around his neck, and pulled him towards her. "I felt the same pull."

Noah set down his glass before leaning in to kiss her. His tongue licked between her lips and she parted them for him. As soon as his tongue entered, it intertwined and mated with hers. Her taste was so exquisite it drove him wild. It was like he was savoring a piece of heaven. He reaches around and grasps her firm ass, pulling her flush against him. His cock twitched at her nearness. He needed to be inside of her. He pulled back from the kiss and got lost in her beautiful, soulful, green eyes. Unlike all the other women he had been with before who were after his money or his family's name, she only wanted to be with him.

The realization of that shook him to his core. "I want you," he said, his voice cracking.

"Take me," Scarlett said as every nerve in her body lit up.

With a possessive growl, he lifted her effortlessly into his arms. As they made their way to his bedroom, he couldn't resist kissing and nuzzling her neck. Once inside, he placed her back on the floor, kissing every inch of her visible skin. Their clothes were a hindrance as they struggled to undress, but their desire was too strong to be deterred. Once undressed, Scarlett crawled onto the bed and laid back, resting on her elbows.

Noah leaned back and basked in the beauty that lay before him. Her beauty was so exquisite that it was hard to look away. He leaned down, eager to savor her, and took one of her nipples into his mouth. As he suckled, he teased the other with his fingers. Her dusty rose nipples puckered with his ministrations.

Scarlett moaned and arched her back. "Oh, God. Don't stop."

Noah's smile grew wider as he listened to her moans and felt her body squirming beneath him. She was so responsive to his touch. He released her nipple and kissed down her breastbone to her stomach. He savored her taste, feeling a sense of euphoria wash over him. It was as if she had consumed nothing but sugar, the way her skin tasted with every kiss. He continued until he reached her soft mound covered by well-manicured red curls. The corners of his top lip turned upwards in a sly grin. Well, there was the proof she was a true redhead. He liked this better than the hairless mounds that many women preferred. The smile widened when he saw the glistening juices on her folds. He took a deep breath, taking in her tangy scent of heated desire. The scent was intoxicating and he had to taste her and could hardly wait another moment. He buried his face between her parted thighs and flicked his tongue along her moist folds. Scarlett arched her back and let out a guttural moan. He raised his head to look into her eyes. "You taste so fucking good."

"Tony, please," she said with a cry. She had only had an orgasm with a battery-operated device. Brooke and Eve gave her one for her birthday. As wonderful as those were, it was plain compared to what she was feeling now.

She moaned as he went back to licking, sucking, and nibbling her clit. He knew exactly how to please her. Her legs fell wider apart involuntarily as her fingers knotted in his hair, yanking on it with each lick.

Her moans became more intense with each passing moment, filling the air around them. He thrust two fingers into her pussy and when he did, her walls clamped down. Her skin broke out in a soft pink hue as her orgasm washed over her. It was beautiful to see and he needed to feel it when she came on his cock.

Scarlett's body convulsed as she cried out in ecstasy. She had experienced nothing like it before, her entire body quivering with pleasure. Her heart was pounding, and her thoughts were racing. Yet, in the back of her mind, she knew she had to tell him she was a virgin.

The desire to be inside her was overwhelming. He moved closer, feeling the heat radiating off her body, and pushed himself deep inside her. The moment he did, he froze in place. She was, no, had been a virgin. "Why?" He asked.

Despite the tears rolling down her cheeks, she managed to smile at him. "It is fine. You did nothing I didn't want."

"But," he said. Why hadn't she told him that she was a virgin? He would have been more careful with her.

Scarlett's hand stroked the side of his face, feeling the contours of his strong cheekbones and jaw. "No buts or regrets."

The pain was subsiding, but a powerful pressure was building again, and she knew she couldn't wait much longer. "Make me yours."

When she looked at Noah with sincerity in her blazing emerald green eyes, he knew she was telling the truth. "Gladly."

He pulled back and thrust again. This time, she vocalized her pleasure with moans of pleasure, filling his auditory senses. He thrust inside of her over and over until he was on the brink of orgasm. However, his passion was for her to climax first. He reached between them and rubbed her swollen clit. Scarlett raised her hips, prompting him to enter her deeper, and the instant he pinched her clit hard, he felt her orgasm commence. He thrust once more, reaching his peak as her orgasm enveloped him. It was an absolute euphoria. It was so powerful that he saw stars.

When they both came down from their highs, he pulled out as easy as possible and saw his dick covered with blood. He had never had sex with a virgin before, even when he was a virgin himself. But the knowledge that he had been the only man to have been inside of her tight pussy made him smile. He rolled to his side and pulled her close. "Scarlett, that was unbelievable."

"It was," she said as she ran her hand across his chest, loving the feel of the coarse hairs there.

"Why me?"

"You made me feel safe when you took care of that server, then you made me feel endeared when you gave me your jacket. Instead of thinking of yourself, you thought of me first," she explained. "As I said, I wanted you and will always remember my first time being wonderful." They lay in each other's arms and soon, they fell asleep.

A few hours later, Noah awoke with an uneasy feeling that something terrible was about to happen. He climbed out of bed, slipped on his underwear, and walked over to the window.

Tonight, there was a supermoon glowing in the night sky. There was something ominous about its grandeur. With a glance back at the bed, he smiled at the naked woman who was asleep in it. No one before her had ever shocked him so much. He would love nothing more than to be back inside of her, but she was too tender and he couldn't bear hurting her. He would have to wait a few days. The thought of seeing her again didn't bring dread as it usually did. One-night stands were what he did, but he didn't want just one night with Scarlett.

His phone rang, and he rushed to get it before it woke Scarlett. He slipped out of the room and answered it without looking to see who it was.

"Noah," his mother cried, her voice cracking with emotions.

"Mom, what is wrong?"

"Your father has been shot. He is at New York-Presbyterian Hospital. Garrett is doing the surgery. Please come home. I need you."

"I will be there as soon as I can. Do we know who did this?" Noah asked, thinking how he could get there as fast as he could. How had this happened? His father had guards around him at all times.

"No, but Connor and Finn are looking into it."

"I will leave in a few minutes and will call you back in an hour. We will get the fucker who did this and make him suffer." No one fucks with the Kelly family and lives.

"I know you will, son. Be careful," she said.

He dashed back to his bedroom and to his closet. He hastily donned the nearest pair of pants, a white button-up shirt, and a jacket. He put on his leather shoes and promptly returned to the room to find Scarlett still in a state of deep sleep. Fuck, he had forgotten about her. She looked so peaceful and he didn't have time to explain why he had to leave. He grabbed a scrap of paper and wrote her a note.

> Scarlett,
>
> I am sorry not to be here when you woke up. There has been an emergency at home and I have to go. This night was beyond words and I really want to see you again. I promise to call you.
>
> Tony

He bent over and kissed her forehead gently. With one last

glance at her, he placed the note on the nightstand beside her. He rushed out of the room.

Noah phoned his security team in the elevator and filled them in on what was happening. He told them he was driving and for them to get there as soon as they could. Getting behind the wheel, he started it and put it in gear. The average person might take four hours to get to New York, but he was way above average.

CHAPTER THREE

The June sun rose, creating a dazzling display of light as its rays pierced through the high-rise buildings. Scarlett rolled over, looked at the clock, and grumbled. Damn, all she wanted to do was sleep a little longer. However, she needed to get up. Sitting up and sliding her legs over the edge of the mattress, her head spun once again. What was with the dizzy spells, and why was this happening, plus she always so tired? With a sigh, she assumed it was because she'd been going full speed for the last six weeks.

It all began when she awoke in Noah's bed after they had made love. Well, maybe in his mind, it was only sex, but it was so much more in her heart. She never imagined her first time would be so wonderful, but it was and more.

When she awoke she was confused about where she was, but the memories of the previous night's activities flashed through her mind. As well as the dull ache between her legs.

She looked to the other side of the bed and found that Tony was not there. Oh well, she thought. Maybe he got up after she slept and went to another room. A pang of sadness enveloped her. She rolled over and saw a note on the bedside table. The note said he had an emergency and he left her sleeping.

It wouldn't have bothered her if he woke me up. Then she read he was going to call her. But how? How was he supposed to call her if they hadn't swapped numbers? Had he only written that to pacify her, or had the emergency been so unnerving that he didn't remember? Not coming up with any answers to the questions, she got up and dressed, put the note in her purse, and left. When she pulled out her phone, she noticed multiple texts from Brooke and Eve. Her response to them could wait until she had her caffeine fix.

Scarlett stepped out of the apartment building foyer and tried to orient herself. She recognized some buildings. Eve and Brooke's favorite boutique was down the street.

A Starbucks sign caught her eye a couple of blocks away. She walked the short distance, trying not to think about last night too much. The smell of coffee and sweetbread floated in the air outside of the shop making her stomach growl. After purchasing a grande coffee and a chocolate muffin, she found an open table by the window. The hot liquid sent a comforting warmth through her body. Only then did she allow herself to reminisce about the night before. The lingering soreness between her legs reminded her that she was no longer a virgin. Her golden virgin card was punched. She didn't regret giving herself to Tony. In fact, she realized she had been carrying the weight of her father's judgment for far too long, and now she felt lighter and unencumbered.

Weston Murphy, her father, was a religious fanatic who founded his church with just twenty followers. His once small congregation has flourished and now boasts over two thousand members. On Sundays, he preached three services since the church was so small. He also held small group meetings four times a week. He warned the congregation of the fiery destruction that awaited those who fell prey to sinful women. Had the apple from the forbidden tree not been picked, life on earth would be without sin. He believed his wife was guilty of wrongdoing because, in his view, she failed to provide him with a male heir. He had been unyielding and severe in his punishment of her.

Scarlett was astonished that she had escaped from him and the man he had arranged for her to marry. God only knew which one her father had selected.

Her phone chimed with an incoming text message, bringing her out of her thoughts.

Where are you? - BM

She couldn't avoid her friends forever, so she replied to Brooke.

Stopped for coffee. On my way home now - SM

She disposed of her wrapper and headed outside to wait after requesting a ride. While she waited, her mind wandered to Tony and what he was doing. She hoped that he was alright, no matter what the emergency was. Even if it was a lie, she had no regrets about last night. It felt like Tony truly cared for her, and he was incredibly considerate after discovering she was a virgin. When she told him to make her his, she meant it. No matter where life took her, he would always be a part of her heart and soul.

She returned to her apartment, which she shared with Brooke and Eve. She inhaled deeply and readied herself for the interrogation. As soon as she stepped in, she was bombarded with questions. Her roommates were unyielding, so she shared with them everything that had happened. She answered every question they threw at her, even the ones that made her blush deeply. Brooke wanted to track him down and find out what was so damn important to leave her asleep in his bed. She urged her not to, and eventually, she convinced her to leave him be.

The following two weeks flew by, and suddenly, they were walking across the stage, their hearts racing with excitement.

Scarlett gave her valedictorian's speech, challenging the graduating class to go out and make a difference in the world.

While the others had their next careers planned out, she was still searching. Brooke was on her way to work for her father's company, while Eve was eager to begin her own design studio.

Before leaving Boston to go to New York, they went out once again to the Club "O" where she had met Tony. She couldn't stop herself from constantly scanning the room. However, he wasn't there. She tucked that night away in her memories with a heavy heart and moved on.

Brooke's dad went above and beyond to prepare the apartment for their arrival. The location was on the forty-fifth floor of one of the newest buildings in downtown Manhattan. He wanted the penthouse, but the owner kept it for himself. The building's security was the main selling point of the apartment. The electronic security system was cutting-edge and was supported by a large, highly trained security team. He knew the dangers of living in New York and wanted his girls, including Scarlett, to be safe.

His love for her was unwavering, and he told her this just as often as he did with Brooke. When he first heard what her father had done to her, he clenched his fists and felt the urge to fly to Washington State to teach Weston Murphy a lesson. However, Scarlett convinced him not to go, not wanting Weston's toxic ideas and abuse to harm him.

Robert Martin was a prominent member of the city's charitable and arts communities, serving on the board of several organizations. He used his influence to help Scarlett land a job as a museum archivist for the prestigious NYC Natural History Museum. Of course, she argued about not getting the job on her own merit. But after Robert explained his confidence in her ability to do the job, she ultimately relented and accepted the position.

Scarlett was uncomfortable with receiving extravagant gifts. She was afraid of making a mistake that would reflect poorly on

Mr. Martin or Robbie, as he insisted she call him. On her first day of work, she was a bundle of nerves. She held her breath, waiting for the moment when she would have to face her colleagues and explain how she got the position. Despite her worries, she excelled and developed a passion for it. The weeks that followed brought newfound confidence.

Every morning, Scarlett woke up with a sense of excitement, eager to start her workday. That was until last week. She was holding up well, but then she hit a wall of fatigue and could barely keep her eyes open. She believed it was just a passing phase caused by the changes and didn't bother consulting a doctor.

After her shower, she dressed in her favorite outfit, feeling confident and ready for the day. She walked out of the room, and the sight of Brooke and Eve laughing over their breakfast at the dining room table made her smile.

"Good morning, sunshine," Eve said.

"Morning," Scarlett said as her stomach lurched. She breathed deeply through her nose, trying to settle it.

"Still not feeling well?" Brooke asked, worried about her friend.

"It is not that I feel unwell. I am just tired," Scarlett answered, pouring a large steaming cup of coffee into her favorite mug.

"Well, if you don't start getting your energy back in a few weeks, I am taking you to the doctor. Got it?" Brooke said in her no-argument tone.

"Yes, Mother," Scarlett said as she bit her lower lip, trying not to laugh.

"Ass," Brooke said with a twinkle in her bright crystal blue eyes.

"Bitch," Scarlett replied, this time with a giggle.

Boston had transformed her into a confident, independent woman, a far cry from the meek girl she was under her father's dominance. The once timid woman was now speaking with confidence and conviction. She was known for her unwavering confidence, which prevented people from pushing her around. Brooke and Eve were the reason behind her change.

"Damn it. I've got to get to the office. That pencil dick Mike thinks he can take over my clients," Brooke said through gritted teeth as she looked at her watch.

"Pencil dick?" Eve asked, one of her brows raised.

Brooke threw her long hair over her shoulder and chuckled. "Well, I might have walked in on him while he was taking a piss."

"You might have, or you did?" Scarlett asked.

"Alright, bitch, I did. I just wrapped up reading a report and walked into the wrong bathroom. The asshole was at the urinal and when I looked up, I saw it. Fuck, it was the smallest dick I have ever seen on a man."

Scarlett shook her head at her friend and smiled. Brooke and Eve had a history of multiple sexual partners, unlike her, who had only ever been intimate with Tony. Oh God, her cheeks warmed at the thought of what a perfect specimen it was in her book, long and thick.

"She is thinking of him again," Eve said, snapping her fingers in Scarlett's face.

"What?" Scarlett asked, coming out of her trance of the memories of Tony.

"You were thinking of him again," Eve said as a giggle escaped her lips.

"Was not!"

"Yeah, yeah. Get your bag. It is time to go," Brooke said, collecting her computer bag and purse. She had a driver that drove her to work each day and since Scarlett's work was on the way, she rode in with her. Eve's studio was only two blocks down from the apartment.

With her jacket over her arm and bag on her shoulder, Scarlett headed out the door after Brooke and Eve. She took three steps into the hall when her world suddenly spun out of control, and everything went black.

Brooke was talking to Eve and when they turned to ask Scarlett a question, they found her unconscious on the floor.

"SCARLETT!" Eve screamed, falling to her knees beside her.

Brooke pulled her phone out, calling 911. They sat beside Scarlett, ensuring she was still breathing and waiting for help to arrive when the door to their neighbor's apartment opened.

The gentleman looked out and saw two women sitting beside a young woman lying on the floor. "What happened here?" he asked, rushing to her side.

"We don't know," Eve said, tears running down her face.

"I'm Dr. Garrett Byrne. Let me get my bag and I will check her out," he said. He ran back into the apartment, collected his physician's bag, and returned to the woman. He lowered himself and began accessing her vitals. Her heart rate was strong and her lungs were clear. However, she was extremely pale. "Has she been sick?"

"She has been complaining about being tired," Brooke replied. "Do you know what is wrong with her?"

"No. You said that you called for an ambulance?" Garrett asked. Not only was he a doctor but also a surgeon. And more importantly, was the Kelly family's physician. In cases where a family member got injured and couldn't go to the hospital, he was the one who provided medical assistance. As a surgeon in good standing, he could utilize the facilities of a hospital when necessary.

"I can't see anything major wrong. However, I think it is best to take her to the hospital and get her checked out. I would be more than happy to assist if you would like, seeing that we are neighbors."

"Thank you, Dr. Byrne," Eve said, wiping her tears.

Brooke phoned her father and informed him of the situation, then contacted Scarlett's workplace and did the same. As she ended her phone calls, the elevator opened and the ambulance crew came out with a stretcher. Garrett explained the situation and let them know he was her doctor. Scarlett was placed with care on the gurney and transported to the ambulance.

"They are taking her to New York-Presbyterian Hospital. I need her full name and any medical history you may know. I also need to know if she has any allergies," Garrett said, pulling out his phone to place the information in his notepad.

"Scarlett Aria Murphy, twenty-two, with no prior medical issue and has no drug allergies," Brooke said as she reached out and grasped Garrett's arm. "Please help her."

Garrett patted her on the hand. "I will."

Thirty minutes later, Scarlett was hooked to the monitors in the ER. A set of blood tests was performed. Other than her slightly low blood pressure, nothing seemed to be out of the ordinary. There had to be a reason for a healthy young woman to faint.

Scarlett opened her eyes but just as quickly closed them. The bright lights made her cry out in pain, her eyes unable to adjust to the sudden brightness.

"Miss Murphy?"

"Where am I?" she asked, raising her arm to shield her eyes.

"You are in the emergency room. I am Dr. Byrne."

"What am I doing here and how did I get here?" she asked.

Garrett switched off the large overhead light, leaving the one soft light over the bed on. "Is that better?"

Scarlett moved her arm and opened her eyes. "Much, thank you."

"To answer your questions. You passed out in the hall outside your apartment and an ambulance brought you."

Scarlett looked around the room. "Where are Brooke and Eve?"

"They are waiting, very impatiently, I might add, in the waiting room. Ms. Martin is definitely headstrong, much like her father," Garrett said, his lips turned up in a sly smile. "And Ms. Landon is downright scary. She had the security guards shaking in their boots."

Scarlett giggled at his comment about Eve. "You know Robbie, I mean Mr. Martin?"

"Ah, I see he has brought you into the family. Only those who are close to him can get by calling him Robbie. We are old friends." Garrett had been so busy lately that he didn't realize his new neighbors were Robert Martin's daughter and her friends.

A nurse walked in with a chart and gave it to Garrett. He checked the blood tests. All seemed okay except for one.

"Dr. Byrne, have you found something that has caused me to pass out?" Scarlett asked, fisting her blanket. What if she was dying? Hell, she had only just begun experiencing life.

"I have found a little something," Garrett said. He felt grateful that her condition was not life-threatening. He had only known her a short time, yet he was drawn to her unique charm. Her fiery red hair hinted that Irish blood flowed through her veins. If the test results had been different and she was single, he would have introduced her to one of Liam's sons.

Scarlett's breathing grew labored as her heart raced like a runaway train. The sound of the alarm filled the room as her heart rate spiked. "What is it?"

Garrett came over to the bed and placed his hand on her arm. "Calm down, lass. You are going to be fine. I predict you should be right as rain in about seven and a half months, give or take a week."

"Seven and a half months?"

"You're going to have a wee one," Garrett declared, and as soon as the words left his mouth, she fainted once again.

CHAPTER FOUR

Noah shifted on the cramped bed his father had kept in the office, rubbing his eyes to stay awake. He could be in his penthouse apartment in his luxurious king-size bed. However, he promised himself he wouldn't truly rest until he found out who was behind the hit on his dad.

He stood and stretched his tight muscles. Damn, he was tired. He walked over to the window and saw the first glow of the morning light in the distance, signaling the start of a new day. At that very moment, he couldn't help but think of Scarlett and wonder how she was doing. The family chaos had prevented him from searching for her, but as soon as it settled, he would start looking.

The day after he left Boston, he reached for his phone to call Scarlett to explain what was happening but realized he had never gotten her number. He couldn't help but wonder what she must have felt when she read his note. He was an idiot for not getting her number or at least leaving his for her.

He checked his watch and groaned in frustration. Four hours of sleep was all he could manage, leaving him feeling exhausted and unrefreshed. Since the night he received the call from his mom that someone had shot his father, he had not gotten any more than that.

His speedy driving skills allowed him to cover the distance between Boston and New York in just two and a half hours, a feat that usually takes four hours. He had been on the phone with Finn and Connor, who were trying to find the scumbag who had shot their father. When he wasn't talking to his brothers, he was left to his thoughts as he sped down the darkened highway. Who would be stupid enough to try to kill his father?

His parents had been at a benefit gala at the Guggenheim Museum. Liam Kelly was a cold-blooded mafia Skipper who controlled New York and New Jersey's guns and rare antiquities. But he also gave a shitload of money to charities to help those in need.

It is not like Liam had a choice in his career. Being born into a family of organized crime means you have no choice but to live and die in that world. Liam had inherited the leadership of our organization from his father, who had taken over from his father before him. This position is often passed down as an inheritance upon death or physical disability.

His seanathair, or grandfather, Noah Anthony Kelly, migrated to the United States in 1921 from Dublin, Ireland. He had few chances to earn a decent living and provide his beloved wife, Deirhre, with the lifestyle she deserved in Ireland.

He considered himself fortunate when Deirhre O'Malley bestowed her attention upon him. With her button nose and scattering of freckles, she looked like a true daughter of the Emerald Isle's Mountain. Her ginger hair shone like the sun on a hot summer day. Despite all the men in the village vying for her attention, her heart belonged only to Noah Kelly. Noah nervously approached her father the day before her eighteenth birthday and asked for her hand in marriage. The Kellys were a family that Patrick O'Malley knew he could trust and respect. He had also noticed the way his daughter's eyes sparkled with joy as she stood beside Noah. The next day, they exchanged vows with his approval. Six months later, they were on a boat to America. Noah's cousin migrated two years prior and helped the couple to settle in New York.

Noah started working in a tire plant, day in and day out, until one day, the men he worked with invited him out for the evening for some refreshments. The bootlegged liquor burned his throat as he took his first sip that night. It wasn't anything like the smooth Irish whiskey he was used to. However, the men were willing to pay their hard-earned money for the vile drink. It was then he came up with an idea. He turned the high demand for quality liquor into a profitable family business by catering to the masses. His large family from New York and New Jersey played a crucial role in his rise to becoming the king of illegal liquor. As time passed, he grew his empire to include not only liquor but also weapons and, eventually, drugs.

His family flourished in America. Deirhre gave him a son, Sean Liam, and two beautiful daughters, Clara and Brianna. They lived in the finest homes in New York and never worried about money. Noah knew how to network and had amassed connections within the city government offices as well as law enforcement officials. He only encountered problems with an occasional rookie trying to advance in the force.

On Sean's twenty-fifth birthday, his father surprised him with news of an arranged marriage to a girl from Ireland. Anger boiled inside Sean when he learned about the arranged marriage. The idea of not being able to marry whomever he wanted faded away when he saw Grace Walsh's youthful beauty. Love hit him like a ton of bricks when he met her. He worked closely alongside his father, aiding him in the trafficking of guns. Seeing the damage drugs had on families, Noah phased out the drug trade and began trafficking rare antiquities. Noah was shot and killed by a rival group in 1949. Sean assumed control of the family business and expanded the empire. He ruled the streets of New York and New Jersey mercilessly, not letting any other family take their territory.

The pain of Gracie's multiple miscarriages weighed on their hearts. Sean thought he wouldn't ever be a father and thought about who would take over if something horrible happened to him. Maybe he was being punished for all the illegal things that he had done. He had killed so many men that he had lost count.

Then, when Gracie was thirty-five, she gave birth to a healthy baby boy, Liam Hayes Kelly. Even though he loved his mother, Liam idolized his father and strived to be just like him. When Sean turned sixty, he was diagnosed with lung cancer. Even though the doctors gave him hope for a full recovery, Sean turned over the family's leadership and the business to Liam.

He had newly married the lovely Eimear Fitzpatrick. It wasn't exactly an arranged marriage, though Sean invited the Fitzpatrick's of Boston to dinner. As soon as Liam laid eyes on Eimear, or Emee as she preferred to be called, his heart was hers.

The Kelly mansion, which was enormous, was intended for the head of the family, the Skipper. Sean and Gracie relocated to their new townhome on the Upper East Side, allowing Liam and Emee to move in. Four years later, Liam and Emee welcomed their first child, a boy whom they named after his great-grandfather and grandfather, Noah Anthony Kelly. The day before he turned one, his family welcomed his Irish twin brothers, Finn and Connor.

The boys were groomed from a young age to take over the family business, thanks to Liam and Emee's guidance. Recognizing the need to adapt to changing times, they sent Noah, Finn, and Connor to college. They would learn skills in business, computer science, and international business, respectively.

Liam and Emee were the epitome of sophistication in the eyes of New York society. Despite the rumors of their family's ties to organized crime, everyone still wanted to be associated with them.

Liam's approach to handling the business was similar to that of his father. He was adaptable and recognized the potential of technology in expanding his business. His father had taught him how to manage local and federal law enforcement. Public records and databases made it easier to use extortion to either make law enforcement cooperate or eliminate the threat.

Noah parked his car in the first spot he saw at the hospital, unconcerned about the possibility of being towed. He stepped out of his car, double-checking that he had his SVI Tiki-T and Desert Eagle .50 cal with him. The level of security would be at its peak until he found out who was after his family and dealt with them. As he approached the entrance, he noticed two family guards standing outside. It was a relief to see Finn as he entered the hospital, along with two more guards by his side.

"Noah, God, man, I am happy to see you," Finn said. Noah could tell from the creases on his forehead that he was distraught.

"Any updates?" Noah asked.

"No. He is still in surgery. Come, let me take you up."

Finn led them up to the surgical wing and to the private room where their mother was waiting.

Before they walked in, he said. "The hospital chief of staff arranged for the room. I think he is kissing up for a hefty donation."

"He'll get it if he keeps everyone except family away from

Mother and Father. Are all the guards set up as I specified?" Noah asked.

"Yes."

"I want one of us with Mother at all times," Noah said.

"I will let Connor know. He is with her now."

The sound of the door opening made Emee jump up, her heart racing with anticipation that Garrett had good news about the love of her life. As her gaze fell on the door, she saw Noah's silhouette standing there, his broad shoulders filling the frame. He looked like he had been through hell, with his wrinkled clothes and dark circles under his eyes.

Noah's eyes scanned his Mother from head to foot to ensure she was indeed unharmed. She wore a long, beaded evening gown that was now marred with blood. He didn't know if it was her blood or his father's. "Mother, are you okay?" He rushed out, pulling his Mother into his strong arms.

"I am fine, baby. This is your Father's blood."

Before releasing her, he gave her a tight squeeze. He motioned for her to sit back on the small couch, and his eyes darted around the room before finding Connor near the door. "Connor, can you bring us some coffee?"

"Sure, brother," he answered, then nodded to Finn, who took his spot.

"Oh, baby, you look so tired," she said as she wiped the piece of hair that had fallen over his eye.

"I am fine, Mother. How are you holding up?"

"By a thread," she confessed. Even though she knew something like this could happen, she never thought it would.

Connor returned with a tray of steaming hot coffee, handing a cup to each of them. Finn surveyed the area outside the door to ensure the guards were present before sitting with his family.

Noah took a big gulp of his coffee. Placing the cup on the table, he turned toward his mother. "Mother, I need to know what happened."

Emee sipped her coffee and got her thoughts together. "We had been at the gala a while and were leaving. When we stepped outside, there was a crowd of people waiting for cars. Declan and Steven were our guards and walked a few steps behind us, as always. Suddenly, I heard two muffled shots, and when I turned, I saw both of the guards on the ground. Liam was taking out his weapon when another shot sounded. He lurched forward and fell to the ground. As I glanced over, I saw a man of average build wearing a dark hoodie and jeans. I didn't see his face. He ran off, and I fell to the ground to check on Liam. When I placed my hand on his back, I felt the sticky, warm blood. He was on his side and groaning. He murmured to call Garrett. No one around us even paid us one bit of attention. Hell, we have three people on the ground and no one stopped to ask if there was a problem," Emee recounted, her hand shaking at the end, not in fear but rage.

"What happened next?" Noah asked.

"Our caddie Owen looked over and he jumped out of the car. He rushed over to us. I told him to call Garrett. Garrett told him he would call an ambulance and meet us here."

"Did Garrett say anything about him before going to surgery?" Noah asked.

"He said that they had shot him in the back and it was bad," she answered as her voice cracked.

Noah wrapped his arm around her. "Mother, Garrett is an awesome doctor and surgeon. He will do everything possible for Dad."

"We must keep our faith," Finn said, reaching out and placing his hand on her knee. "Now, why don't I get you home and get you some clean clothes?"

Emee looked down and just now noticed her state. It wasn't until this point that she realized how poorly she looked. She was always put together with stylish clothes, makeup, and her hair perfectly styled. "Oh my. I can't leave him. Can someone go get me something?"

"What would you like, Mother?" Connor asked. "I will go get them myself."

"Thank you, my sweet," Emee cooed and told him what she wanted and where to find them. Edward instructed Connor to also arrange for breakfast to arrive in two hours.

Two hours later, Emee was freshly showered and changed into a comfortable yet fashionable pantsuit. Even at this time of great pain and uncertainty, she had to keep up with appearances. She was Emee Kelly, wife to the great Liam Kelly.

When she left the bathroom, she found Connor waiting for her. She smiled at him and took his arm. They went back to the private room. As they stepped in, Noah was barking out orders on the phone. She smiled while listening to his conversation. It was as if his father was in the room with them when he spoke. Emee was proud of the man he had become and his readiness to take over if necessary. Liam would be so proud and she couldn't wait for him to awake so he could see for himself.

Noah called his Father's Clan Chief, Seamus. His list of demands included the requirement to investigate the video surveillance footage of the museum to identify the man in the black hoodie. Holy shit, he thought, running his hand through his hair. He couldn't help but chuckle quietly to himself. As soon as he returned, he slipped back into his Irish heritage, speaking with an accent and using the Gaelic language. While studying in Boston, he kept his native accent and Gaelic language to himself to avoid unwanted attention.

Garrett appeared in the room and removed his surgical mask, with blood visible on the front of his gown. Everyone was on their feet and rushed over to him.

"Garrett, how is he?" Emee asked, wringing her hands.

Garrett took a deep breath in. "He is alive and in the ICU. He is not out of the woods yet, but we all know how strong of a man he is."

Despite hearing everything Garrett said, Noah couldn't shake the unease he felt from the look in his eyes. "Garrett, what is it?"

"Damn, you are so much like Liam," Garrett said. "As you know, they shot him from behind and the bullet damaged his spinal cord."

"What does that mean?" Connor questioned.

"He may never walk again," Garrett replied.

"But he will live?" Finn asked.

"Yes. He has a long road ahead once he wakes up and we all know it won't be easy for him," Garrett said.

"As long as he is alive, we as a teaghlach will handle whatever comes our way," Emee said, her voice strong and determined.

Noah knew she was right. The Family would handle whatever came their way.

CHAPTER FIVE

With a loud huff, Scarlett flung the pants across the room, falling onto the bed in a heap. None of her clothes fit over her ever-growing belly. She couldn't believe that she was pregnant, especially since she had only had sex once before. If that wasn't bad enough, she wasn't just having one baby. Oh no, she was having twins.

Brooke and Eve had provided comfort with their reassuring words. Hell, they were elated. Eve was busily creating an entire wardrobe for the little bundles of joy while the decorator was busy designing the nursery.

After the initial shock dissipated, Scarlett realized she needed to inform Tony about the baby. Without his contact details, she relied on the scraps of information she had to start her search. He had been a student at Boston University.

She called the school and they refused to give her information about him, citing their privacy policy. Brooke was enraged and phoned her dad, Robbie, who then called the President of the University, an old buddy he used to drink with. It was surprising that Anthony Hayes's name, social security number, and address were the only things President Fuller found in their records. There were no parents' names, prior addresses, phone numbers, or email addresses. Robbie checked Tony's social security number by tapping into his resources. He discovered it belonged to someone who died thirty years ago.

Scarlett was heartbroken by the news. She believed she and Tony had a connection that was tangible like a magnetic force pulled them together. However, it appeared that he had a specific goal in mind. Sex. She was too innocent to see his true nature and gave him everything, and now she's carrying his child. No correction, babies.

Their neighbor, Dr. Garrett Byrne, had been so compassionate, breaking the news to her about her pregnancy. Then, he arranged for her to meet with the best OBGYN in the entire city, Dr. Rachel O'Neill. Dr. O'Neill and her staff had delivered ninety-five percent of New York City's elite. Usually, you could never get an appointment unless you knew someone and Dr. Garrett Byrne was that someone.

Not many people knew that Dr. O'Neill's dad had been the Kelly family's personal OBGYN for years before his retirement. Dr. Alstair O'Neill delivered all three of Kelly's sons, two of whom were twins.

Scarlett, Brooke, and Eve were so grateful to Garrett for all his help that they asked him to come over for dinner. Brooke invited her father, and he eagerly anticipated spending time with his old friend. The fact that Garrett lived on the same floor as his "girls" gave Robbie peace of mind in case they required a doctor.

Garrett wondered about the father of Scarlett's baby. Given her young age and recent college graduation, he wondered if it had been a boy from school or a boyfriend. He offered to accompany her to her initial consultation with Dr. O'Neill, and Scarlett accepted. In the car, he chose to inquire about the father of the baby.

"Scarlett, you don't have to tell me, but where is the baby's father?"

She was silent, her breathing shallow and rapid, as she struggled to keep her composure. The silence stretched on until she finally cleared her throat, breaking the tension. "He was a guy I met in a bar," she said, her voice whisper soft. She then turned toward Garrett. "Please don't think that I did that a lot. To be honest, it was my first time and I had thought he was special."

"Does he know?" Garrett asked, feeling sorry for her.

"I tried to find him, but he gave me a fake name," she said, brushing away tears. "Foolish me. I thought he would have given me his real name."

"You are not foolish. He is just an immature asshole who needs to be taught how to treat a lady." Men like him should be taken to the warehouse and skinned alive. He was sure Noah would help him.

Scarlett couldn't help but feel grateful as she smiled warmly at the protective comment. Whenever she was feeling down, her friends would lift her up, and she felt lucky to have such a supportive group of people in her life.

Dr. O'Neill was terrific, with a quick wit and a thick Irish brogue. Within a few moments of talking, Scarlett felt completely at ease with her. She informed her about the upcoming months and provided her with prenatal vitamins.

Two months later, Scarlett had her first ultrasound to check on the development of the baby. She was lying on the table while Dr. O'Neill used the wand over her stomach. She described what she saw to Scarlett as the image appeared on the screen. Dr. O'Neill abruptly stopped and repositioned the device for a clearer view.

Scarlett was watching her face and became concerned. "Is there something wrong?"

"Scarlet, there is nothing wrong, but someone likes to play hide and seek."

"What?"

"You are having twins," she replied, pointing to the screen at the second little head.

Scarlett was utterly shocked. Her heart pounded in her chest and her mind buzzed with a flurry of emotions. She had never imagined having one baby, let alone two, and the realization left her feeling both excited and terrified. "How didn't we hear two heartbeats?"

"It happens. The one baby was hiding behind the other," Dr. O'Neill explained. "Causing us only to hear one heartbeat."

"Are they both okay?" Scarlett asked.

"They are both perfect and seem to want to show us their sex if you want to know," Rachel giggled.

She was excited to find out when she would give birth, but the overpowering urge to know was far more significant. She wanted to know.

"Congratulations, you are having two feisty boys," she said, then pointed to the screen. "And they are both showing off their penises."

Dr. O'Neill pointed at the screen. Scarlett's gaze followed his finger and landed on the unmistakable image of their penises. It was like they were proud of them and if this was what was to come. She was going to be in real trouble. Girls would swoon at their feet if they inherited their father's looks and the size of their private parts. Dr. O'Neill printed off several copies of the ultrasound for Scarlett.

Scarlett arrived home and immediately called her friends over to share the news. The excitement in the room grew as she shared the images with them. They were equally surprised but overjoyed, just like her.

She was only four months pregnant, but her body had undergone significant changes, leaving her nothing to wear. The thought of shopping filled her with dread, leading her to procrastinate until she had nothing that fit. The door to her room opened up and Brooke walked in.

"Having a little problem?" she asked. One side of her lips curled up.

Scarlett sniffled. "I have nothing to wear."

Brooke came over to the bed and sat down. "You wouldn't be lying on the bed naked if you had gone shopping like we asked. Now get your ass up, and put on a pair of yoga pants and a T-shirt. We are going to get you some clothes," Brooke said, her tone leaving no room for argument.

"I have to be at work in an hour," Scarlett said, as tears burned her eyes. Dr. Neill explained her distress was due to her hormones, but she still despised feeling powerless.

"Alright, get your face and hair done. We will rush into the boutique and select something for today," Brooke said.

Wiping her eyes, Scarlett sat up and gave Brooke a little smile. "Thank you."

Twenty minutes later, they were at a boutique down the street. Scarlett was changing into a cute black dress in the dressing room. The classic style with a rocker chic edge by the Tunisian neckline and glamorous gold zipper detailing on the sides. The fabric was a soft stretch jersey that hugged her bump. Brooke tossed in a pair of black pumps with an accent of cream and gold studding.

Scarlett left the dressing room beaming. Not only did the dress make her feel like a professional, but it also highlighted her baby bump.

"Shit, you look great," Brooke said, then looked up at the clock. "You have to leave now. I will take care of the bill."

"I can pay," Scarlett said. Her job paid her well, but she was trying to watch her spending because raising two babies would be expensive.

"I know, but you need to get to work. Be prepared for some major shopping when you get off."

"Alright," Scarlett said as she reached out, took Brooke's hand, and squeezed tightly. "Thank you."

"You are very welcome. NOW GO!"

Scarlett arrived at work on time and received compliments all day about her dress. By the time she was off, she couldn't wait to shop. Brooke didn't lie when she said significant shopping. When Brooke and Eve, who had to be there to ensure that Scarlett looked fashionable, left the last boutique, their arms were covered in bags full of clothes. The clothes were tailored with fabrics that would adjust to her growing belly. In addition, they bought new bras, panties, slips, and nightgowns.

Scarlett's pregnancy was progressive normally for someone who was carrying twins. With her small frame, her belly appeared to be ready to give birth at any time, even though she was only nearing her fifth month.

One of her jobs was to organize a gala to collect funds for the museum. It was the biggest event of the year, with attendees from the upper echelon of society, most with deep pockets. The museum's survival relies on its donations, which were highlighted in the gala through exhibits.

Eve designed a gown for Scarlett to wear at the event. It was a stunning, strapless, floor-length gown in a delicious shade of cappuccino. It had a boned bodice, which gave Scarlett the perfect shape in confidence and comfort. The softly shimmering acetate jersey boasted a little stretch to accommodate her changing body. A pretty sweetheart neckline emphasizes her bare shoulders above a full-flowing skirt. Eve designed a vintage sash with matching cappuccino tails that added a touch of sparkle in front for the essential hint of bling.

Robbie wanted his girls to look their best on the day of the event, so he booked them for an exclusive day spa excursion. Every inch of them would be pampered. Robbie arranged for a driver to take them to the spa and back. When they arrived, they walked up to the reception desk.

"Good day. Welcome to Oasis Day Spa. My name is Rebecca."

"Hello. We have an appointment," Brooke said.

"Certainly. Your name, please?"

"Brooke Martin."

"Oh, Miss Martin, we have been expecting your party. Bridget, please take these ladies to the executive suite," Rebecca said.

She and the staff had been waiting for the Martin party to arrive. Mr. Martin had prepaid the services in advance as well as the hefty tip to all the staff. The only other guest who exceeded his generous tips was Mrs. Kelly.

"Follow me, please," Bridget said with a warm smile. They made their way through the lavish building towards a set of double doors. "This suite is designed for four patrons. It is the best suite in the house."

When Scarlett looked at the doors to the suite, she noticed two large men standing on either side of them. She was curious about who they were and why they were there. Bridget opened the door and gestured for them to go in.

As soon as they entered the room, they were enveloped in its cozy atmosphere, which was created by four camel-colored chaise loungers, dark brown walls, and light stone floors with red rugs scattered around. The warm, glowing lights cast a soft, inviting glow throughout the room, creating a soothing ambiance. Scarlett noticed an older woman occupying one of the chaise loungers. She had on a camel-colored robe with slippers to match. She stood and her face broke out in a wide smile.

"Hello. My name is Emee. You must be my suite mates today."

"Yes, we are," Eve said. "This is Brooke, Scarlett, and I am Eve."

"Glad to make your acquaintance," Emee replied in her thick Irish brogue.

"God, I love your accent," Scarlett said. She had heard it before in her childhood, but she couldn't remember where.

"How sweet of you to say so. Irish born and bred," Emee said, then glanced at Scarlett's midsection. "Oh my goodness, you are carrying a precious little angel."

Scarlett's hand went to her belly. "Actually, two."

Emee looked intently at her belly. "Then you must be about five months."

"How did you know?" Scarlett asked. Everyone who saw her thought she was about to give birth.

"Because that is about the size I was with my twins. God, I can't believe that was twenty-one years ago."

"Wow. You don't look old enough to have children that old," Brooke said.

"Thank you, leannán," Emee said. "But they are not my oldest. My Noah is twenty-two. They are Irish twins."

"Leannán? Irish twins?" Scarlett asked.

"Sorry, I keep forgetting that not everyone knows Gaelic. Leannán means sweetheart. Irish twins mean that they were born within one year of each other. Finn and Connor were born the day before Noah's first birthday," Emee explained.

"I can't imagine having three children so close together. Hell, I can't imagine having one," Scarlett said, rubbing her belly. "But here I am pregnant with two."

Emee studied Scarlett's face. The hurt and loneliness in her beautiful green eyes were heart-wrenching to witness. She wondered why she looked that way. This should be the most precious time in her life.

Four staff members entered and diverted Brooke, Eve, and Scarlett to the dressing room to get ready. Shortly after, they returned to the suite and relaxed on their loungers. Everyone got mimosas except for Scarlett. They gave her just plain orange juice.

"So ladies, is there a special occasion for you being here today?" Emee asked.

"We are going to this huge shindig over at the museum tonight that this one organized," Brooke said, pointing at Scarlett.

"The gala? That is where I am going," Emee said. "Scarlett, you work at the museum?"

"Yes, ma'am."

"Oh, my stars. We are one of your donors."

"Really?" Scarlett asked. "I am sorry, but what is your last name?"

"Kelly. Emee and Liam Kelly."

HOLY SHIT! Scarlett thought. She had been conversing with one of the top donors to the museum.

CHAPTER SIX

"Damn it, I ruined another suit," Noah said through gritted teeth as he looked down at the blood splatters and pieces of brain matter staining his jacket and pants.

"How many does this make?" Finn asked, holstering his gun and giving his brother a smirk.

"Nine, ten. Shit, I don't know," Noah answered. He hoped he had found the person who had shot his father. But this imbecile was clearly unskilled and incapable of making the precise kill shot of two guards, then his father, before he could pull his gun.

For five months, he and his brothers supported their father's adjustment to life in a wheelchair. They also investigated who had been responsible for the hit. When Liam woke up in the ICU, his family was by his side and Garrett broke the news about his spinal damage.

"Liam, the bullet nicked the Thoracic Nerve T-12 close to the Lumbar Nerve L-1," Garrett said. "Currently, you have no nerve stimulation to your lower extremities."

Liam's mind was reeling as he tried to process what he was hearing. How could this have happened? "Will I walk again?"

"I don't think there is a possibility." Garrett's heart was heavy with telling the leader of the family this news.

"Sweetheart, we are going to get through this together. You are alive and strong," Emee said, taking his hand and bringing it to her mouth to kiss.

Liam smiled at Emee, the love of his life. "Oh my, love, I am not ready to leave you yet."

Noah placed his hand on his father's shoulder. "Dad, we will find out who did this and make the fucker pay."

"Noah, I'm confident you and your brothers will do everything possible. However, I want all of you to know I am not giving up. I cannot run the family from this bed or while I am trying to regain the use of my legs. It was a matter of time before this happened, anyway. It appears the timetable has just moved my decision into the present."

After Liam came out of surgery, Garrett ensured to place his ring back on his finger. No one else in the family saw their Skipper without it.

Liam slid the ring from his right-hand ring finger and he held it up. Even though his body was weak, his voice was strong as he spoke in the language of his family, Gaelic. "As the leader of the Kelly family, I hereby pass the leadership to my blood, my firstborn, Noah Anthony. Do you promise to always put the family first?"

"I do."

"Lead, my son, with head and your heart. Never allow any injustice to go unpunished." Liam slid the ring on Noah's right-hand ring finger.

Connor approached and presented his father with the knife. Although he had never witnessed this aspect of the ritual before, his father had described each procedure to his sons. The knife was given to Connor on his eighteenth birthday and he was instructed to carry it with him at all times. For generations, the same knife was used during the ceremony where the Family's Skipper handed over the reins to the next leader.

Liam cut his hand and then made a matching cut on Noah's hand using the knife. Clasping the bleeding hands together. "Blood of my blood, rule and protect the family at all costs."

After his father released his hand, Noah looked down at the ring that now resided on his finger. From a young age, he knew he'd be wearing this ring one day. However, it was supposed to be in the distant future. Was he nervous about assuming all the responsibilities of becoming the Skipper? YES. Was he prepared to be the Skipper? YES.

His father had been preparing him for the longest time and would be behind him as he began his reign as Skipper. He immediately knew who would be his second and who would be the Warlord when he looked at his brothers. "Finn, I name you Clan Chief and Connor, I name you Warlord."

"I am honored, Skipper," Finn and Connor stated at the same time.

Skipper. He was now Skipper of the Kelly Family.

From that day, he took over the business of running the family, both the legal and illegal aspects, as well as dealing with every fucking attempt to kill him. He knew this was how the other families tested a new leader, but man, it was getting old. And it was taking up valuable time to discover who had called the hit and who had carried it out.

Looking down at his watch, Noah grumbled. "Shit, we are going to be late for this gala thing."

"Fuck, Mom is going to kill us," Finn groaned. "God, Save Us!"

"Alright, there is no reason for all of us to be in the doghouse. I will call the cleaners and stay until they get here," Noah said.

"Thanks, brother," Connor and Finn said in unison. Their dissimilarity in appearance didn't stop them from often speaking in unison. They had a mysterious connection, a sixth sense that kicked in whenever one of them was in trouble or needed support. It was a source of constant annoyance for their parents.

His brothers left, chatting away in Gaelic about finding some hot pussy tonight at the gala. Noah and his brothers were raised bilingually, speaking both Gaelic and English fluently. Gaelic was the language they spoke when they were at home or around family. Otherwise, they spoke English, except when whispering nasty nothings into a woman's ear as they pounded into them.

Tonight's event always had the usual group of women looking for some rich man to sink their nails into. He won't be looking for any pussy tonight. He had been celibate since the night his father was shot, and he was determined to find the culprit before he slept with anyone else.

Tonight, he had taken on the role of the observer while his brothers enjoyed some much-needed relaxation. His mind drifted to Scarlett, and he wondered if she was thinking about him, too. Did she find a job that perfectly fits her skills and interests? Was she happy? Was she dating? The thought of another guy touching her made his blood boil.

"Skipper," Morgan called out, carrying in the large roll of plastic wrap, followed by George and Matthew.

These men were a critical part of the family. Their attention to detail was unparalleled regarding disposing of a body and covering their tracks. Noah was lucky to have such an excellent team as part of the family. Reaching into his pocket, he pulled out the white envelope, handing it to Morgan. "Thank you."

Morgan nodded in acknowledgment. It was an odd feeling for him when the Skipper expressed his gratitude, especially since he was just a cleaner.

As he watched Morgan, Noah noticed a range of emotions flickers across her face. His father had always been able to read people with ease, but he never expected to develop the skill himself. Lately, however, he had noticed the slight hints in people's expressions. He was able to read Morgan's thoughts. "Morgan, without you and your team, the family would be vulnerable to rival families and law enforcement authorities. Never feel that you are just the cleaner."

Morgan was shocked. Had he said his thoughts out loud?

"Yes, Skipper. I promise to ensure that not one drop of blood or speck of evidence will ever be found."

"I do not doubt that. Now, I must get out of here." Noah walked out and saw Rory by the back door of his car.

After he had become the Skipper, he hardly ever drove anywhere. His caddie, Rory Bell, drove him around to his desired locations and he was constantly shadowed by two guards, Luke Mullan and Thomas Kane. Security would remain on high alert until they could determine who was responsible for ordering the hit on his father.

His armored Bentley, Bentayga, incorporates the same heightened level of ballistic protection, also achieving a B6 rating. But this bulletproof beauty was opulent, thanks to the Bentley badge. The all-black brute can withstand two of the German military's DM51 hand grenades exploding simultaneously from beneath its floor and take a barrage of bullets from assault rifles, such as an AK-47 or AR-10. It was a beast. His parents were chauffeured in a Rolls-Royce Cullinan limo. They needed the added space for Liam's wheelchair, but they were just as protected.

After spending a week in the hospital, Liam was now under home care and had to undergo physical therapy. Garrett visited three times a day and discovered that three of the wives of family members were nurses. He set up a meeting with himself and Noah. Noah's ultimate say determined if the women would be deemed acceptable. Noah met with each prospect individually. His Counselor, Rowan Fitzpatrick, conducted a thorough background check on each person and their entire family. He didn't want to leave anything to chance, especially since his father was in a vulnerable state. The nurses passed with flying colors, each taking turns working shifts at the Kelly mansion.

Since no one in his family was qualified in physical therapy, Garrett searched for the most skilled person in the field, believing that no one else could suffice. The name that was repeatedly mentioned was Rebecca Morris.

She was on top of her field, working with people with spinal cord injuries. Garrett contacted her and asked if she would take on a patient with Liam's injuries. She wanted to see his file and x-rays before making a final decision. It took a few days, but she eventually agreed. Noah didn't interview her, though he had Rowan do his usual background. Rebecca moved into the Kelly mansion. She worked with Liam daily on advanced trunk, pelvic, and leg functions, focusing on improving movement, coordination, strength, and balance.

Without any expenses being spared, all the necessary equipment was purchased. The lower-level bedroom suite was converted into a new gym. Thanks to the mansion's elevator system, Liam could navigate between floors more easily.

Liam was usually in high spirits, but occasionally, he would feel depressed and frustrated, fearing he might never be the same man he used to be. Emee refused to coddle him on those bleak days. She reminded him they were a family and would face the situation together.

Noah reached the garage of the building where his penthouse apartment was located. He had only spent a few hours a day here. Nevertheless, it was still home.

He had only slept in the bed one night when he was too exhausted to make it across town to his office. The apartment was furnished and decorated by his mother. Her taste was incredible and she knew exactly what he liked.

His closet at the office held his suits for everyday business. But his casual attire and tuxedos were housed in the penthouse's closet. He took the elevator from the garage, which seemed to take forever to get to the top floor. It finally stopped, and he stepped out into his foyer. He quickly made his way through the apartment, discarding his bloody suit into a designated hamper for disposal. One of the cleaning crew would be called to collect the basket tomorrow.

After his shower, he cleaned away all the blood before spraying bleach on the walls, floor, and drain. He brushed his teeth and worked on taming his hair. Though it was useless, it had a mind of its own.

"Son of a bitch," he grumbled, throwing the brush on the counter.

Stomping into the bedroom, he slipped on a pair of boxers, socks, a white tailored shirt with French cuffs, and one of his black Armani tuxedos. Pulling off the shelf, the Derby cap toe shoes with double buckles and the Testoni belt to match. After getting dressed, he opened the cabinet door and picked up his Kelly crest cufflinks and Hublot Big Bang watch from the collection. He loved this one because of the 1,280 diamonds that circled the face. He adjusted his family ring and was ready to go. After a text to Rory, he left the apartment using the public elevator. His guard waited on the ground level unless a security breach or an unauthorized person was trying to access the upper floors. All tenants of the building were thoroughly investigated before allowing them to purchase an apartment. Before guests were allowed on the floors, they went through a metal detector and family recognition.

As the elevator descended, it stopped on the floor just below him. A middle-aged man was waiting, holding a beaded bag, looking very uncomfortable. The man looked familiar, but he couldn't place him. Noah hadn't seen him before in the building, but that might have been the case since he had only been here a few times and that was usually late at night.

This floor had three apartments. Garrett, the family doctor and surgeon, and Victoria, the family arbiter, lived in two of them. The third and largest belonged to Robert Martin, the CEO of Martin International. The company was an import/export company that the family had used occasionally. Robert didn't live in the apartment, but his daughter and two of her friends did. He never got their names, though Rowan said they were clean, with no ties to other families or Police. It was then Noah remembered who the man was.

The older man stepped into the elevator. Once the doors were closed, Noah cleared his throat. "Nice bag."

Robert smiled nervously. "It is not mine."

"I figured."

"Aria forgot her bag and demanded that I come to pick it up," Robert said. Scarlett had only agreed to call him Robbie if he would call her Aria. He loved her as much as he did his feisty daughter, Brooke.

"Wife?" Noah asked.

"No, daughter. Sorry, I am Robert Martin," he said, holding out his hand.

"Noah Kelly," he replied, shaking his hand.

"Kelly? Liam Kelly's son?"

"You know my father?" Noah asked, knowing he did, but wanted to see what he would say.

"Yes. How is he doing? I heard about the incident."

"Getting better every day. I am in control of the family business now," Noah said, his face blank from emotions.

"I hadn't heard," Robert replied.

He didn't have first-hand knowledge, though the rumors suggested the Kellys were a mafia family. The business dealings that his company had with the family had been on the up and up. His text message tone sounded from his phone. He looked down, and he saw it was from Aria. She was craving a chocolate bar. He chuckled as he read the text. "Aria is having another craving."

"She's pregnant?"

"Yes, and doing it all by herself," Robert said through gritted teeth.

"The father not around?"

"No. She had a one-night stand, and the asshole gave her a

fictitious name. We have looked everywhere for him, but he just disappeared."

"Baligeard," Noah snarled. He didn't know the man who had done this, but if he did, he would take him to the warehouse and teach him how to treat the woman carrying his child.

Robert didn't know what Noah had said, though the look on his face told him it wasn't nice. The elevator bell chimed, indicating that they had arrived. "Mr. Kelly, it has been a pleasure."

"It has, and I will be in touch if I need your services."

Robert stepped off the elevator and headed to the town car that was waiting for him. As he opened the back door, he glanced back and noticed Noah getting into a Bentayga, damn he didn't know they were available in the States. Noah Kelly was a dangerous man, but the look on his face when he told him about Aria showed that he also had a good heart.

S carlett checked in with the donors to ensure their happiness while circulating through the crowd. Despite the place being packed, she heard nothing but praise about the exhibits. She slipped away from the crowd to text Robbie about her forgotten purse and ask if he could pick it up.

Brooke and Eve had already arrived, but she hadn't seen them since. She figured they had found a couple of guys and were flirting their asses off. They had been complaining this morning that it had been a long time since they had seen some action.

As the minutes ticked by, she felt a strong desire for a chocolate fix, leading her to message Robbie for a chocolate bar. Throughout her pregnancy, he was her rock, anticipating her every need and desire.

With her chocolate fix text sent, she breathed a sigh of relief and rejoined the lively crowd. She came around the corner of the Moai statue, or Dum Dum statue from the movie Night at the Museum, and came face to face with Emee Kelly.

"SCARLETT!" she squealed, putting Eve to shame on hyper-activity and volume, then wrapped her arms around her, giving her a tight squeeze.

"Mrs. Kelly."

Emee pulled back and shook her head. "What did I tell you earlier? I am Emee. Mrs. Kelly is my mother-in-law. I like her, but we fight over who makes the best colcannon," she said, her green eyes sparkling, then leaned closer and whispered. "Mine is better."

Scarlett couldn't help but giggle over the confession. "Alright, Emee."

It was then she noticed a man in a wheelchair beside Emee.

"My heart, this is the young woman I was telling you about," Emee said as she placed her hand on his shoulder. "Scarlett, this is Liam."

Liam took Scarlett's hand, bringing it up to his lips and kissing her knuckles. "It is a pleasure to meet you. Emee hasn't stopped talking about you and your friends."

"Mr. Kelly, the pleasure is all mine."

"Liam," he said, giving her a wink. "It's only fair, don't you think?"

"Okay, Liam, and thank you both for your generous donations to the museum."

"Oh, we love the museum. We brought our boys here as soon as they were old enough to enjoy it," Emee said.

"You have three boys, correct?" Scarlett asked.

"Yes. Our oldest is Noah and our twin boys are three hundred sixty-four days younger," Emee proclaimed with a smile.

"Yes, the Irish Twins," Scarlett said.

"Ah, yes. Are you Irish?" Liam asked.

"Maybe. My grandparents passed away a long time ago,"

Scarlett shared.

"Where are Brooke and Eve?" Emee asked, looking around the room for them.

"I don't know. They disappeared a few minutes after they got here."

"Finn and Connor did the same thing when they arrived. I am sure they are at the New World Mammals exhibit. Connor is as big as a bear and Finn loves the cougars," Emee said with a smile. They are grown men now, all with influential positions in the family business. Nonetheless, in her eyes, they were still her little boys.

"And Noah?" Scarlett asked.

"He is late," Liam said with a smirk. Emee had emphasized to Noah the importance of punctuality for the event. The family had not been out in society since the shooting, and Emee wanted to use this opportunity to show their strength together.

Emee looked around at Scarlett and grinned, raising her arm and waving. "Here he is now. Noah, come meet the lady who put this event together."

Noah stepped around the deep red-haired woman, not looking at her, instead kissing his mother on the cheek. Then he reached down and gently squeezed his father's shoulder. He turned to greet the woman with his parents when his world came to a complete stop. "Scarlett?" She was even more beautiful than he had remembered. He couldn't believe he had finally found her.

Scarlett's heart stopped at the sight of him. "Tony," she murmured. The memories of their night together washed over her, his touch, his kisses, the energy that flowed between them as they made love. Suddenly, Emee's voice broke into her memories. She referred to him as Noah. He wasn't Tony Hayes, but Noah Kelly. He deceived, exploited, and abandoned her like garbage. The truth dawned on her like a sudden blow, and that's when her hormones took over. She stepped back and smacked him across the face. "YOU FUCKING LIAR!"

CHAPTER SEVEN

Noah couldn't believe Scarlett slapped him and called him a liar. Well, he did tell her his name was Tony, but that was for both of their protection. He felt his arm pulled back and his mother stepped around him, placing her arms around Scarlett's shoulders before he could even ask where she had been.

"Sweetie, is there a room we can go to that is more private to straighten out this situation?" Emee asked, keeping her voice calm even though she was pissed as hell. Being the quick thinker she was, Emee had surmised that her son left this lovely young woman carrying his children and gave her his alias, Tony. She had raised him and his brothers better than this.

Tears streamed down Scarlett's face as she nodded and gestured to the back of the room.

As they walked away from the crowd, Emee turned to Noah and gave him a look he had only seen a few times in his life. One of those incidents was when he broke her grandmother's treasured vase. Despite her warning not to do so, he threw a football in the formal living room, which she had explicitly prohibited. The football hit the vase square on, causing it to wobble before crashing onto the floor. He deserved an ass-whooping, fully expecting it, but she gave him something much worse. With unshed tears, she picked up the largest piece and looked up at him. Her expression towards him was one of disappointment. He promised himself that he would never see that look again. However, he had today.

He followed Scarlett and his mom down a hallway, longing to be the one with his arm around her shoulders, comforting her. Memories of their night came flooding back as he glimpsed her face, and she somehow looked even more stunning than he recalled.

They arrived at a door. He noticed her name on a plate next to it. Scarlett Murphy, Curator. A faint smile graced his lips. Despite being worried about finding employment, she had a job in her field and was excelling in it. Tonight's event was evident.

Emee opened the door and assisted Scarlett inside. Once inside, she saw a sofa against one wall. "Scarlett, let's have a seat and talk."

"Alright," she said in a small voice.

She searched for Tony for months to inform him about the babies but found no trace of him. Now, to find out he was in New York the whole time. Why had he lied about his name? Emee and Liam were so warm and caring. Why was Noah so cold and cruel? Damn it, did he do this with other women? A shiver ran down her spine. How many children are there who lack a father and means of support?

"Scarlett." Noah began but was quickly cut off by his mother.

"Bastard shut the fuck up," Emee yelled in Gaelic.

Scarlett wondered what she said, though the tone told her it was not pleasant.

Emee sat beside Scarlett, wrapping her arm around her again, pulling her close. "Scarlett, I promise Liam and I will be here for you."

"You will?" Scarlett asked, sniffling and needing a tissue. She saw the box on the corner of her side table, so she stood and reached over. At that moment, she heard Noah's intake of a deep breath.

"YOU'RE PREGNANT!" he yelled.

Scarlett turned towards him, giving him a better view of her protruding stomach. "No shit, you Irish dick."

"Who's the daddy? Some other guy you picked up at the bar, where you picked me up?" Noah threw out the insult with no regard, his jaw taut with anger. She had allowed someone else to touch her and he didn't like it one bit. He looked intently at her round belly. He didn't know much about pregnant women, but she looked like she could give birth at any minute. That meant she was trying to trick him. "I'm not falling for it. You are too big to be only five months. So that means you were pregnant when we had sex."

Scarlett was about to answer his extremely hurtful insinuation when she saw Emee jump to her feet, pull something from her bag, and point it at Noah's head.

Shit, it was a gun. Why did Emee have a gun? Scarlett thought.

"One more word, asshole," she hissed in Gaelic, pointing her Jessie James Unlimited engraved 45 caliber 8-shot handgun at her son's head. "She is five months pregnant with your twins."

Noah's gaze shifted back and forth between his mother and Scarlett. Could this really be true? How did his mother know so much about her?

"My heart, put the gun down," Liam said, wheeling close to Emee and placing his hand on her lower back. He knew Emee wouldn't shoot Noah. But his concern was for Scarlett. Her face showed she didn't understand why Emee had a gun or if she would use it on Noah. Liam was still reeling from what had taken place, but he could also see that Noah had feelings for this woman.

Emee had come back from the spa this afternoon, relaxed and smiling. She told him about the three young ladies she met at the spa. It was apparent she had formed a bond with Scarlett and her friends. She shared with him how she felt this overwhelming need to help and protect the girl.

He had remembered his grandmother telling him the tale of Anu, the Irish Goddess from whom all life emerged. She graced each good Irish mother with the ability to sense when their children or grandchildren needed help. Looking at what was transpiring before him, he thought maybe it was true, and that was why Emee had felt this connection to Scarlett.

Emee's heart was still racing with fury, her mind consumed with the memory of her son's hurtful words to Scarlett. Despite that, Liam was right, and she lowered her weapon. Her eyes met Scarlett's, who was staring at her intently. "Scarlett, dear, sorry about this. My Irish temper gets the best of me sometimes."

She placed her gun back in her purse and moved over to Scarlett, helping her back onto the couch. Liam motioned for Noah to sit. From the look on his father's face, Noah knew to hold his tongue.

It took a few tries, but Scarlett eventually found the words to say. "Why do you have a gun?"

Emee glanced over at Liam, who gave her a slight nod. Even though he was no longer Skipper of the family, he still held a role as the Counselor. Only people who were or would be part of the family were ever to know the truth. Scarlett was carrying the next generation that he was sure of. Because of that fact, she had the right to know.

"She has it for protection," Liam answered.

"I don't understand," Scarlett said, looking between Emee and Liam. She had only glanced a few times at Tony, no, Noah, since he had sat down. The anger she saw in his eyes when he noticed her belly was gone and its place was a look of what looked like worry.

"What I am about to tell you, you can't tell anyone else without permission from Noah," Liam said.

"Why, Noah?" Scarlett asked, her brows knitted together.

"Because he is the Skipper of the family," Liam answered.

"Skipper? Are you part of the Navy or a boat club?"

Emee couldn't help but giggle at the comment. The Irish mafia family had different names for their members than the greasy Italian dickheads that were idolized in the movies and tv shows.

Liam smirked. "No, Scarlett. Do I have your promise not to reveal to anyone what you are about to learn?"

Scarlett thought for a moment, deciding that she was already tied to this family because of the babies. "Yes, I swear."

"Good. Noah is the Skipper of our family, as I was before I passed the duty to him, like my father, his father before him, and so on. From this day forth, you will be protected, as will our grandchildren that I am sure you are carrying," Liam said, then took a deep breath. This next part was going to be the hardest. "The Kelly family is part of the mafia. We control New York and New Jersey, running guns, racketeering, gambling booking, art theft, and rare car theft."

Scarlett's mouth fell open. It was as if the world had turned upside down, and she couldn't believe what was happening. The museum's largest benefactors were the Kellys. They were not ordinary citizens. They were gangsters or murderers. Her gaze shifted to Noah and she stared. Had he given her a false name for this reason? Perhaps it was not enough to excuse him for leaving without so much as a goodbye. They had shared something special. She felt it in the depths of her soul. She searched his soulful green eyes, hoping to find any trace of the feelings they had shared that night.

Emee placed her hand on top of Scarlett's, squeezing it. "Scarlett, do you have any questions?"

"Only about a million."

"Just know that even though we make a living a little differently than most people, the main thing to remember is that family comes first in all things," Liam said.

"Scarlett," Noah said, his voice cracking. "I'm sorry I haven't been there for you."

"Sorry? Really?" She said. "All you had to do was to wake me up that morning or leave me your phone number."

"I left a note."

Scarlett rolled her eyes. "Yeah, stating that you would call me."

"I didn't realize I didn't have your number until I could think straight after the accident. By then, I tried to find you, but you had already graduated and moved away. The only address the university had was the one in Washington State. I had one of my men snoop around, but they only found your parents at the address we had."

Scarlett's eyes grew large and her hands shook. "They talked to my father?"

"No," Noah answered, running his hand through his hair. He was thinking the best way to say the next part without hurting her feelings. "From the information I have received, your father is...different."

"No, shit. The man is an egotistical, religious zealot."

Noah's shoulders relaxed as he let out a long-held breath. Luke had returned with a comprehensive account of Pastor Weston Murphy. He attended a tent meeting where he surreptitiously recorded Pastor Murphy's sermon. He spewed hateful words about women being responsible for mankind's downfall since Adam and Eve. According to God's commandment, women were to be regarded as property and submissive to their husbands. Women were to keep silent and submit to their husbands without question. It was hard for Noah to imagine that the woman he met in a bar had grown up in such a strict environment. Scarlett's vivaciousness had drawn him in, and when she gave herself to him, it was with complete abandon, telling him how special he was.

"Yes, he is," Noah chuckled.

"Scarlett, the reason Noah left the way he did was because I was shot that night. Someone shot me, putting me in this chair,"

Liam said, patting the arms. "It doesn't excuse what he did, but I wanted to let you know the reason he left you in such a hurry."

"Thank you, Liam. Be that as it may, where does this leave me now?"

Before anyone could answer, she heard raised voices outside her door.

"Out of my way. My daughter is in there and you are not stopping me," Robbie yelled.

Noah stood and went to the door, opening up to find Robert Martin standing toe to toe with Luke. "Mr. Martin, what are you doing here?"

"What are you doing in my daughter's office?" Robert said, trying to look around Noah. "Aria, are you okay?"

"Scarlett, is your daughter?" Noah asked, then looked back at Scarlett. "I thought you said your last name was Weston. Did you fucking lie to me again? What else are you lying about?"

Robert reached out to grab Noah but was quickly wrapped up in Luke's massive arms. Scarlett jumped to her feet and rushed across the room.

"Let him go NOW!" she yelled.

Luke looked at Noah, who gave him a nod. Once Robert was free, he ran to Scarlett. "Are you okay?"

"I'm fine, for the most part." She looked over at Noah and narrowed her eyes.

"Do you care to explain?" Noah growled.

"Not to you, asshole," she said, turning her back toward him. "Robbie, come meet Liam and Emee Kelly."

Scarlett went back to where they were sitting. "Liam, Emee, this is Robert Martin or Robbie. He is my best friend's father, who adopted me in a way. Without his support, I really don't know what I would have done."

"Robert, good to see you again," Liam said, holding his hand, which Robert took and shook.

Scarlett was stunned that Robert knew Liam.

"Mr. Kelly, a pleasure as always," Robert said. "Mrs. Kelly, it's a pleasure to meet you finally."

"Robert, what did I tell you? Call me Liam and this is Emee. Please have a seat."

After Robert sat down beside Scarlett, he handed her the purse. "What you wanted is inside."

Scarlett opened her bag, pulling out the chocolate bar. "Thank you so much." She unwrapped it and took a large bite the of chocolate goodness, then remembered she wasn't alone. She placed her hand over her mouth as a pink hue formed across her cheeks.

"Go ahead and eat it, dear," Emee said. "We wouldn't want our grandkids deprived of their urges."

Robert gasped. "Grandchildren?" He wondered when and how Scarlett had found the asshole who got her pregnant. Then the realization hit him. The father of her children was part of the mafia. He wondered which one of Liam's sons was the son of a bitch who left Scarlett with a fictitious name and no way to get a hold of him.

"Yes, Scarlett is carrying our grandchildren," Emee said with a bright smile.

"Who is the father?" Robert asked through gritted teeth.

"I am the father," Noah answered.

"You are nothing but the sperm donor," Scarlett hissed. She had enough of his two-faced attitude. One moment he was the sweet man she had made love to and the next, he was a fucking bastard.

"THOSE ARE MY CHILDREN!" Noah yelled. "You can't keep them from me."

Scarlett stood, stepped in front of Noah, and looked into his eyes. "You want to try me because I assure you I won't be bullied into anything I don't want to do." She crossed her arms over her chest, then turned back to Emee and Liam. "Liam, Emee, it was a pleasure. Please leave your number with Robert. I have to leave before I do something I will regret."

Robert stood and handed her the purse. "I'll call for your driver. Text me when you get home, please."

"I will," she replied. Taking one last look at Noah, she couldn't believe she had wasted so much time trying to find him. Stepping around him, she proceeded to the door.

Noah couldn't believe what was happening. He had found Scarlett and found out she was pregnant with his children. Instead of a joyous reunion, she was walking out on him. No woman had ever stood up to him like she had. They needed to talk and work this all out because there was no way he would not be the father to his children. Just as she was about to open the door, he called out in a pained voice. "Scarlett."

She didn't look around or stop, knowing that if she did, he would see the hurt in her eyes.

CHAPTER EIGHT

Noah stood frozen, his eyes glued to the empty doorway where Scarlett walked out. The shock of what happened left him reeling, struggling to find his bearings. It was a complete nightmare. What the hell was wrong with him to treat her so badly?

"Noah, son," Liam said, coming alongside him.

"Dad."

"We will work this out, but she needs protection," Liam said, concerned for his son and for the mother of his grandchildren.

Fuck, he was right. Why had he allowed her to leave without one or fuck a contingent of guards following her? His mind was racing about how he could find her. Then he remembered Scarlett had told Robert to give her number to his parents. He turned towards Robert. "Where does she live?"

"Get your head out of your ass and think." Robert didn't care that he was poking the bear. The rumors had it that the Kelly family was ruthless when it came to anyone hurting a family member. Scarlett deserved a man who treated her well, taking care of her and her children. And above all else, protect them from the world.

"Don't you think that if I knew where she lived, I would have been with her before now?" Noah said, his hand itching to grab his gun and put a bullet between his eyes. Did he not know who he was speaking to?

"Where did you see me first this evening?" Robert asked.

"Here, you asshole," Noah growled, then he glanced at Robert, who held up his hand like he was holding something. The memory hit him like a knife to the gut. "Are you telling me that Scarlett lives in the apartment one floor below me?"

Robert nodded his head with a grin. "I purchased the apartment for my daughter and her two friends. I have known Aria for years. She came home with Brooke from school during the first break freshman year. If she hadn't, she would have been all alone for holidays and school breaks. When I was searching for a building for them, I wanted the safest building in New York and came across your building. It had the best security system and for that reason, I bought it."

"What?" Emee said, her hand covering her mouth. "She lives on the same floor as Garrett?"

"Dr. Byrne?" Robert asked.

"Yes. He is the family's doctor," Liam answered.

"He has been helping Scarlett, finding her an OB and checking on her several times a week," Robert replied. "He has formed a special attachment to her. She has a way about her that makes people instantly fall in love with her and want to protect her."

"Who is her OB?" Emee asked, her mind still racing with the news. She formed a special connection with Scarlett earlier today at the spa. Then she finds out that this lovely woman is carrying her grandchildren. This had been a tough year, and this news was the bit of sunshine the family needed.

"Dr. Rachel O'Neill."

"Thank God," Emee wheezed.

"Is she the best?" Noah asked. Scarlett and his children deserve the best, no matter what it costs. Money was no object to him. The family's legal enterprises had placed them in the top one percent of the country's wealthiest. Then you add in their illegal operations they could possibly be on top of that list.

"Yes," Emee confirmed with a reassuring smile. "Her father was my doctor."

"Alright. But why didn't Garrett tell us about her?" Noah asked.

"He probably didn't know you were looking for her," Liam said.

"Yeah, you are right. Sorry, my mind is going in every different direction," Noah said as he tried to calm his racing thoughts.

"My darling, please come sit down with me," Emee said, using her pet terms in Gaelic. She patted the cushion beside her. Noah came over and sat down. "I want to say that I am sorry for letting my temper get the best of me."

"I deserved it, Mother."

Emee patted his knee. "You were just shocked."

"What am I going to do? The way I yelled at her tonight, she will never forgive me." The realization of his actions weighed on his heart.

"You are going to apologize to Scarlett," Emee replied.

"Do you think that will do it?" Hope flooded him. He would get down on his knees and apologize if it meant Scarlett would forgive him.

"No, but it is a start. She has been hurt, and she feels like she has been deserted. That is something that doesn't just go away with just words. Prove to her you will be there for her no matter what," Emee said, concerned by Scarlett's comments about her father. Was it just her father, or was it her mother as well? "You will also have to remember that right now, her body has an unusual amount of hormones pulsing through her. One moment she will be happy, the next she will be in tears."

"And the next, she will threaten to cut off your balls," Liam said. He remembered the many times that Emee had said that same thing to him when she was pregnant with both Noah and his brothers.

Emee's lip turned up and her green eyes sparkled. "Well, you deserved it a time or two."

"I know how to run the family business and kill a man a hundred different ways. However, I know nothing about being a father." Hell, he had never held a baby before. What did he do if the baby cried?

"Being a father is something that you learn as you go, but some aspects will come naturally," Liam said. "I know you will be great father, son. You just need to trust your intuition and instincts."

Noah lowered his head and rubbed his neck. The tension of the night seemed to settle there. "I hope so."

As Robert eavesdropped on their conversation, he was relieved to hear Noah's heartfelt sincerity. It seemed like an insurmountable number of obstacles had been placed between them, making it difficult for him to find her. He knew Scarlett would eventually forgive him and give him another chance. On the back of his business card, he wrote Scarlett's cellphone number. He rose and gave it to Noah. "This is her cell number. I know what you do and what you are capable of. You could take me out with a blink of an eye, but if you hurt her again, I will make you wish for death."

Noah took the card and cleared his throat. "And I would allow you to do it. I promise you, sir, that I will do everything I can to make her happy. Her wish is my command. She will want for nothing."

Robert nodded his head. "I know you will. Liam, Emee, if there is anything you need from me, just call."

Emee stood up and wrapped her arms around Robert. "Thank you for taking care of her."

"I consider her as my own flesh and blood," Robert said with conviction. Emee released him from her tight hug, allowing him to walk out of the room. Robert felt Scarlett was going to be okay.

"We should leave as well. People are going to get suspicious about us being in Scarlett's office," Liam proposed. "Noah, you need to get Conner on her security detail ASAP."

Noah looked around the room one last time, the smell of her perfume still in the air. With slow steps, he walked over to his desk and grabbed a piece of pink paper and a pen. He took a moment to think, then wrote.

I never meant to put you through pain. I promise to never to do it again.
Noah

He went over the note multiple times before scribbling his name. To ensure that she would see it immediately upon sitting down, he placed the note right in the middle of her desk. He inhaled deeply, and as he looked around her desk, he gasped. In a small silver frame, there was an ultrasound image of his children. He couldn't help but feel a sense of love and warmth enveloping him as he stared at the little ones. They were a part of him and Scarlett. A product of the evening they shared. He knew that night that it wasn't just sex but something special. It was then he noticed the writing. Baby 1 - Boy, Baby 2 - Boy. He was going to have a son, no sons. With a quick motion, he pulled out his phone and snapped a photo. The thought of becoming a father was terrifying him to the core.

"My little darling, what are you looking at?" Emee asked. She had been watching him as he wrote something, then picked up the frame.

"Mother, it is a picture of my sons," he said, his voice cracking with emotions.

Emee wrapped her arm around him. "They are lovely. Please send me a copy of the picture. I will print them out for the family members to have, though I will wait until Scarlett permits us to do so."

"Thank you," he said, clearing this tightened throat. "I am ready to leave now."

They walked back over to Liam and proceeded out the door. Their guard fell into step as he alerted the other guards of their movements. Noah looked at Luke. "We are leaving. Have the cars brought around."

"Yes, sir," Luke answered, then relayed the information to the others. The amount of security surrounding the family was massive. Even the President didn't have this much security.

Upon re-entering the museum's central atrium, they immediately spotted the person they had hoped to steer clear of.

"Liam, it is so good to see you up. No, I mean out and about," Eleazar Ortiz said with a grin.

"Eleazar," Liam said, his tone void of any emotion.

"Oh, Noahie," Marta said as she rushed over to wrap her arms around him, placing a kiss on his lips before he stopped her. She ran her hand down between them until she reached his cock, palming it through his pants. In the past, his cock would stand at attention. However, he didn't want any other woman. Scarlett owned him now and forever.

Noah jumped back, pulling himself away from her. "Marta," he said, his tone hard and unyielding.

"Oh, Noahie, I am so happy to see you. I've missed you so much," she purred, undressing him with her eyes.

"Liam, they make such a lovely couple. It would be so lucrative for both families if they would marry," Eleazar said.

He'd been scheming for years to grab Kelly's turf and their control of the docks in both NY and NJ. He had to have them to make shipping his heroin and cocaine cheaper. He was still pissed that the hit on Liam had failed. The fucker was still alive, though, in a wheelchair. Instead of the family crumbling, Liam put Noah in charge of it. In his book, Noah was nothing but a pretty boy and could easily be controlled if he could get his daughter married to him.

Liam itched to pull his gun and blow this fucker away. He might be in a wheelchair, but he was always carrying, including tonight. He had his Ed Brown 1911 Signature Edition. It was the Liberace of handguns with the detailed metalwork on the flat surfaces on the frame, the slides, the grip screws, the slide stop, the mag release, and the mag itself. It was a sight to behold. He loathed Eleazar Ortiz, the drug mogul and wanna-be mobster from Columbia. For years, he had been trying to slime his way into his territory, and now it seems he thinks that marrying his slutty daughter to Noah would make it happen. "Sorry, Eleazar, Noah is already taken."

Eleazar was stunned. He hadn't heard Noah was seeing someone. He knew he had to get in touch with his mole in the Kelly organization to extract information about the woman. Once he had what he needed, he would ensure the bitch disappeared.

"Noahie, tell me it is not so," Marta said, sticking her lip out in a pout and wiping away imaginary tears.

"I am very much in love," Noah said. The moment he uttered the words, he realized their truthfulness. Fuck, how the hell did that happen?

Marta was determined not to let any woman take Noahie away from her. She was confident that if she could get him alone in bed, she could prove to him she was superior to anyone else. As she moved closer to him, a wide chest suddenly obstructed her path.

"Take a step back," Conner said, with his arms crossed over his massive chest.

He and Finn had met two women in the New World mammals exhibit. They began talking and suddenly found themselves planning a date. He was mesmerized by the feisty brunette's soulful, brown eyes and couldn't look away. He was intrigued by the woman's knowledge of the exhibit, which rivaled his own. They were coming out of the exhibit so he could introduce her to his parents and Noah when he saw Eleazar Ortiz and his family. He didn't trust them. He swiftly navigated through the throngs of people, reaching his brother just in time before Marta, the vicious bitch, could pounce. She was so focused on Noah that she didn't even see him until he stepped between them.

Marta blinked several times before scurrying back to her father's side. Eleazar glared at Conner. "Well, Liam, it seems we need to move along. I will be in contact with you soon."

"As you know, I am no longer the head of the family, so if you have anything to say, you need to contact the Skipper."

Eleazar clicked his tongue, took Marta by the elbow, turned and walked into the crowd. He was determined to take them down, and the sound of their blood spilling would be music to his ears. The docks were his priority, regardless of how it would affect his daughter.

Conner watched the Ortiz trash disappear into the crowd. He turned to Noah. "What the fuck was that all about?"

"I really don't know, but we need to monitor him. There is something in his eyes that I don't like," Noah explained. "I also need a new security team."

"For who?" Conner asked.

"Not here. Come, let us get Mother and Father in their car. Where is Finn?"

"He is with the girls," Conner answered.

"What girls?"

Conner looked around the room and gave a nod upon seeing Finn. When he saw Eleazar he whispered to Finn not to follow. He would protect Brooke and Eve. They would remain clueless about their identity. A smile automatically surfaced on his face at the sight of Brooke approaching him. He was about to say something suave to her, but she dodged him and went over to Emee.

"Emee, we were looking everywhere for you," Brooke said, wrapping her arms around Emee.

"I am so glad that you found me."

Finn and Conner stood wondering how the hell they knew their mother. They were talking over each other, and it was pretty much impossible to get a word in edge-wise. At last, they halted and Emee glanced at her boys. "So you found two of three lovely ladies that I had the pleasure to meet today."

"Two, who was the third?" Finn asked.

Noah stepped up with a sly grin. "That would be me. I found Scarlett."

CHAPTER NINE

"What do you mean you found Scarlett?" Eve asked, her eyes narrowing. Scarlett had never mentioned someone named Noah before. The only guy she had been with since they met freshman year was the asshole who took her virginity and left her pregnant.

She and Brooke had been there for Scarlett every step of the way. Even before they knew she was pregnant, they saw how much this man meant to her. Should Tony ever be found, she would ensure he experienced the same pain as Scarlett. No one hurts her sister. Ever. Their connection went deeper than blood. They were soul sisters.

Noah looked around and realized this was not the ideal place for this conversation. These two women were Scarlett's friends and, for all intents and purposes, her family. He knew he had to find somewhere else to break the news, as they would probably not react well to the fact that he impregnated Scarlett and then vanished. "Why don't we give you ladies a ride home?"

"We can't leave yet," Brooke explained, then looked around the room to see if she could find Scarlett. She wasn't leaving without her.

"Brooke, dear, Scarlett left a little bit ago," Emee said, hoping to curb another incident that would garner them more attention. "Why don't you allow my boys to take you home?"

Brooke looked at Emee, who gave her a knowing look. "Alright, but we're ready to leave now."

Conner stepped up and offered his arm to her. "Our driver is waiting out front."

Once Eve had her arm around Finn and walked towards the door, Noah looked at his mother. "Thanks. I feel this will not be a pleasant ride, but at least we will be out of the public."

"I am sure once you explain, they will be okay," Liam said.

"You mean the way Scarlett was, okay?" Noah asked.

"She was the one who was hurt. These are just her friends," Liam said.

"Just let them get the anger out and remain calm," Emee said, shaking her head at her husband. Even with gunmen surrounding him, he could handle tense situations with expert ease. However, he knew nothing about how to handle a mad woman. The jewelry box at home held his attempts to calm her down.

"I think I can do that. Thanks again and I will call you later."

Noah hugged Emee, then headed out of the museum. His security team surrounded him as he exited and led him to the armored car, where Rory was waiting by the back door. Rory opened the backdoor and Noah entered, seeing his brothers on one side and Brooke and Eve on the other. With a calm expression, he waited for Rory to enter the car before calling out. "172 Madison Avenue."

Eve's eyes grew large. "HOW THE FUCK DID YOU KNOW OUR ADDRESS AND WHAT THE HELL HAVE YOU DONE TO SCARLETT?!?"

"She is fine. Mr. Martin had her taken home after our meeting."

"What meeting?" Eve said in a clipped voice.

"We hadn't seen each other for several months and it was a surprise to run into her here in New York," Noah said vaguely.

Eve and Brooke looked at each other, revealing their shared apprehension for Scarlett. Emee had been friendly and courteous at the spa, and it was clear that Finn and Conner had inherited her pleasantness. Though Noah's cold demeanor added to their apprehension. "Where do you know her from?" Eve asked.

Noah knew that lying to them would only exacerbate the situation, and the truth would come out sooner rather than later. "Boston."

In a split second, Eve let out a blood-curdling scream and launched herself at Noah, her fist contacting his dick. "YOU BASTARD!"

Noah groaned, covering his throbbing dick with his hands. "Holy hell."

In a sudden moment of clarity, Brooke realized the reason for Eve's anger. Noah was Tony, the man who had gotten Scarlett pregnant and disappeared. She was ready to beat the shit out of Noah, but Conner caught her and pulled her into his arms.

"Let him explain," he whispered into her ear, his hot breath sending shivers down her spine.

"Why should I? He hurt her so badly."

"Because there was a reason why he left, and I'm not saying it just because he is my brother."

"Fine," she said, crossing her arms over her breasts.

Finn moved beside Eve and gave her tiny hand a gentle squeeze, reassuring her. He leaned down, his warm breath tickling her ear as he murmured. "I do so love feisty women."

Eve looked up at him, his deep green eyes causing her panties to become damp and her core tightened with the evil thoughts of what he could do with those full pouty lips. Quickly clearing her head and returning to the topic, she obliged. "Alright, spill."

Noah took several deep breaths and waited for the pain in his groin to subside before recounting that evening, including how he had searched high and low for Scarlett. "I even sent a private investigator to Washington."

The moment those words left his mouth, he saw Eve and Brooke's faces contort in terror. Noah knew he needed more information on Scarlett's father.

"Damn. Did he find her father?" Brooke said with a gasp.

"Yes. He is a fucking blaigeard," Noah said.

"What did you say?" Eve asked.

"Sorry, my Irish blood comes out when I am upset. I called him a bastard."

"Irish?" Brooke quizzed.

"Yes, a chumann," Conner said, his smile breaking out, showing off his dimples.

"A chumann?" Brooke quizzed, her heart racing. Dimples were her weakness, and she couldn't help but wonder if his backside had them. As soon as she saw him standing with his back to her, she couldn't help but appreciate how his tuxedo pants hugged his athletic build.

"Not telling," Conner replied, raising his eyebrows in amusement.

"Hmm, I guess I will have to ask Siri later," Brooke said as her eyes danced with mischievousness.

"I wouldn't have left her that night if my father hadn't been shot," Noah said, hoping they knew he was speaking the truth.

"Oh my God. Is that why Liam is in a wheelchair?" Brooke asked.

He wouldn't tell them the truth on that matter. Only family knows the truth. The outside world bought the fictitious story with no hesitation.

"Yes, but the cops haven't apprehended the person yet. They stole his wallet and threatened Emee. Dad went to protect her and they shot him," Noah answered, with a straight face.

"It really destroyed Scarlett when you left and when she found out she was pregnant, the pain intensified," Brooke explained.

"I will make it up to her and assure her I will never do it

again," Noah said, looking into their eyes, hoping his sincerity showed through.

Brooke met Eve's gaze and gave her a subtle nod. There was something about the way he looked at her that made her believe him, despite her doubts. "If you hurt her again, I will sic Eve on you for a repeat performance."

"And I will stand by and allow her to do as she wishes," Noah declared. As the car navigated the congested streets, Noah's thoughts were consumed with Scarlett and their sons.

Scarlett's mind raced as she navigated through the sea of people, trying to maintain her composure until she could escape to the car. As soon as he noticed her, Harry positioned himself by the back door and offered her a beaming smile before opening the door. Instead of addressing the issue, she gave a half-hearted smile.

"Thank you, Harry," she murmured, climbing into the back of the Town car. Harry went around the car and they were soon driving home.

She focused on her breath, inhaling deeply and exhaling slowly to calm her nerves. She was aware of the fact that her distress could be detrimental to the health of the unborn children. With her eyes closed, she could still hear her heart pounding as she thought about the evening's events and the shocking revelations about Tony, or rather, Noah. He was not only involved in the mafia. He was the head of the mafia; hence, her children's father was a criminal. With each passing second, her heart was beating faster, and her breaths were becoming shallower.

As soon as Harry saw Scarlett, he knew something was amiss. He monitored her through the rearview mirror, trying not to draw attention to himself. When he saw her in distress, he quickly typed a text to Mr. Martin, carefully keeping it hidden from Scarlett's view. Mr. Martin sent a message instructing him to keep a close eye on her and alert him immediately if he noticed any health concerns. As he approached the building, he looked back and noticed she was having difficulty breathing. "Miss Scarlett, are you okay?"

Scarlett was gasping for air, her chest heaving with each breath when a sharp pain suddenly stabbed her lower belly. "No," she cried, tears pouring down her face.

They had arrived at the apartment. Harry parked the car and in an instant, he was around the car and opened the door. Pain was etched on her face, and her breaths were labored, making it clear that she was not well. He fumbled for his phone and hastily punched in Mr. Martin's number, the urgency in his voice apparent. "Sir, Miss Scarlett is not well."

"What is going on?" Robert asked, his brows tense with worry.

"Her breathing is wrong, and she is having pains," Harry explained.

"FUCK!" He regretted not following her when she walked out of the room. "I am on my way. Keep her calm."

"Yes, sir," Harry said, then turned to Scarlett. "You just stay put. Mr. Martin is on the way."

"No, I should be fine," she said as she gasped between words. She swung her legs from the car and stood. She barely took a step before a piercing pain shot through her abdomen, causing her to hunch over.

Harry quickly came to her aid, guiding her back into the back seat of the car. He sat opposite her and retrieved a cold water bottle from the small refrigerator. "Here, take a drink."

Scarlett brought the opened bottle to her lips and took a small sip. She couldn't stop the tears from falling down her cheeks. She couldn't help but wonder if there was a grave issue with her babies. Her anxiety spiked at the possibility of losing them. "Please, God," she said in a prayer.

Garrett was about to enter the building after dinner. When a woman's distressed voice caught his attention, he turned and saw Scarlett sitting in the back of a Town car. Her face was streaked with tears and her body contorted in pain.

"Scarlett," he yelled and ran towards her. He climbed into the car and immediately checked her pulse to assess her condition. He could see the fear in her eyes and knew he had to act quickly to get her to the hospital. "Call 911," he said to the man standing by the car. Garrett figured he was her driver.

"Who are you?" Henry asked.

"I am Dr. Garrett Byrne, CALL NOW!"

Henry dialed 911 and five minutes later, they heard sirens coming down the street.

"Scarlett, sweetie, I need you to take some deep breaths and try to calm down. I am here and won't leave your side," Garrett said in an even voice.

"It hurts," she cried. "I am scared for my babies. Please…"

"Shh. They are fine. Now, take some deep breaths for me, please."

Despite Scarlett's efforts to control her breathing, the stabbing pain persisted. The paramedics arrived quickly, and in just a few minutes, she was strapped onto a stretcher and loaded into the ambulance. Garrett had called Scarlett's OB, Rachel O'Neill, and explained the situation. He climbed into the rig's back and settled onto the hard metal bench.

Just as they were preparing to leave, a sleek black Town car pulled up, followed closely by a black SUV. Three imposing figures stepped out of the SUV, and he immediately knew they were Noah's protection detail. Noah, Finn, and Conner stepped out of the vehicle, followed by Brooke and Eve. Why were they with the Kellys? Scarlett's driver rushed forward, his finger outstretched, pointing urgently towards the ambulance. Everyone's color drained from their faces, but Noah's expression was the most stunning. He looked visibly distraught. As the ambulance pulled away, Noah started running towards it. What the hell was that all about? Did Noah know Scarlett? The many times they were together, Noah never said her name.

The EMTs attached the blood pressure cuff, O2 sensor, and heart monitor. A bag containing saline was hung, and the needle was placed on the top of her left hand.

His eyes widened in concern when he saw her blood pressure on the monitor. It was way too high, and she was still in pain. He was uncomfortable doing a pelvic exam in the back of an ambulance, so he opted to wait until they arrived at the hospital. Rachel messaged him, letting him know she had already arrived at the hospital. She would meet them in the ER. The ambulance screeched to a halt in the ER bay seven minutes later. The crew carefully wheeled out her stretcher, ensuring she did not jostle the monitors or IV. Rachel was just inside the bay doors. She led them to a room that had been prepared with a fetal monitor and a portable ultrasound machine.

"What are her stats?" Rachel asked as she helped them move Scarlett from the stretcher to bed. Concern etched her face as she heard the stats from Garrett. She didn't like this one bit. The nurses swiftly transferred the equipment from the ambulance units to the hospital units. They carefully removed Scarlett's gown, replacing it with a plain hospital gown. "Scarlett, are you still having pains?" Rachel asked

Through tears that were running down her face, she answered. "Yes."

"Did something happen that could have caused them?" Rachel asked.

"I had a stressful evening."

"Alright. I am going to do a pelvic exam and an ultrasound."

"Please don't let me lose my babies," Scarlett said with a sob.

"Calm down. It is not helping your blood pressure," Rachel said, looking over at Garrett and giving him a concerned look. They needed to calm her down.

He stepped closer and took Scarlett's hand in his. "I am not leaving your side. Lass. We both know that Rachel is the bomb. She and I will do everything possible to ensure those little munchkins stay put for another four months," he said, his Irish brogue thicker than usual. Scarlett had told him how much she loved his accent and that it seemed to calm her.

She tried to calm down, but the sharp pains were making it impossible. She loved her babies so much and couldn't imagine a world without them in it.

Rachel examined the cervix to see Scarlett was dilating and sighed when it found was intact with no signs of thinning. This was the first piece of good news.

Garrett made sure her O2 was properly adjusted. Rachel removed her gloves and attached the fetal monitor. As soon as she finished, she turned up the volume, and the room was filled with strong, fast heartbeats.

"Listen, how strong they are," Garrett urged, squeezing Scarlett's hand.

The sound of their steady heartbeats was a soothing rhythm that helped Scarlett find peace. They were fighters. Her gown was lifted, and she shivered as the cold gel was smeared on her belly. With the ultrasound wand in hand, Dr. O'Neill applied gentle pressure.

As Rachel started the monitor, she was relieved to see that everything was looking good. Scarlett's blood pressure had decreased from its initial reading, yet it was still elevated. "Scarlett, your babies are fine. I am not sure what happened. I want to keep you a few days and keep you on the monitors."

"But, my job. I have only been there a few months."

"Your job right now is to take care of your babies and yourself," Garrett said.

Scarlett nodded, realizing he was right. All of a sudden, she heard someone shouting from the hall and it sure sounded like Noah. "What is happening?"

"I don't know, but I'll go check it out," Garrett said, giving her hand a squeeze before walking to the door. The moment he stepped into the hallway, he heard the sounds of a scuffle, and his eyes landed on Noah. Two muscular security guards were restraining him. Noah's security guards were engaged in a heated battle with three other guards.

"Sir, you are not going in there," a hospital security guard said.

"I fucking will. She is carrying my babies," Noah said through gritted teeth.

Garrett paused. His brows furrowed as he tried to make sense of Noah's comment. He must be confused. "Noah, calm down. This is Scarlett Murphy's room."

"I fucking know that. I have to see if she is okay," he said.

As Garrett reflected on his conversations with Scarlett, he remembered discussing the father of her children. It suddenly occurred to him that Noah's alias was Tony. She told him the father's name was Tony and she couldn't find him to tell him about the babies.

Holy shit, Scarlett was carrying the next heirs to the family.

CHAPTER TEN

As Noah and the girls arrived at the apartment building, Scarlett's driver, Harry, informed them of the situation. It felt as though his heart had been ripped out, leaving him numb and empty. He had just located her, and he could not bear the thought of them being separated again or the lives they had created together during that memorable night. When he looked into the ambulance and saw Garrett, he was reassured by the knowledge that she was not alone. He turned back to Conner and Finn, beckoning them to come over to where he stood. He needed a little privacy.

"Get Scarlett's security detail lined up and to the hospital immediately. She is not to be left unsecured for a second. I want at least three guards assigned to her at all times. Two to be stationed outside her door and one on roving patrol. Also, make sure that the security in the building is increased, especially on her floor. Call the hospital president and tell him I wanted it done immediately."

"Skipper, what are we going to tell Brooke and Eve?" Finn asked.

"Nothing."

"They are not stupid and are very protective of Scarlett," Conner said.

"Are you prepared to make them more than a quick lay?" Noah asked with a raised eyebrow. Scarlett had been told about the family. However, she was carrying his children, who were the princes and heirs to the Kelly family. One of them would be the next in line to take over when it was time for him to step down.

The way Eve and Brooke cared for Scarlett was what made him like them. But they had no ties to the family other than his brothers wanting to get into their panties.

Conner and Finn paled and shifted weight from one foot to the other. "Ahh, hmm, ahh," Conner stuttered.

"We just met them," Finn said, peeking over his shoulder at the gorgeous, petite woman who had captured his attention at the museum. She had his interest, but he didn't know if she was the one.

"Then they are not to be told about our family business. If they ask, give them the information that we allow the press and cops to know," Noah said, his mouth set in a hard line.

Before they could agree, Brooke and Eve walked up. "We need to get to the hospital," Brooke said, her face full of fear for Scarlett and her babies.

"We are going as well," Noah said, his voice rigid and authoritative.

"Brooke, Eve, if it is okay, I will ride with you," Finn said.

"We would like that," Eve whispered, her stomach churning with fear of the unknown.

Noah and Conner strode with determination toward their car. Finn assisted the girls into Scarlett's previously used vehicle. "Rory, get us to the hospital as fast as possible."

"Yes, Skipper," Rory answered, putting the car into drive and gunning down the road. As they traveled, Conner scrolled through the list of family members who were trained for security. They were all experts in various forms of protection, including weapons and hand-to-hand combat. They had also shown their allegiance to the family beyond doubt.

"Noah. What do you think about placing several female guards on Scarlett's detail?" Conner asked.

Noah knew a handful of female guards. Each one was just as qualified as their male counterparts. "Who?"

"Claire, Cora, and Gianna," Conner replied.

Noah knew them well, not sexually, but with their abilities. They were just as skilled as the men, some even surpassing them. "I like that idea. I believe it would make Scarlett feel more comfortable having females look out for her. Which men are you looking at?"

"Jonah, Scott, and Mark," Conner answered.

As he thought about each person, Noah weighed their unique strengths and weaknesses. They were both skilled in various forms of hand-to-hand combat and weapons, proving themselves to be deadly killers. "Alright, I want the first shift to be at the hospital in an hour."

"Sure thing," Conner said, sending a text to each one explaining their assignment. The enormity of the task of protecting the mother of the next heir would not be lost on them, and they would embrace it with reverence.

As they pulled up to the emergency room, Noah didn't bother to wait for his security team. The car screeched to a halt, and he wasted no time jumping out and rushing through the doors. God, he hated hospitals. The pungent smell in the air brought back vivid memories of the night his father was shot. He rushed over to the desk and saw a young girl, who couldn't have been over sixteen, sitting behind it. "An ambulance brought my fiancee in. Can you tell me which room she is in?" he asked, giving her one of his panty-dropping smiles.

"Her name?" the girl asked, looking up at the fucking handsome man before her. Damn, whoever the girl was, she was one lucky bitch.

"Scarlett Murphy," Noah answered, watching the girl type Scarlett's name on the computer.

"It looks like she is in exam room six," she replied.

"Thank you," Noah said, turning to walk through the doors that lead to the rooms.

"Sir, you can't go in there," the girl called out.

Noah carried on through the door as if he hadn't heard a word she said. He needed to get to Scarlett, and no one would stop him. As he looked around, he noticed the numbering system of the rooms and set off toward the back. Just a few feet from the door, two rent-a-cops grabbed him from behind.

"LET ME GO, ASSHOLES!" Noah yelled as he struggled against their grip.

"You are not allowed back here," one of the security guards said, pulling Noah's arm back.

"I don't fucking care. My fiancée is back here."

"Sir, you are not going in there."

Noah's voice rose as he argued with the guard until Garrett emerged to investigate. Noah watched Garrett's face as it went through a series of expressions. He finally settled on one of understanding. He had figured it out.

Garrett's eyes darted to the two burly guards, their grip on Noah unyielding. He needed to defuse the situation before Noah pulled his gun. "I am Dr. Garrett Byrne and if I assure you I can control Mr. Kelly, will you let him go?"

The two guards looked at each other, then back at Dr. Byrne. "Fine, but one more outburst and he will be escorted out of the hospital in handcuffs."

"Mr. Kelly, do you agree to their terms?" Garrett asked, hoping Noah's Irish temper wouldn't get in his way.

"Yeah." His blood was still boiling with the fact that they were blocking him from getting to Scarlett and his children.

Noah adjusted his suit as the guard released him, and he trailed Garrett to a room located two doors down from Scarlett's. Before walking in, he turned and motioned for Alec and Thomas to guard Scarlett's door. As soon as they stepped into the room, Garrett closed the door behind them, shutting out the noise from outside.

"Noah, why didn't you tell me about Scarlett?" Garrett asked.

"Because I didn't know until earlier this evening. I lost track of her when I had to rush home after the hit on DAD. When things settled, I began searching for her but came up empty. It was as if she had just disappeared from the face of the earth," Noah explained.

"God, I wish I had known," Garrett said.

"How are she and the babies?" Noah asked, running his hand against the tight muscles of his neck.

"Her blood pressure is high, and she is having irregular contractions. She said she had had a stressful night, which is probably the cause."

"Fuck." Noah slammed his fist down onto the wooden table beside him. He had caused this. He kept hurting her over and over again.

Garrett reached forward, grasping Noah's hand that he had just smashed, seeing redness across the knuckles. Although he didn't believe it was broken, he knew the pain would be excruciating later on. "Noah, you need to calm down. Scarlett will be able to feel your anger, and she doesn't need that."

"Can I see her?" Noah asked.

"Not now. Dr. O'Neill is admitting her for observation and once she is settled, we will see if she wants to see you."

"But."

"Right now, it is important to keep her calm. It is way too early for the babies to be born and you need to do everything possible to ensure they stay secure in her womb," Garrett said.

Numbness infused his body. "She hates me."

"I doubt that. She and I have become close over the past few months and she hoped to find Tony to tell him about the babies," Garrett said.

Noah was surprised to hear that, but it also gave him a faint glimmer of hope. The thought of making it up to her filled him with a sense of determination. "Alright, but I am not leaving the hospital and promise to wait in the waiting area. Her security team will be here in a little bit and I need the hospital security not to get in their way."

"I can do that and will keep you updated on her condition," Garret said. "Why don't you stay here and I will come to get you when she is moved to her room."

"Alright," Noah said, hating the fact he couldn't be the one who was giving her the support and comfort that she needed. As soon as Garrett was out of sight, Noah took out his phone and dialed his parents' number. He could feel his heart racing as he recounted the past hour's events. Emee informed him that his father was tired from the night's activities and once he was settled, she would come to the hospital. Once he hung up with his parents, he stood and looked out the glass door. He saw Eve and Brooke being ushered into Scarlett's room. Although he longed to be by her side, at least she had her friends to lean on.

Finn and Conner kept in touch by texting, keeping watch on the emergency room's entrance while their guards secured all the other doors. Claire and Jonah had arrived, relieving Noah's guard at Scarlett's door. They returned to their duty of protecting the Skipper.

Thirty minutes passed before Scarlett's bed was wheeled out of the ER room and transported to her room on the labor/delivery floor. Wanting the best for Scarlett, Noah called the hospital's Chief of Staff to arrange for her to stay in the top suite on the floor. Her guard followed and no one really paid attention to them, which was perfect. Noah departed from the room and moved to the waiting area outside Scarlett's room ten minutes after they moved her. He texted Finn to bring up their mother when she arrived. He found a chair that gave him a clear view of her door and settled in for the long wait, his heart heavy with worry.

Scarlett was finishing up her lunch two days later. There were fluctuations in her blood pressure readings, although it was much lower than when she arrived. The contractions had ceased, bringing a sense of calm over her. As she rubbed her belly, she felt reassured that the babies were healthy and growing strong. As she savored the last bite of the gourmet chocolate layered cake, memories of Noah flooded her mind.

He had organized for her meals to be brought in by restaurants from all corners of the city. Brooke and Eve provided him with a list of her favorites. The room was alive with the vibrant colors and sweet smells of the many vases of flowers he had sent her. She initially declined the flowers, insisting they be given to other patients in the hospital. But he persisted, leaving heartfelt notes and eventually convincing her to accept them.

She was surprised when Emee appeared, offering to keep her company while Brooke and Eve could return to their jobs. Brooke returned in the evenings after work and Eve stayed overnight since she proclaimed she fit the chair that turned into a bed.

Emee's caring motherly nature was something she always longed for, having grown up with a mother who showed her no affection. Emee cringed as she felt the rough texture of the sheets and pillows on her bed. An hour later, the bed was dressed with Charlotte Thomas sheets. They were made of high-quality Merino wool fabric with a subtle shimmer from the small amount of pure gold thread woven into them. Scarlett had felt nothing like it before and didn't think she could ever sleep on anything else. However, Emee didn't stop there. She upgraded her pillows from hard, flat hospital pillows to ones of luxurious soft European White Goose Down. They were so fluffy Scarlett felt like she was sleeping on a cloud.

When the meals arrived, Emee took them out of plastic containers and placed them on real china plates. She poured the purified water into a crystal glass. She laid her fork on the plate and whipped her mouth on the cloth napkin. When she looked towards Emee, she saw another package.

"Emee, this is too much," Scarlett said. Emee shook her head and pushed the bag towards her. She knew that she couldn't refuse the gift as she pulled out the beautifully crafted pajamas and robes from the bag. They were so comfortable and stylish that they would even impress Eve.

"Nothing is too much for the mother of my grandchildren," Emee said with a warm smile and a kiss on her head. "Can I help you change?"

"Yes, but we might need a nurse to help with putting all the monitors through the pajamas."

A bright smile broke out across Emee's face. "You are wired up, aren't you?"

Scarlett giggled as rang for the nurse. A few minutes later, Tracey came in with a smile.

"What does my favorite patient need?" she said.

"Emee brought me these lovely pajamas and we need help getting all my lead wires put through them," Scarlett said. All the nurses on the floor had been extremely nice, but Tracey was the one who made her feel most at ease.

"They look so soft," Tracey said as she helped Emee change Scarlett. Tracey checked Scarlett's temperature, O2 saturation, and blood pressure after she changed into her new pajamas. She jotted down the reading on Scarlett's electronic chart after removing the cuff.

"What is it?" Scarlett asked, hoping that it was once again normal. Dr. Neil had said if it stayed normal for twenty-four hours, she would consider releasing her. However, she didn't want her to return to work full-time until after the babies were born.

"122 over 82," Tracey answered. "Much better than what it was when you came in."

"Scarlett, that is fantastic. It looks like you might get home tomorrow," Emee said.

"Yes, except I can't go to work full time, only a few hours a day. How will I be able to afford all these doctor bills?" Scarlett said as the color drained out of her face. She was saving her salary to pay for the ever-mounting bills she would have when the babies were born. She didn't have to pay for rent since Robbie refused to take any money for the apartment.

"Don't you get upset over the bills. Noah has already taken care of them. He will also continue to take care of any expenses for you and the babies," Emee said. She took hold of Scarlett's hand and leaned close to her ear so Tracey couldn't hear her. "Please, my child, don't argue about it. You are part of the family and we take care of family."

Tears shimmered in her eyes. Could she really take so much? She had always taken care of herself. Only in the past year had she allowed Brooke and Eve to buy the things she needed when she couldn't afford them. "Alright."

"If you need anything else, please just ring," Tracey said, wanting to give the two of them some privacy. She was informed by her supervisor that Scarlett was a VIP patient and that two armed guards would be stationed outside her door at all times.

She was new to New York, coming from Charlton Heights, West Virginia. Before becoming a nurse, she worked as an ambulance driver and EMT in her hometown. She aspired to work in a large hospital where she could have a positive impact. When she saw the job listing at New York-Presbyterian Hospital's maternity ward, she never believed she would get it. However, she was offered the position. She moved in with two other nurses from the hospital and found herself in the midst of a city that never rested. The news of Scarlett spread, as well as the rumors of who the Kellys actually were and what they did for a living. Tracey found it hard to believe that Emee or any of her family members she had met were involved in illegal activities.

Emee sat beside Scarlett, who was visibly overwhelmed by the money, and waited patiently for her to process the gift. Scarlett was a strong, independent woman, and those were traits that Emee admired and would be needed when she became his wife. Yes, she was getting ahead of herself, but she could see the spark of love in her son's eyes.

"Emee, thank Noah the next time you see him for all he has done while I was here," Scarlett said, waiting breathlessly for her reply. Her thoughts were continually on Noah.

"Scarlett, he is here," Emee said.

"Here, as at the hospital?" Scarlett asked.

"He hasn't left since you were brought in. The staff has allowed him to take showers and change clothes in the doctor's lounge. His brothers and I bring him food every day."

"Where does he sleep?"

"Hardhead won't leave the waiting area, so he has been cramming himself on one of those hard loveseats."

"Why won't he leave?" Scarlett asked. Her heart ached for him. She was still upset with him, yet she couldn't quit remembering how she felt when she was in his arms.

"He wants to be near if you ever need anything," Emee explained.

"Oh." This bit of news caused Scarlett to wonder if she had misjudged Noah. He might just be the man she thought he was when she left with him from the club.

Hours later, Brooke called to state that there was an emergency at work and wouldn't be able to come until much later and Eve had a show.

Emee insisted she could stay, but Scarlett assured her she could manage one night alone. After dinner, Emee stood up, leaned down to kiss her on the forehead, and said goodnight.

Dr. O'Neill came in with smiles over the vast improvements

in her vitals and if they continued through the night, she would release her at noon.

"I am going to take off the monitors. The babies' heartbeats haven't changed in the last twenty-four hours, remaining steady at a healthy 150. Tonight, I would like for you to get up and take a walk down the hallway and back. The nurses will take your blood pressure afterward to see what changes happen, if any."

"Alright," Scarlett said.

"You are doing great, Scarlett and I feel that if you avoid stressful situations, in four months, we will deliver two healthy little boys."

"Thank you, Dr. O'Neill."

Thirty minutes later, the night nurse, Jessica, entered the room and removed all the leads to the fetal monitor. They had turned down the sound, but Scarlett could look at the monitor and see the rhythmic peaks.

"Dr. O'Neill wants you to take a walk," Jessica said in a clipped tone.

Scarlett couldn't quite put her finger on it, but there was something about Jessica that rubbed her the wrong way. It wasn't as if she had done anything wrong, but the way her high-pitched voice echoed in the room or her cold manner when it came to doing her job. "Yes, she told me."

"Well, let's get going. I have a ward of patients."

Scarlett swung her feet over the bed, slipped on her slippers, and put on her robe. Jessica's hand wrapped around Scarlett's elbow, supporting her as she stood. She was unsteady on her feet, and her movements were slow and cautious. She had only been up, placed in a wheelchair, and wheeled to the bathroom to relieve herself. As they reached the door and stepped out of the room, she was startled by the sight of two people standing on either side of the doorway.

"Come on, Miss Murphy," Jessica said, leading her further out the door.

Scarlett shuffled her feet as she continued forward. As soon as she was in the hallway and saw Noah sitting in a chair in the waiting area. He looked pale, with a light beard on his chiseled jaw, and his white shirt was open at the neck.

Noah was thinking about what present to send Scarlett next when he heard her name. He looked up and saw her standing with a nurse, holding her elbow for support. His eyes scanned her body before settling on her face, where instead of anger, he saw a small smile.

"Jessica, I know you are busy. I am sure that Noah would be happy to assist me down the hall," Scarlett said, looking at Noah.

Noah was by her side seconds after jumping to his feet. "I would be honored."

"Fine, but if she gets dizzy, make sure she sits down and call the nurses' station," Jessica said.

"I promise," Noah said, taking Scarlett's arm and linking it over his. He hoped their walk down the hall was a step in the right direction.

CHAPTER ELEVEN

Noah tried to hide his lovesick demeanor, but he couldn't resist the feeling of Scarlett leaning on him as they walked down the extended hallway. He took small steps to make it easy for her to follow. Scarlett stopped halfway down the hall.

"Are you okay? Do I need to get the nurse?" Noah asked, concern written on his face.

"No, I am fine. I just wanted to ask why you stayed at the hospital all this time?" Scarlett asked, her eyes searching his. That was when she observed the dark circles under them. He wasn't sleeping well, and she was the cause. Initially, upon discovering his name was a lie, she was mad, hurt, and disappointed. However, her temper has since calmed, and she's now ready to discuss the future of their relationship.

His deceit had caused her stress, and Noah wanted to be honest with her. He saw two chairs at the end of the hall and thought it would be best to sit and confess. "Let's sit down so I can give you my full attention," he said, pointing to the chairs.

After a few more steps, they finally reached the chairs and Noah helped Scarlett sit down. Once she was settled, Noah moved a chair to sit in front of her. He was uneasy that their conversation was out in the open for anyone to overhear. Before he sat down he looked around to ensure that both his and her guards were in a position to handle any issues. Confident in the security placement, he took a seat. He couldn't believe how nervous he was. Noah Kelly, Skipper of the Kelly family, was never worried.

Scarlett noticed him struggling and saw him nervously raking his hand through his hair. She placed her hand on his knee, feeling the tension in his muscles. "Noah, just tell me what you want."

He closed his eyes, inhaling deeply, and then looked up to meet her gaze, offering a gentle smile. He gently placed his hand on top of hers and gave it a reassuring squeeze. "When I arrived at your apartment building and was told you were in the ambulance, my heart stopped. I knew it was my fault because I had treated you so badly at the museum. I arrived at the hospital and needed to see that you and our babies received the best care possible. Damn guards wouldn't let me through and Garrett came to my aid," he explained. He saw the look of shock when he said Garrett's name. It was then he remembered she didn't know that he knew him. "Garrett is the family's physician."

"Oh, he is a great doctor. He seems to have very liberal office hours since I often see him around the building," Scarlett said.

"Scarlett, he is not your typical physician. He is the 'family' doctor," he said, stressing the word family.

"So, your parents and brothers go to him as well?" she asked, confused by how he stressed the word 'family'.

Noah glanced around. "Scarlett, he is part of the Kelly family. When something goes wrong, Garrett takes care of us since we can't go to a traditional doctor because they are bound to inform the police of gunshot wounds."

"Oh," she said as a shiver ran through her body. She couldn't believe Noah was part of the mafia and was still trying to process the information.

As Emee sat with her over the last few days, she readily

answered any questions Scarlett had. She learned the Kelly family's illegal activities were the primary source of income but the legal businesses were gaining on them. Emee shared every dirty detail yet stressed that family was always first. This brought her back to why Noah had left her that night. His father had been shot and he had to get back to New York to be with his family. She felt abandoned, and she couldn't help but wonder if it was just her hormones playing tricks on her. Pregnancy will do that.

"Scarlett, I know you probably have hundreds of questions about the family. I promise to answer every one of them I can," Noah said as he turned her hand over and rubbed his thumb over her palm. "I couldn't leave you here, not knowing whether or not you and our children would be alright. If you needed something, I wanted to be the one to give it to you. Your health and happiness are my number one priority. I can't promise that I won't fuck up again. But I will try my damnedest to always be there for you and whatever you need, no matter what time, day or night, I will ensure you get it."

Scarlett's hand tingled from the electricity of his touch. The feeling was familiar, just like the night they had made love and created the tiny blessings she now carried. "Noah, I am sorry for not allowing you to explain, but you said some very hurtful things."

"I know and I will forever regret every vile, disgusting word I muttered," he said, dropping his head in shame.

Her fingers slipped from his hand and traced a line up his arm until they rested under his chin, lifting it so she could see his sad green eyes. "I accept your apology, Noah. Now, help me up so I can finish my walk. I want to get out of here tomorrow."

Noah stood and extended his arm, offering support as she pulled herself up. Once she was steady on her feet, they began the slow walk toward her room, his arm wrapped around her waist. As they approached her door, she saw the woman and man flanking it. She had seen them before and couldn't shake the feeling that Noah was somehow involved in their presence.

"Who are they?" Scarlett asked in a whisper.

"They are your guards," he answered.

"Guards?"

"Let's get you settled and allow the nurse to take your blood pressure, and then I will explain," Noah said, giving her one of his heart-stopping smiles.

"Stop that. I need my heartbeat to be normal."

Noah leaned down and whispered in her ear. "You make my heart race as well."

Scarlett gasped. His hot breath sent shivers down her body, making her nipples harden and an ache in her core. "Noah," she moaned.

"I promise to make you feel better after your vitals," he said, placing a kiss behind her ear.

Scarlett glared at him as she removed her robe and sat on the bed. "That did not help the situation one bit."

Noah bent over and took off her slippers. "I'm," he began, giving her a wink. "Not sorry."

"Asshole!" Scarlett said with a growl. Her laughter filled the room as she playfully hit him on the arm. She reached over and pressed the nurse button.

Ten minutes later, Jessica walked in. "So, how did you fare with the walk?"

"Good. I am a little tired, but I think that is because I haven't walked much in the last few days."

"Fine," Jessica said, coming over and hooking the O2 sensor back on Scarlett's finger and placing the blood pressure cuff around her arm. She allowed it to pump up, putting pressure on Scarlett's arm. As the cuff deflated, she watched the numbers.

"What is it?" Scarlett asked, turning towards the screen.

"125 over 75," Jessica answered.

"Really!" Scarlett said. "Noah, it stayed down."

"It did, my Cuishie," Noah drawled, his voice gravelly with emotion.

Jessica couldn't believe a man as handsome as Mr. Kelly was

with someone as plain as Scarlett. Hell, she didn't even allow him in her room until today. If Jessica had her way, she would pull him into the nearest closet and suck him off, then fuck him. He looked like he needed a release, and she was just the woman to give it to him. "Is there anything else you need?"

"No, I am fine," Scarlett answered narrowing her eyes. She didn't like the way Jessica was looking at Noah.

"Mr. Kelly, is there anything I can do to you, no, I mean for you," Jessica asked, straightening her back so her chest stuck out more.

"I have everything I want or need right here," Noah said, wrapping his arm around Scarlett and kissing her temple.

"Hmph," Jessica huffed, spinning around and stomping out of the room.

Even after the nurse left the room in a huff, Noah didn't remove his arm from around Scarlett. There was no way he would ever give her a second glance when he had a chance with Scarlett, and it wasn't just because she was carrying his children. She fulfilled everything he desired in a woman.

Scarlett's heart was still racing from Noah's declaration to Jessica and the kiss on her temple. It was a feeling that couldn't be put into words. Also, she didn't know what he called her earlier, but the way the Gaelic words dipped off his tongue was sexy as hell. As she turned her head, she found herself face-to-face with him. Her eyes widened and her breaths became shallow.

"Noah," she whispered, her lips mere inches away from his, and instinctively her tongue came out, licking her dry lips.

He could feel the warmth from her breath and the sweet smell floated up to his nose, causing him to groan. He struggled to maintain his composure, feeling his self-control slipping away as she continued to tempt him with her presence. Then it happened. Her sweet tongue came out, licking her full lips. His self-restraint vanished, and he kissed her fiercely. The softness of her lips brought back vivid memories of their intimate night together. Despite the wonderful feeling, he craved something more. He angled his head and deepened the kiss, causing her to wrap her arms around his neck and tug at his hair. Then he felt her tongue on his lips, demanding entrance to his mouth. The feeling was so intense he couldn't contain his moans of pleasure. They continued to swirl their tongues around each other until they were both gasping for air.

As she struggled to catch her breath, Scarlett's body ached with the longing for his lips on hers. When she could finally focus, she stared deep into his emerald-green eyes. She could see the passion, but there was something else there, though she didn't know what it was.

As he gazed into her deep, enchanting eyes, he knew he had found the one for him. No one else would ever come close. Scarlett Murphy had captured his heart completely, and he couldn't imagine life without her. She was Mo fhiorghra. "A chulsle, a chroi."

Scarlett pulled back. "What did you say?"

"One day, I will tell you, not now, because I don't want to scare you," Noah said, his mouth twisting into a smirk.

"You may be the Skipper of the family, but I am not afraid of you," she said, raising her eyebrow in amusement.

Noah leaned down and placed a quick kiss on her lips. "I am glad you are not afraid of me. Now, let's get you back in bed." He gently guided her back into the bed, arranging the pillow just so and tucking the blanket snugly around her legs. Once she was situated, he sat in the chair beside her. "I promised to tell you about the two guards who are at your door. They are part of a team that will be with you from now on."

"I don't need guards," Scarlett said, her mouth in a hard line.

"Yes, you do. Scarlett. I hate it is necessary, but since you are the mother of my children, my enemies could try to harm you. I couldn't live if something like that happened. I don't know if I could survive. Please don't fight me about this."

Scarlett thought for a moment. "It kinda sucks that I am thrown into danger and we haven't even had a date."

"Well, I can't have that. Miss Martin, would you give me the great honor of going on a date with me?" Noah asked, taking her hand in his.

"I would love that," she replied.

"Perfect. Once you are back home, we will plan something special."

They continued to hold hands in blissful silence. Then it hit Scarlett. She had seen a woman by the door. "Noah, is one of my guards a woman?"

"Yes. Connor thought you would be more comfortable having female guards. There will be one on every shift," he explained.

"Thank you. It makes me feel better," Scarlett said, placing her other hand on top of his.

Noah loved the feel of her delicate hands on his. "Now, what would you like for a snack tonight?"

"I don't need anything," she whispered, even though she had an intense craving.

Noah's tender touch on her cheek sent shivers down her spine. "I know that there has to be something that my little boys are craving."

"Nope, nothing at all," she smirked, her eyes dancing.

He took his hand away from her cheek and rested it on the curve of her stomach. The nurturing mound which housed their precious offspring. He leaned down and started talking in a hushed tone. "What do my little boys want for a snack?"

As Scarlett watched Noah talk to their children, tears pooled in her eyes. Her heart swelled with joy at the sight before her. It was the most precious thing she had ever seen. "Chocolate cake."

Noah looked up and smiled. "Chocolate cake, it will be." With a few taps of his fingers, he texted Rory, asking for the most delectable chocolate cake in New York. "It will be here soon."

It was amazing how quickly the cake arrived. Noah fed her bite after bite and Scarlett's moans grew louder with each taste of the chocolate goodness. After finishing, Noah lent her a hand and walked her to the bathroom. She quickly freshened up by using the bathroom, brushing her teeth, and washing her face. She was surprised by the healthy glow in the mirror. Was it the relief from her illness or the presence of the green-eyed god sitting by her bed that made her feel better? She opened the door and Noah rushed towards her, offering his arm as a steady support for her. She crawled back into her bed and the exhaustion of the day washed over her.

"Thank you for all you have done for me this evening," she said, ducking her head, allowing her hair to fall in curtains around her face.

Noah brushed it away, cupping her face in his large hand. "I am so happy that you allowed me to help. Is Eve coming soon?" he asked, knowing she was the one who stayed the overnight shift.

"No. She cannot come tonight. I will be fine without her."

"Would it be alright if I stayed?" Noah asked, his heart leaping over the thought of it.

"Are you sure?"

"If not in here, I will sleep out there," he said, pointing to the waiting room.

"Oh. Okay. The chair actually pulls out into a bed."

"Great. I will be right back. I have a bag with some clothes in a hall closet. The hospital staff has been very nice to allow me to keep it there," Noah said. He exited the room and retrieved his bag from the closet. He paused and informed his guard that he would be spending the night in the room, coordinating with Scarlett's guard for surveillance. Upon returning to the room, he observed Scarlett staring at the door. Was she waiting for him? Did his staying make her excited? He took a quick shower after using the toilet. He put on a T-shirt and pajama pants before leaving. When he walked out he found Scarlett fast asleep. He put his bag next to the chair and then pulled it out to use as a bed. Even though it was small, it was better than the small couch he had been sleeping on. He grabbed a pillow and blanket from the nook by the window and laid them on the bed.

He looked at Scarlett's sleeping face and was overflowed with love for her. As quietly as possible he moved close and leaned over, planting a sweet kiss on her forehead. "Goodnight, my love."

After turning off the light, he climbed onto the bed and covered up. A few minutes later, he was fast asleep, dreaming of the woman who was now in his world.

CHAPTER TWELVE

The early morning sun filtered through the hospital windows, landing on Scarlett's sleeping face. As she opened her eyes, she felt confused about her surroundings until she remembered she was in the hospital. Since her arrival, this was the first night of peaceful sleep.

She looked over and saw Noah sleeping on the chair that converted into a small bed. The cramped space didn't fit his massive body. He was forced to lie on his side with his feet dangling over the end. It wasn't until that moment that she realized how large his feet were, causing her to remember the old saying. It was a very accurate assessment in Noah's case, as she vividly remembered his impressive endowment. Her mind replayed the sensation of his cock filling her, and her pelvic floor muscles responded automatically. She could still feel the heat of his body against hers, his weight pressing down as he moved with primal intensity in and out of her pussy. Damn, she was horny and she needed relief that wasn't battery-operated.

"Scarlett," Noah said in a low moan as he rolled over on his back.

Scarlett was surprised to hear him moan her name, but it was nothing compared to the shock she felt when she saw the unmistakable tent in his sleep pants. The fabric was so tight that it had to be uncomfortable for him. She watched as he rubbed and pushed his pants down until the head of his cock slowly came into view. It was magnificent, with a pearl of cum dripping from the slit. She felt a shiver run down her spine as Noah started stroking his cock.

Many times she awoke from a dream to find her hand down her panties and her fingers stroking her pussy. But she never imagined men did the same thing.

"Scarlett, sweetheart, I need you so badly. I only want you, now and forever," Noah moaned. His eyes were closed and he was clearly still asleep.

Scarlett felt a lump form in her throat as a cry threatened to escape. He wanted her forever. Would he be able to break down the walls around her heart and let him in? Could she rely on him to be honest with her? Her hand rested on her belly as she remembered Noah's voice, full of love, as he spoke to them. It was clear he loved their sons.

They were their sons, a combination of the two of them. A product of a magical night of passion and love. Yes, love. She felt complete when she was with him as if he was the missing piece of her puzzle. As she thought about the truth of that statement, she was gifted with two powerful kicks. She leaned down, her voice a whisper. "You are going to be so loved."

She swung her feet over the edge of the bed and stood, watching as Noah continued to stroke himself and moan her name. Her eyes darted toward the door, and she let out a sigh of relief when she saw it was closed. She quietly removed her pajama bottoms and underwear before stepping over to Noah. With a gentle touch, she swept his hair from his eyes and caressed his face.

"Scarlett, baby."

She put her hand over his and stroked his cock in unison with his movements. The perfection of his cock was exactly as she remembered.

"Fuck, baby. I need your wet pussy squeezing my cock."

HOLY SHIT! The words wet pussy from his lips almost made her almost combust. She needed his cock to fill her so completely. She climbed over his legs and positioned her slick heat over his engorged member. With feather-like kisses, she kissed his neck, moved up to his jawline, and ended up at his ear. "Noah, my love, wake up."

Scarlett's voice was so vivid in Noah's dream that it felt like she was right next to him. He could almost feel her hot breath on his ear. He never had his dream felt so real.

"Wake up. I have a wet ass pussy waiting for your cock," she said.

Upon hearing those words, he groaned and opened his eyes. Scarlett was straddling him. She had silky brown hair hanging down, and then he felt her hot and wet sex rubbing against his dick. "What are you doing?"

"I need you to plunge deep into my wet...hot...pussy," she said, drawing out the words.

He pressed his lips against hers, kissing her deeply, his tongue exploring every inch of her mouth. As he pulled away, he planted gentle kisses up her jawline, eliciting a shiver down her spine. "Are you sure, my love?"

With a soft touch, she cupped his cheek and met his crystal-green eyes. "Since arriving at the hospital, you have ensured that all of my needs have been met. I enjoyed the soft, comfortable bedding, delicious meals, cute pajamas, and decadent chocolate cake. But I need something else. My body is screaming for release, and I'm relying on you to help me keep it under control." She wanted him to want to be with her.

"Well, I can't have you wanting something when I can give it to you," he smirked, reaching between them and aligning himself at her wet opening. Her desire was so intense that it was soaking him. As he entered, he let out a loud moan, savoring the sensation.

"YES!" Scarlett said with a groan as every nerve in her body lit up with desire.

"God, I have missed you so fucking much," Noah said, overwhelmed by the feeling of being inside her once again.

"Better than I dreamed," she said, leaning back her body, matching his thrust. The sound of her voice chanting his name echoed through the room as the pressure of her release grew stronger.

"So fucking good. Never again will I lose you." He would never let her go. She held his heart in her hands.

Waves of pleasure consumed Scarlett as her orgasm took over upon hearing that. She scraped her nails up his chest and twisted one of his nipples. "COME FOR ME!"

Noah was always in charge. The Skipper of the family, the man whom everyone complies with his every command. Yet, hearing Scarlett scream for him to come, his body followed hers, releasing deep inside of her. She collapsed against him, and he felt his sons kicking against her large belly. "Is that what I think it is?"

As she leaned back up, Scarlett savored the sensation of his semi-hard member still inside her. God, what that man did to her. She watched his face in amazement as he felt the kicks through her belly. "Yes, they are very active in the morning."

Noah wrapped his arms around her and sat up. "Did you sleep well?"

"Yes. I'm sorry you didn't have a comfortable bed," Scarlett answered. "I hope Dr. O'Neill lets me go home today."

"Home? Do you think it is wise to go home alone?" He asked, not wanting to be apart from her now that they had made progress.

"I won't be alone. I live with Eve and Brooke."

"They work all day and you will be alone. What if something happens and they are not there? I can't imagine something happening to you or our precious little ones," he said.

"I'll be okay." She could see the worry on his face.

"Stay with me," he blurted out.

Scarlett gasped over the comment. "I can't. Brooke and Eve have been so supportive, and I don't want to be far from them."

He reached up and gently caressed her cheek. It was so smooth and flawless. "Fate or destiny used to be just a phrase for me, but now I can see how it can shape our lives. Robbie bought your apartment in my building and one floor above yours is my apartment. You would be close to your friends, and my mother would be happy to assist you in deciding how to decorate the nursery. Damn, you can redecorate the whole place, make it a home for you, the babies," he stated, then in a much lower voice, almost a whisper. "And me."

"Noah, we just found each other and we still have a lot of things to work out," Scarlett replied, as her heart rate was increasing.

"We can do that with you in my, no, our apartment. I will work as much as I can from home," he whispered, his voice filled with longing as he gazed into her eyes. He craved to be close to her, fulfilling her every want and longing. As he spoke, he felt the warmth of her body against his, and the sensation of her skin against his caused his cock to grow harder once more. His hips shifted, and he began moving inside her with a slow, steady rhythm.

"Fuck, Noah." Scarlett gripped his shoulders as she met his moves, stroke for stroke.

"Anytime, anywhere you want this, I will be there," he said. "I will never leave you wanting."

"Yes."

The door opened suddenly. "Scarlett, sweetie, I didn't see," Emee began as she walked in, then stopped. She broke into a huge smile and turned quickly. "I'll just go freshen up my coffee."

When the door opened, Scarlett turned and her face turned red with embarrassment. She turned back to Noah and hid her face in his shoulder. Once she heard the door close, she remained there. "I can't believe that happened."

Noah chuckled. "It is fine. She is probably out there planning our wedding."

"How can you laugh at a time like this? She saw us having sex."

Noah into her eyes. "She already knows we had sex." He placed his hands on her belly.

Scarlett slapped his arm. "That is not funny."

He licked his lips and traced his fingertips down her belly, finally settling on the bundle of nerves at the apex of her sex. With every stroke and pinch, she felt her passion returning to its previous intensity. "Stop thinking and just feel."

She obeyed his command and pushed aside the thought of his mother, focusing solely on the sensation of his touch. With each thrust, the intensity grew until they finally succumbed to their powerful orgasms. Once their spasms had ceased, he stood up and offered her his hand, leading her to the bathroom. "We better hurry before Mom comes back or a nurse comes in. It would be quicker if we showered together."

Scarlett gave him a smile with a raised eyebrow. "Yeah, right."

The hot water felt like a warm embrace as they stepped in, and Noah gently rubbed the soap-covered rag on her skin, lathering it up. He meticulously washed every inch of her body, giving special attention to her breasts and pussy. As he gazed at her, he could sense the smoldering passion within her reigniting his own. As much as he would love to take her once again, they didn't have time. Once he was done bathing her, he turned his attention to washing his own body.

His hands were going to be the death of her. Her skin tingled with desire after just one touch. She watched as he washed and turned off the water. He grabbed a towel, not one of the sterile hospital ones, but one he had chosen for her, and dried her off. He gently wrapped her in a soft, dry towel and grabbed another one to tie around his waist. "Fuck, I forgot our clothes are in the room."

"Oh well, she has already seen us having sex. At least we are covered with towels," Scarlett giggled.

"Minco," he said. He took her hand and brought it to his lips, where he planted a delicate kiss on her knuckles.

"I am going to have to get a translator if you keep speaking Gaelic."

As Emee kept her company the last few days, they talked about the family. After learning about their history, Scarlett came to appreciate the importance of their heritage. The Gaelic language was a big part of that, and she wanted to learn.

Noah wiggled his eyebrows. "I'll give you Gaelic lessons. But only if we are both naked."

Scarlett's jaw dropped in surprise. With a disapproving shake of her head, she frowned at him. "You are one dangerous man."

"Oh, baby, you have no clue," he smirked. They opened the door, looked around, and breathed a sigh of relief that no one was there. They dressed quickly and Noah helped Scarlett into the bed and then cleaned up the blankets from the chair. The fucking thing was the most uncomfortable contraption ever invented. Just as he was finishing tying his shoes, there was a soft knock on the door.

"Come in, Mom," he called out as he looked over to Scarlett, whose face had turned a bright shade of red.

"Good Morning, I brought breakfast for you both," Emee said, trying to hide the smile. She was both shocked and elated to see them together this morning. She knew they were meant to be together and had already started envisioning the wedding, down to the smallest details. The celebration would be an intimate affair but with a grand reception following the birth of her grandsons.

She imagined the event taking place at St. Peter's with Father Michael presiding over the ceremony. The delicate petals of the gardenias and hydrangeas would adorn the chapel, adding a touch of elegance to the ceremony. It would have to be soon before Scarlett was too large to enjoy the day. "You both look very refreshed. Did you sleep well?"

"Mom," Noah groaned.

"What?" she asked, giving him a pointed look before turning to Scarlett. "I brought you a wonderful omelet." She placed the container on the table and went over to pick up the plates and silverware. Noah helped her to serve up the omelet, fresh fruit, hot non-caffeine tea for Scarlett, and coffee for Noah.

The smell of the food was so enticing that Scarlett forgot all about her embarrassment. She dug in hungrily, relishing every morsel of food.

"So happy to see that your appetite has returned," Emee teased as she looked at Noah, who had also devoured his food. Hmm, sex makes you hungry, remembering the many times that she and Liam had been ravenous after a night of lovemaking.

Noah sighed, shaking his head as he finished his breakfast. When they were done eating, he took all the plates and silverware, giving them to one of the guards to be cleaned in the kitchen. He excused himself and went out to make a few phone calls to check on the business. He had been diligently tracking the shipments, making sure he was always up to date.

While Noah was out of the room, nurse Tracey came in and took Scarlett's vitals.

"Wonderful, they are all normal and your little ones' heartbeats are normal as well," Tracey explained. "Dr. O'Neill will be here in a few minutes."

"Great, I'm hoping to leave this place today," Scarlett said.

"I'll miss you but I am so happy you are feeling better," Tracey said. "I'll be back after Dr. O'Neill's assessment."

Noah returned after Tracey left and sat on the bed beside Scarlett. Taking her hand, he kissed it. "Is everything normal?"

"Yes. We are just waiting for the doctor."

"Scarlett has agreed to move in with me," Noah said to his mother.

Scarlett whipped her head towards him. "I did not."

His lips brushed against her ear as he leaned in and whispered. "You cried out yes just a little while ago."

Scarlett then remembered. Damn, his magical cock. "Alright, though, we still need to work out a few things."

"Gladly, as long as I get to see you every day," he said, placing a soft kiss on her lips.

"This is fantastic news. I would love to help you decorate the place to blend both your tastes," Emee said.

"See, I told you," Noah joked.

Scarlett just shook her head. Noah Kelly was one cocky bastard. But he was her cocky bastard and she loved that."

Dr. O'Neill entered the room ten minutes later and carefully examined Scarlett before allowing her to go home. The doctor cautioned Scarlett to take it easy for the next two weeks. If her condition remained stable, would additional restrictions be lifted? Noah wasted no time and immediately made calls to ensure a vehicle and an extra guard were ready to move them from the hospital to home after Dr. O'Neill left.

Scarlett was grateful for Emee's help. She changed into stretchy maternity leggings, a sapphire top that made her feel elegant, and black ballet flats which were easy on her feet. Emee packed Scarlett's bags and arranged to have the excess floral arrangements sent to other patients throughout the hospital. An hour later, Scarlett was surrounded by four guards as she was wheeled through the hospital in a wheelchair.

When they reached the front door, a black limo with dark windows and four more guards was waiting. Noah aided Scarlett in getting out of the chair and supported her with his arm, moving towards the car at a slow pace as he surveyed the area for any danger.

As he helped Scarlett into the car, he didn't see the woman across the street. Her face was full of rage. Noah Kelly was hers and no one would stand in her way.

CHAPTER THIRTEEN

Scarlett's thoughts raced as the black limo moved through the busy city. They were on their way back to his, no, their apartment. Would he have any quirks that would drive her crazy? Her OCD tendencies would be set off by things like leaving the toilet seat up, dirty socks on the bedroom floor, and dirty dishes all over the apartment.

"Whatcha thinking about so seriously, my love?" Noah asked, reaching out and placing his hand on her leg. He had been observing her since their departure from the hospital. Her inner beauty shone just as brightly as her outward appearance. He knew she would make a great mother, as she possessed many of the same qualities as his own mom. He knew he had a lot to make up for and silently vowed to show her how much he valued her from that day on.

She shrugged her shoulders. "Things."

She struggled to find the right words to articulate her fears about the sudden changes. Last week, she lived with Brooke and Eve, planning to have her babies without having their father around. He appeared out of nowhere, and all her carefully laid plans went up in smoke. It wasn't like she wasn't happy that

Noah wanted their babies as much as she did. But it was the fact that everything had changed so fast.

He reached out and held her delicate face, turning it to meet his gaze. "Please tell me."

Scarlett's eyes met his and she let out a sigh. "I am afraid you will hate living with me."

"How could I hate having you near me all the time?" he asked hesitantly, noticing the sadness in her eyes, unsure of her thoughts. With nothing else to do, he spent the past few days lost in thought about Scarlett and their future. He was uncertain about the depth of his feelings for her in the beginning. Was it because she was carrying his children, or was it something else? After his father's visit on the second day, he gained clarity on what he was feeling and why.

He had been watching Scarlett's door, hoping for a chance to catch a glimpse. Thankfully, Garrett kept him appraised about Scarlett and their children's health. He also had the insider information his mother provided. He had her every food carving delivered and any other necessities she needed while confined to a hospital room. His father's wheelchair rolled up to him unnoticed as he was lost in thought.

"Son," Liam said.

"Dad, I didn't hear you." In his line of work, even a momentary lapse in concentration could have dire consequences, making it essential to stay aware of one's surroundings.

"Thinking about a green-eyed beauty who is over there in that room?" Liam asked, even though he knew the answer. The look in his son's eyes was the same he had when he first met his lovely Emee.

"I just worry that she and my sons will be okay."

"You love her," Liam said.

"I can't. We have only known each other for just a few days and one of them, I was accusing her of whoring around," he said as he lowered his head and pulled his hair. "She will never forgive me. I am nothing but a fucking monster."

"You are not a monster and I feel sure once she calms down, she

will forgive you," Liam said. "And, yes, you do love her and I can tell you how I know and how you can tell."

"How?" Noah asked as he lifted his somber face towards his father.

"When you look into her eyes and the only thing you see is your future with her, that is how you will know."

"Did you see that in Mom's eyes?" Noah asked. It was clear to anyone who looked at his parents that they were completely and utterly in love with each other.

"Yes. Unlike your grandparents, who had arranged marriages, I had the freedom to choose my bride as long as she was Irish. Well, that being said, your grandfather and grandmother still had their hands in me meeting your mother. They had gone to great lengths to organize a dinner party for an old friend of the family who had unexpectedly arrived in New York. The family had been locked in a bitter power struggle with the Italians on the docks in Jersey for weeks. I stood shoulder to shoulder with the sentinel and buttonmen for weeks, determined to protect what was rightfully ours. Mother had made it clear that the dinner was important and had even taken the time to lay out one of my best suits for me to wear. I was late getting home and by the time I showered and dressed, the party was in full force. As I entered the living room, the sweet melody of My Lovely Brooke of Clare filled the air, and my eyes were drawn to her across the room. Her emerald green gown was so tight that it accentuated her every curve. Her hair was a deep shade of auburn, and it hung loosely down her back and over her shoulders. The song had a hypnotic effect on me, and before I knew it, I was standing in front of her. The unexpected happened. She looked up at me. I met her gaze and I was lost in shamrock green eyes. At that moment, I knew I would love her until my dying breath," Liam said with a sigh.

"Are you sure?" Scarlett asked as she held her breath.

Noah leaned down and placed a soft kiss on her lips. He pulled back and smiled at her. "I don't want to scare you, but Irish men know who their soulmates are rather quickly. Scarlett, as I sat in the waiting room waiting for news of your condition, I couldn't think of anything else but you. My dad came to visit, and he helped me understand the feelings I was having. You see, he instantly fell in love with my mother when he met her. And I feel the same way. I love you. Not because you are carrying our children but because you are the only woman I will ever want. I want to share my life with you through good times and bad. I want to go to bed with you every night and wake up in the morning with my arms wrapped around you. I know there will be times when we will disagree, but I promise never to go to bed mad. You are my life, my soul, and you are the owner of my heart. Please give me a chance to show you," Noah pleaded, then placed his hands on either side of her belly. "I also promise to be here for these precious little boys and the other children you will give me."

Scarlett couldn't believe what she was hearing. Unbelievably, she wanted it all with Noah. Quickly leaning forward, she placed a kiss on his lips. Pulling back, she whispered. "I love you, too."

Noah's heart soared, and he pulled Scarlett onto his lap and kissed her with all the love he had for her. Her hands went to his hair, tugging him closer as their tongues tangled in an erotic dance. Scarlett couldn't sit still. Her little ass moved restlessly as she tried to gain some friction, which caused Noah's cock to harden. God, he needed to be inside of her again. Suddenly, the car stopped and when he pulled back from the kiss, his breath ragged from the lack of oxygen, he saw they were in front of their apartment building. Well, it wasn't technically hers yet, but it would be as soon as he contacted his lawyer. She would be the co-owner of everything that he owned. "Let's finish this later in our bed," he murmured against her lips.

"Please," she begged. Her hormones were raging, and she wanted some relief. She didn't care where they were. She needed release.

"Fuck, I can't deny you anything," he groaned. Knowing Rory wouldn't open the door until he was given the signal and the windows were darkened so no one could see in, he would take care of her needs. Moving her ass back a little on his lap, he slipped his hand inside her leggings and panties, finding her folds wet and her clit swollen with need. "Oh, my little girl is so wet. Do you need to come?"

"Yes, I need to come so bad," she cried.

Noah stroked her wet folds and then took her clit between his fingers, rubbing and pinching. He could hear her panting and knew she was close. Moving close to her ear, he ran his tongue around the shell and took the earlobe between his teeth, biting down. "COME FOR ME!" He demanded.

She heard his command and the tension that had been building released with wave after wave of euphoria. It pulsed through her body, which seemed to go on for hours. Finally, the spasms stopped, and she opened her eyes and faced Noah's blazing green orbs. She watched as he pulled his fingers from her leggings, bringing them up to his lips, sucking the juices from them. "Fuck me," she gasped.

"So fucking yummy, and I plan on dining from the source when I get us to our bed," he said, giving her one of his devilish smiles.

"Our bed?" Scarlett asked.

"What is mine is yours, so get used to it. Come, woman, let's get upstairs and invite your friends and our family over," Noah chuckled as he helped her back to the seat. He tapped on the security glass, signaling Rory to open the door.

Rory exited the driver's seat and surveyed the area to verify that Noah's and Scarlett's guards were in position. His primary duty was to drive the Skipper and keep him safe while in the vehicle. Over the years, he had also participated in a few assaults with rival families using "The Beast." It is a hand-built monster SUV named Knight XV that weighs over thirteen hundred pounds and has a gas tank that holds sixty-three gallons of gas. With a V10, 6.8-liter engine and sits on a commercial class chassis, it provides 400 hp and 498 lbs of torque. The Skipper didn't skimp on money and it was decked out with luxury carpeting, leather seating, a custom flat-screen television and a TracVision satellite system. It also had indirect LED lighting, AM, FM, CD, DVD, navigation, Bluetooth equipment, overhead tandem bullet-proof sunroof, TV monitors, night vision, and a rear op camera system with a PlayStation 3 and Xbox personal digital entertainment. He had only driven it a few times since the Warlord claimed it for his own private vehicle. The Skipper just laughed and ordered another one, not wanting to take away his brother's toy.

When Rory felt everyone was in place, he opened the back door. Noah stepped out, inspecting the area for any dangers and when he thought it was safe, he offered his hand to Scarlett. Helping her from the vehicle, he offered his arm to her and they walked arm in arm to the door held open by Thomas while the others surrounded them. Once inside, they walked toward the elevator used only by the apartments' residents. Each resident had a passcode that had to be entered before the doors would open. Guests were escorted in by one of the security teams to be vetted before gaining entrance. Once they were in the elevator, Noah pulled his key fob from his pocket and pushed the unlock button.

"I will get you a key fob today," Noah declared as they began their ascent.

"You don't have to," Scarlett reasoned.

Placing a kiss on top of her head and he pulled her close. He knew she was very independent and would fight him concerning money. But she would have to get used to their wealth. Soon, they arrived at the penthouse and the double doors of the elevator opened to the front foyer. The epitome of luxury, with the most breathtaking views of Central Park, the iconic Manhattan skyline, and all points north, south, east, and west.

Scarlett stood, looking around with her mouth wide open. She thought that the apartment she shared with Brooke and Eve was spectacular. But it dwarfed in comparison to this opulent space. Hell, she was impressed with just the foyer. The walls were a soft gray with a white marble floor with a black star inlay. As they walked toward the living room, there were floor-to-ceiling windows that had dramatic views of the city. Looking around, she saw that everywhere seemed to be the same gray color.

"I haven't stayed here much," Noah said.

"Why?" Scarlett asked.

"There is a small bed in the back room of my office, and I usually crash there after a long day," Noah explained. "However, I promise I will not be sleeping there anymore. How do you like it so far?"

"It's nice," Scarlett answered, even though the color and furnishings weren't her taste.

"Change whatever you want," Noah instructed.

"No, it is fine."

He placed his finger under her chin and raised it to look at him. "Scarlett, this is our home, a place where we live, a place that we will bring our boys back to after they are born," Noah implored.

"I know nothing about design," she muttered. Brooke and Eve had designed their apartment.

"Mom would be more than happy to help you. She lives to decorate."

"Okay," Scarlett said as she thought about what she wanted to do to the room.

Sweeping her up into his arms. "Come, let me give you a quick tour."

"Put me down before you hurt your back," Scarlett laughed, slapping his arm.

"You are as light as a feather and we don't want you to exert yourself since we have plans after everyone leaves," Noah said, wagging his eyebrows.

The library was next to the living room, which overlooked the park and had pocket doors to close off the space. Next is the formal dining room, which also had the same mesmerizing views and pocket doors, allowing the entertaining area to flow. There is an impressive windowed eat-in kitchen with a separate corner windowed breakfast room; both rooms have stunning views of Central Park and the city skyline. The kitchen is outfitted and has state-of-the-art appliances, including a Subzero refrigerator with two freezer drawers, two Miele dishwashers, a Miele oven, a Miele speed oven/microwave, a Miele warming drawer, a Miele wine refrigerator, a Wolf double oven, a Wolf range with six burners and a griddle, a Wolf vented hood, and two sinks. Besides the breakfast room, there is an island with seating for four and a large pantry closet with built-in storage. An elegant, full bathroom clad in onyx with a shower and coat closet completes the public spaces.

Noah walked them into the extraordinary master suite. The corner of the bedroom faced the south and east, allowing brilliant sunlight to illuminate the room throughout the day. Attached was an enormous dressing room and a separate over-sized closet. The suite had two lavish, windowed en-suite master bathrooms. Both bathrooms have radiant heat in the floors, marble slabs, and polished nickel fixtures. The second bedroom suite faced the south, with a large closet and an en-suite with a floor-to-ceiling marble shower with radiant heated floors. The third bedroom was a corner suite that faced south and west, with beautiful views of Central Park and the Midtown skyline. When Noah finished the tour, he returned to the living room and placed her on one couch near the window. "So, do you think you can live in this humble abode?" Noah asked with a smile.

"Are you crazy? This place is unbelievable. I'm going to need a map just to get around."

"I thought the third bedroom would be a splendid room for a nursery," Noah said.

Her lips turned up in a toothy grin. He was thinking about the nursery. "Me too."

"Alright, let's call our family and invite them up," Noah said, placing a quick kiss on her sweet lips. He knew Brooke and Eve were more than just friends to Scarlett.

"Okay," Scarlett said, even though she was worried about how her friends would take the fact that she was moving in with Noah.

"**D**addy, there is some whore that's saying she is having Noah's baby," Marta whined, twirling her hair around her finger.

"Oh, my love, I will take care of the issue," Eleazar said, placing his arm around his daughter.

Marta sobbed on her father's chest. "I want to be the one to give Noah his son."

"You will, sweetheart, you will. I have someone on the inside and they will bring the bitch to us," he chuckled darkly as he sent a text.

CHAPTER FOURTEEN

"You have a cook and a housekeeper?" Scarlett asked. After receiving a text from everyone that they would be there at six o'clock, Scarlett got up to go to the kitchen to see if there was any food. That was when Noah informed her about the household staff.

"Yes, we have a cook and a housekeeper."

"Who are they, and do they live here?" Scarlett was unsure about them being around all the time. The apartment was large, but not that large.

"Molly is the cook and Angela is our housekeeper. They live five floors down in their own private apartments. Most of the family live here in this building," he explained.

Scarlett looked around and saw that the place was immaculate, with not a speck of dust anywhere, which calmed her OCD tendency. "Is Molly a good cook?"

"She is a formally trained chef from the Culinary Institute of America here in New York."

"Wow. So, are they part of the family, or are they just an employee?" She was still coming to grips with the whole mafia thing.

"I allow no one this close without being part of the family.

Both of their families have been part of the family in some capacity for decades," he answered, taking her hand in his. Her touch was so captivating that he knew he could spend his entire life holding her hand and feel complete. He brought it to his mouth and kissed each knuckle before turning it over and kissing her palm. "So you can stop worrying about the dinner. Molly will be here in about an hour to begin preparations. However, we need to discuss a few things before they get here."

Scarlett's posture stiffened as she sat upright, mentally preparing for the challenging conversation. She wondered if she had already offended him.

Noah immediately noticed the change in Scarlett's body. "My one and only, lean back and relax."

Scarlett did as Noah told her and he reached down, picking up each of her feet, slipping off her shoes, and placing them onto his lap, where he massaged each one. The sensation was so intense that she couldn't help but moan softly.

"God, baby, you can't make those sounds. I am hanging on by a thread from not christening each and every room in this apartment," he said, adjusting his hardened cock. "Now, you can't tell Brooke and Eve about the fact that my family is part of a mafia."

"I know. Why me and not them?" Scarlett asked.

"You are family. Brooke and Eve are not."

"We are not married."

"Not yet, but soon," Noah said with a tone of assurance.

"Married? You are crazy. We have only known each other a few days," Scarlett said, her voice squeaking.

"Do you love me?" Noah asked.

"Yes, but."

"No buts. You love me and I love you. We are going to be parents in a few months."

"Don't you need to marry someone with Irish blood or something?" Scarlett asked.

Her reluctance to marry Noah wasn't due to a lack of love. It was the fact she was scared. She was clueless about how to be a wife. Where little girls learned from their mothers to be wives, there was no way she would be like her mother. Hell, she was just coming to terms with the fact that she was going to be a mother.

"Do you know anything about your family history?" He asked, hoping she wouldn't be upset over the intrusion that he had investigated her lineage.

"Not really. My mother's parents died when I was very young. I don't know when my father's parents died. Neither one of them ever really spoke of them. But I think they visited a few times when I was little."

"Don't be upset. I looked into your family history. Your great-grandparents from your father's side came from Ireland in 1905. Both of them were in their early twenties and established themselves in Boston. They had three children; however, only one survived the Spanish flu. Your grandfather got married to his childhood sweetheart and moved to Washington State from Boston. They had one child, your father. They were killed by a drunk driver when you were five," Noah said.

"So, I am Irish?" Scarlett asked, excited to find out her ancestry. That explained her red hair and green eyes. Throughout the years, she was frequently asked if she had Irish heritage, and she now knows that Irish blood runs through her veins.

"Yes, but it is not the reason I want to marry you. I love you and can't wait to spend the rest of our days together," he said as he lifted her feet and slid off the couch. On one knee, he held her left hand. "Oh, shit, wait right there."

He jumped and ran to his office, quickly opening the safe and collecting the green velvet box. It was a family heirloom passed down to him from his grandmother. He couldn't resist smiling as he lifted the lid and saw how perfect it would look on her finger. After shutting the lid, he rushed back to his love. He opened the box, kneeling beside her once again. "With the heart, love is shown. With the hands, friendship grows. With the crown, loyalty is given. With all three, it's best to live. The symbol of the Claddagh, for all to behold, is a symbol of my faith and my love." Taking the ring from the box, he slipped it on her left finger. "When you wear the Claddagh on this finger with the heart pointing outward, it means you are engaged. This ring has been passed down to every firstborn son. Scarlett Murphy, will you give me extreme pleasure in agreeing to be my wife?"

Scarlett's tear-filled eyes glistened as she looked down at the beautiful ring on her finger, then turned towards Noah. "Yes."

Noah leaned in, his hands cupping her face as he captured her lips in a searing kiss. After they finally broke apart, she noticed how his smile lingered on his lips, as if he didn't want to let go of the moment. "You have made me the luckiest man on the earth."

He moved her over to him on the couch, and they sank into the cushions, his arm cradling her as she nestled her head on his shoulder. Her hand rested on his chest, with the sun catching the diamond, shooting a dazzling prism around the room.

"It is breathtaking and heavy," she said, not taking her eyes from the ring.

"That's because it is platinum with a two-carat diamond. Do you like it? Because if you don't, we can go to the jeweler's and pick out one you do."

"NO!" she screamed, bringing her hand to her chest as she wrapped her other hand around it. "I love it. It is perfect."

"Good. When we get married, you will turn the ring around so the heart is facing you."

"When do you want to get married?"

"Is tonight too soon?" he asked, his lips turning up in a wicked grin.

"Yeah. I think your mother would have a fit," Scarlett giggled.

"Máthair would cut off my coileach," he said, shifting uncomfortably.

"I really need a translator for you. What did you say?"

"Máthair is mother," Noah said as he accented each syllable.

"Máthair," Scarlett repeated. "And the other word?"

"Ah, well," he said, rubbing his neck.

Scarlett turned to face him and raised an eyebrow.

"Coileach means cock," he whispered.

A giggle escaped her lips. "Cock?"

"Yes, cock."

With the meaning of the two Gaelic words in mind, Scarlett thought about the statement. "I believe you are right. So we can't have it tonight. How does a month from now sound? I will be six months pregnant and big as a house and I don't think they make a wedding gown to cover all this," she said, motioning to her pregnant belly.

"I am sure they do. Isn't Eve a clothing designer?" He asked.

"Damn, I completely forgot about that. This pregnant brain is the worst. I just don't know if a month is long enough for her to make something and we don't have a priest or a license or a church."

"Calm down. Máthair will take care of everything. I promise," he said, placing a kiss on her head.

They spent the rest of the afternoon talking about the wedding and possible changes to the apartment. Molly arrived and Noah introduced Scarlett to her.

Molly had gone to the market when she received Noah's text about cooking dinner for eight. The gossip grapevine had been abuzz with the news that the Skipper was going to be a dad to someone outside the family. When she walked into the apartment, she was welcomed by her boss and a stunning redhead with a large pregnant belly. Like most single women in the family, Molly had dreamed that Noah would fall in love with her. However, one look at Noah as he looked down at Scarlett, and it was crystal clear that he was head over heels in love with her. She was dating one of the guards and even though it was new, she had high hopes.

"Molly, follow Scarlett's instructions as you would my own. She is now the Lady of the House," Noah said, his tone absolute.

"Of course, Skipper," Molly answered.

"Molly, how often do I have to tell you to call me Noah when we are here?"

"And please call me Scarlett."

"Thank you. I need to start dinner, especially since Mr. Connor is coming."

After Molly entered the kitchen, Scarlett wanted to slip downstairs to pick up a few things before Brooke and Eve got home.

"You have been up since you came home. Don't you think you might take a nap or something before everyone gets here?" Noah asked. She had just been released from the hospital and he hoped the next time she was there was to give birth to their sons. He didn't think his heart could take another health scare.

"It will only take us a few minutes. I know what I want to grab, please," she said, sticking out her lower lip in a pout.

"Grrr. I can't deny you. Alright, let's go get your things and when we get back, we are going to bed."

"Bed?" Scarlett said in a husky voice as she thought about them naked in their California King bed.

"To sleep, for now," he answered with a smirk, then ran his finger up her arm, causing goosebumps to break out. "But after everyone leaves, I promise to take care of your every need and desire."

"Damn, I think I need a cold shower."

"Baby, you and me both. Now, let's get that cute ass moving," Noah said, slapping her butt.

Noah sent a text informing their guard that they were going down to Scarlett's old apartment and to do a security check before they arrived. When he received a text saying it was secure, they got in the elevator and traveled down one floor.

"I still can't believe that we lived so close to each other and never ran into each other," Scarlett said.

"I didn't stay here much. Ever since that night when I left you."

"Don't," she said, smoothing her hand along his jawline. "I have forgiven you and we are moving forward."

"Ever since that night, I have been looking for the person or persons who shot my father. All the while, I had the family business to take care of as well. I was putting in twenty-hour days, crashing on the small bed in my office."

"How awful. You still don't know who did it?" Scarlett asked, concern written all over her face. She didn't know what she would do if something happened to Noah.

"No, but I won't stop until I find out who."

They arrived at her door. Scarlett unlocked it and turned off the alarm system once inside. Noah followed her in and looked around. Brooke and Eve did a fantastic job decorating the apartment, as Scarlett had mentioned. His mother might even request their help for his and Scarlett's place. He hoped they would take the news okay, as Scarlett didn't want them to be upset. He followed her through the apartment and into her bedroom. It surprised him that it was not a "girly" style bedroom. Instead, it was decorated in shades of green and brown.

"Noah, can you get the suitcase down from the top of the closet?" Scarlett asked.

"Sure," he answered, walking into her closet to find it impeccably organized. It reminded him of his closet. Lifting down the case, he placed it on a table along the wall. "Is there anything else I can help you with?"

"No, I am going to grab several things and after we break the news, I am sure that Brooke and Eve will pack up the rest," Scarlett said with a sad smile. It wasn't the fact that she was moving in with Noah that made her sad. It was because she had been roommates with Brooke and Eve for almost five years. They had been with her through all the ups and downs, never faltering in their loyalty.

Noah sat down on a small bench and watched Scarlett pull

items off the hook, then meticulously fold the article of clothing. He had been concerned that she would think he was an obsessive asshole who liked to have his boxers ironed and his t-shirts folded in a perfect rectangle.

Scarlett was so engrossed in packing that she barely noticed Noah, but when she finally looked up and saw him gazing at her, she grew anxious about his thoughts. Maybe she should open her underwear drawer, grab a handful of panties, and throw them in the suitcase. However, she couldn't do it. Tears flowed as she bowed her head. She was such a weirdo.

Noah jumped to his feet as soon as he noticed tears beginning to fall. He embraced her tightly with his strong arms. "Why are you crying?"

It took several minutes of her trying to control her tears before she whispered. "I am such a weirdo. I mean, seriously, who folds their underwear into perfect rectangles?"

Noah placed his fingers under her chin and raised it to look at her lovely, tear-stained face. "If I didn't think we were a match made in heaven, this confirmed it. I have to have my boxers ironed before they are folded into rectangles and placed in the second drawer by color."

"Really?" Scarlett said, amazed by his confession.

"Yes. I am so happy that we both love things being in their place. Growing up, Connor and Finn were both pigs. They drove me crazy with how they kept their rooms and how they threw their toys around. Now, let's dry those eyes and get finished."

Ten minutes later, two suitcases were perfectly packed and were being carried by Mark and Luke. Scarlett remembered her laptop bag as she was heading to the elevator after locking the door. Turning around, she headed back.

"Where are you going?" Noah asked.

"I forgot my laptop bag."

"I can get it for you," Thomas said. "But I will need your key and the alarm code."

"Thank you," Scarlett said, handing him her keys and telling him the code.

Thomas returned a few minutes later, bag in hand, and returned Scarlett's keys to her. "We can take it from here, Thomas," Noah advised, taking the bag from him. "Go back to your station."

Thomas nodded and gave him a forced smile.

Once they were back in their apartment, Noah helped Scarlett unpack her suitcases. He ensured each item was perfectly positioned in the right drawer, shelf, or hanger.

"Your clothing looks mighty fine next to mine," he said, wrapping his arms around her and placing his hands on her belly.

"They do," she said, placing her hands on his. She loved the connection that they shared and prayed that it would never end.

"Time for a nap," Noah said, placing a feather-light kiss on her neck.

She turned, reaching up and running her fingers into his hair, and began scratching the back of his neck. "I'm not tired."

"Please behave. I already made you a promise for later."

She looked up at him. "Fine, as long you lay down with me."

He nodded at her, took her hand, and led her to the bed. She sat down and he removed her shoes and then his own. He had no intention of sleeping. He would stay with her until she drifted off. Once they were lying down, he pulled the covers over them. They lay on their sides, the softness of the bed enveloping them as they whispered their confessions of love and drifted off into a peaceful slumber.

Eleazar's phone buzzed, and a malevolent smile formed on his lips. The mole had managed to acquire a significant piece of the puzzle, a valuable asset that would aid in their mission. Noah Kelly's time as ruler was about to come to an end. Now was the time to call in a marker. Dialing the number, he waited for them to answer.

"Hello."

"Get prepared because soon you will have your lost sheep home and she is in need of purification," Eleazar said with an evil chuckle.

CHAPTER FIFTEEN

As Scarlett's eyes fluttered open, the first thing she saw was her handsome fiancé, sound asleep beside her. She could still see the bags under his eyes, and she knew he must have been just as exhausted as she was. It seemed like fate had brought her together with a man who loved her unconditionally and made her feel cherished.

Her father, Weston, habitually belittled her and reminded her of her worthlessness as a child. She was a disappointment and disgrace to her father. God, she was glad she didn't listen to him.

"Hey," Noah said, his voice husky, full of sleep.

"Hey. Nice nap?" Scarlett couldn't help but grin over her comment.

"Fuck, I can't remember the last time I slept in the middle of the day," he said. "Did you sleep well?"

"Oh my, yes. This bed is so comfortable," Scarlett moaned, shifting her body deeper into the plush goodness.

"Fuck," Noah said with a groan.

"What is the matter?" Scarlett asked, lowering her voice to a sexy, deep throat tone as she ran her finger down his exposed neck as desire percolated between them.

He never broke eye contact as he brought her finger to his lips and sucked on it, sending a jolt of electricity through her body. He saw her eyes grow wide, and she let out a whimper as a rush of warmth spread from her head to her toes. He released her finger from his mouth, and his lips curved into a smile. "Now, you know how it feels."

"Tease."

"Giodróg, don't be mad. We don't have time because what I want to do to you will take hours," Noah said with a wicked smile.

"When are you going to start teaching me, Gaelic," Scarlett said, sitting up in the bed and crossing her arms over her chest.

"When we are both naked," Noah said, his eyes twinkling in mischief.

"You are a pig. Since we are not going to have sex, we better get up and get ready for our company," Scarlett said.

Noah reached out and pulled her into his arms. "I promise I will make it up to you."

"Okay."

"Noah, Scarlett, are you awake?" Emee called out, rapping softly on the door.

It didn't surprise him that his mother was already there. "I knew she would be at least an hour early. Máthair, we are sleeping."

Scarlett slapped his arm. "Stop lying to your mother. Emee, we will right out."

Noah nuzzled her neck, placing kisses up to her ear. "Fuck, hearing you speak Gaelic makes me so fucking hard."

It was undeniable that her panties were soaked with desire. She was counting down the hours until they were alone tonight. Just as she ran her hand down his chest, Emee's voice interrupted them from outside the door.

"Okay, dear. I brought over some decorating books I thought we could look at before dinner."

"See, I told you," Noah whispered, then leaned in, capturing her lips with a kiss of promise. His heart raced with anticipation as he imagined kissing, licking, and sucking every inch of her body. As he released her lips, he felt like his lungs were about to burst. "I fucking love you so much."

"I love you."

They got up and began getting ready for their company. Noah wore Kiton dark wash jeans, a white button-down shirt, and Salvatore alligator oxford shoes. Splashing on his favorite Dior Homme cologne, he opened his drawer that held his collection of watches.

"MY GOD, Noah!" Scarlett said, looking down at the drawer. "How many watches do you have?"

Noah shrugged his shoulders. "A few."

"A few, my ass," Scarlett said, her focus on rows and rows of watches. "Are those diamonds?"

"Yes," he answered matter factually.

"Do I want to know how much money these are worth?"

"Probably not," Noah answered, his mouth turning up in a smirk. He picked up the Louis Monet Meteoris and strapped it onto his wrist. This watch alone was 4.3 million dollars.

Scarlett shook her head and went into the closet to pick out something to wear. She selected a pair of skinny stretch pregnancy dark-washed jeans and paired them with a white blouse featuring a twisted cross design. Since Noah was dressing down she put on a pair of comfortable ballet. With a quick flick of her wrist, she gathered her hair into a low ponytail and secured it with a gem clasp. She normally didn't wear much makeup, so she only applied a bit of mascara, some blush on her cheekbones, and her favorite lip gloss.

Noah just watched in fascination as his delicate yet feisty fiancée got ready for the evening. Before Scarlett, he had never really paid attention to the nuances of a woman. He had a pattern of using women for his pleasure but never committed to a relationship. He was always honest with them, ensuring they understood he wasn't interested in anything romantic. It was sex with no commitments. Then, five months ago, he walked into "O" and saw her. Scarlett captivated him like no other had ever done. He lost his heart to her that night, though he was just too stupid at the time to realize it. Even though he screwed up in the beginning, fate intervened and helped him make it right. Scarlett was his life now, a part of his soul and he would do anything to protect her.

Scarlett had just finished applying her lip gloss when she noticed Noah staring at her. "What?"

Stepping forward, he wrapped his arms around her and pulled her close. "I just love you so much and I can't believe that you are here."

"I love you too." She loved hearing him say I love to her.

"We better get out there," Noah said.

Noah took her left hand and they walked out of the room. Emee bounded to her feet and rushed to them.

"Leanbh milis," Emee said, pushing Noah out of the way and pulling Scarlett into a hug. "Don't you look lovely? I love those jeans on you."

"Thank you, Emee," Scarlett said. Emee's hug was full of love and warmth, something her mother had never done. Displays of affection were not permitted in her family, ever. Her father said it was a wasted effort on a girl. In God's eyes, men were the ones to be pampered and loved. "What does leanbh miles mean? I'm trying to learn Gaelic."

"Oh, how wonderful. It means sweet child," Emee said as unshed tears filled her eyes. She couldn't believe just how perfect this woman was, not only for her son but for the family. "I have brought over some magazines and paint samples. Have you decided which room will be the nursery? Because I thought the third guest room would be perfect," Emee said without taking a breath.

Noah stood back and watched his mother embrace Scarlett. It was a beautiful sight as she showered Scarlett with her motherly love. He couldn't be happier to see how his parents had accepted her into their lives and family. "Hey, what am I, chopped liver," he said, with his hand over his heart.

"Son, it looks like you have been replaced," Liam said, wheeling around the corner.

"Yeah, but I am okay with that," Noah said, kissing Scarlett's temple.

"OH MY GOD!" Emee screamed, holding up Scarlett's left hand. "Liam, look at what hand your máthair's Claddagh is on."

"Well, it looks like we have something to celebrate tonight," Liam said, his lips turning into a massive smile. "Do you have good champagne here?"

"I have two bottles of Armand de Brignac Brut Gold Champagne," Noah answered.

"Oh my word, that would be perfect," Emee said. She couldn't be happier unless her other two boys would find women who would complete them as well as Scarlett had done for Noah. She believed in her heart that Brooke and Eve were those women.

"I'll have to go down and get them from the wine vault, along with a few bottles, for dinner," Noah said.

"I am sorry you won't be able to drink the champagne, though when these little ones appear, we will have a bottle to toast their birth," Emee said.

"It is okay. I am not a big drinker, other than Jameson occasionally."

Noah leaned into her ear. "It was such a surprise. I will remember you ordering it for the rest of my life."

Scarlett turned, her lips inches away from his. "As do I."

Liam smirked at Scarlett's admission to drinking Jameson. There was no doubt she was Irish through and through.

Noah came back twenty minutes later with several bottles in his hands. It was nice to have the wine vault in the building. When he built their next home, they would have a wine cellar. His mom pulled out the ice buckets and placed ice in each. He put the champagne in them to chill, waiting for the rest of the family to open them. He opened the wine to let it breathe. Once he was done, he joined Scarlett and his mother on the couch. Even the short time away from her, he needed her touch. He took her hand in his and sighed.

"So, have you discussed a date?" Emee asked, her mind racing on the images of a grand wedding fit for The Skipper and his wife.

"Yes. We want a small ceremony in a month," Noah answered, smiling at Scarlett.

"A MONTH!" Emee yelled. "Impossible."

"Máthair, we want to be married before the babies come," Noah said.

"Emee, I am growing by the day and would love to walk down the aisle, not waddle."

Emee was silent for a few moments. She knew a small, intimate wedding would be best because of Scarlett's delicate situation. "I think we can do that," she said. "But once you are back on your feet after the wee ones are born, we will have a grand reception."

"That sounds perfect. Thanks, Emee," Scarlett said.

"None of that, and I hope you will consider calling me Máthair."

Tears formed in Scarlett's eyes. "Really?"

"Of course, my treasure, I have always wanted a daughter," Emee said, wiping a tear off Scarlett's face.

"THE PARTY CAN START NOW, CONNOR IS IN THE HOUSE!" Connor boomed, walking into the living room with Brooke on his arm.

"You big goof," Brooke said, pushing his arm.

"Hey, don't damage the goods," he said, all the while wagging his eyebrows.

Brooke just shook her head and turned back to everyone in the living room.

If someone had asked her at the beginning of the week what

she thought of Noah, she would have told them he was pond scum. However, as the week progressed, he demonstrated how much he cared about Scarlett. Brooke knew Noah was a wealthy, powerful businessman. Instead of only visiting the hospital after work, he stayed in the waiting room the whole time. He even slept on a small hard loveseat in the waiting area. Noah also took care of all the little things to make Scarlett's stay more comfortable. Maybe there was more behind the story and she needed to trust her friend's judgment.

"Scarlett, you look wonderful," Eve said, rushing over and pulling Scarlett into a tight hug.

"I feel wonderful. It is so nice to be out of the hospital and Noah has been taking care of me all day," Scarlett answered as she looked up at Noah, her eyes full of love.

"Welcome, Brooke and Eve. Finn, Connor, would you mind opening the bottles and getting everyone a glass of champagne, well, except for Scarlett?" Noah said.

"I'll get her a glass of sparkling water," Emee said, rushing to the kitchen.

"Damn, brother, you broke out the good stuff," Connor said as he popped the cork of the gold bottle of champagne. Noah must have something important to announce if they were drinking sixty-five hundred-dollar bottles of champagne.

Once everyone had a flute of champagne, Noah wrapped his arm around Scarlett's waist and raised his glass. "As you all know, I made a huge and painful mistake regarding this wonderful woman. Every day since that night, I have thought of her and prayed that I might find her. Then fate stepped in and I was given another chance. Of course, I screwed up again by speaking before thinking. Despite all my mistakes, this beautiful woman still gave me a chance. She is giving me and our family the greatest gift of all by carrying our sons. I can't wait to spend every day together for the rest of our lives. So today, I asked her to marry me and she said yes."

Brooke and Eve's mouths dropped open as they gasped. "You're engaged?" Eve murmured.

"Yes, and please be happy for me. I love him. I have always loved him. From the moment we touched at the bar, I knew then that I would love Noah for the rest of my life," Scarlett answered, her eyes never leaving Noah.

Noah took her face into his hands. "I felt too, mo chroí."

"What did he say?" Brooke asked. She had heard Connor mumble a few words she didn't recognize.

"Brooke, Eve, if you keep hanging out with these boys, you will need a Gaelic translator," Scarlett laughed.

"He called her his heart," Connor answered.

All the ladies in the room sighed deeply at the explanation.

"Oh, ladies, I would be more than happy to give you Gaelic lessons. Actually, Scarlett, it is a tradition that the bride and groom say their vows in Gaelic to one another," Emee explained.

"I can see a lovely wedding in June," Eve said, her mind racing with dress designs.

"Can you see a lovely wedding in thirty days?" Scarlett asked, biting her lip.

"NO WAY!" Eve yelled.

"Eve, we want to get married in thirty days. Nothing large, just family and close friends in a private ceremony. After these two little ones are born, we will have a large, over-the-top reception," Scarlett explained. "I want to be a Kelly when I give birth."

"And you will be," Noah said, placing a kiss on top of her head.

"I will call the priest tomorrow at St. Patrick's church," Emee said.

"Alright, but I still get to design the dress," Eve said.

"There is no one else I would want to design it," Scarlett said, reaching out to take Eve's hand. "But also, I have moved in here. We have lost so much time together and don't want to lose anymore."

"You are moving out?" Brooke cried. She thought of Scarlett as a sister, not as just a friend.

"Brooke, I won't be far away, just one floor up. You are welcome here anytime and I will need your help to help decorate this place. As you can see, it is a little drab," Scarlett giggled.

"Yes, Brooke and Eve, I have heard that you have a fantastic eye," Emee said. "After dinner, we will sit down and start putting our heads together."

"Alright, let's drink to the happy couple," Liam announced. "To Noah and Scarlett."

"Noah and Scarlett," everyone said together, then drank the very expensive and extra delicious champagne.

L ater in the night, Molly was in bed, her lover wrapped around her. They had just finished having sex and were enjoying the post-orgasmic high.

"How was your day?" he asked, running his hand up and down her arm.

"Good. The Skipper had a dinner party for his family and Scarlett's friends. He announced tonight that she was moving in and that they were getting married," Molly disclosed.

"Married?"

"Yes. He gave her his grandmother's Claddagh ring," Molly answered.

"So when is the joyful event?" he asked, needing as much information as possible. "Sometime next year? I mean, I am sure planning such a grand event takes a while."

"No. I heard they want to get married in the next thirty days. They will hold a grand reception after the babies are born," Molly answered.

"Oh," he muttered. "Well, goodnight, my sweet."

"Goodnight," Molly whispered, closing her eyes and quickly falling asleep.

Sometime later, he carefully removed himself from their embrace, gathering his clothes and slipping out of the room. It wasn't uncommon for him to leave after sex, so he knew Molly wouldn't be upset if she woke up alone. He was a guard in the family and being so meant he was called out at all times of the day or night.

Once he was in his vehicle, he picked up his phone and made his essential call.

"Do you have any news?" Eleazar answered.

"Noah is getting married within the next thirty days."

"THIRTY DAYS!" Eleazar yelled.

"Yes."

"We have to move fast. Call me with any details you discover. If you get a chance to take her, do it and I will take it from there."

"She is heavily guarded at all times. Noah is staying close and that puts his guard in the mix as well."

"I am sure she is, though we might have to enact some diversions to diminish the numbers," Eleazar said. "Keep me updated and remember the prize when you take her."

After Eleazar hung up, he had to smile. He would make this happen and soon, he would be the downfall of the Kelly family.

CHAPTER SIXTEEN

"Damn, Scarlett, you have a shit pile of clothes," Connor said as he carried another large box labeled clothing into the bedroom.

"You can blame Brooke and Eve," Scarlett said, carefully folding her t-shirts and stacking them in piles by color. She didn't know why she placed them in the drawers since she couldn't fit into them. "Though Brooke has three times the amount of clothes and you don't even want to know how many pairs of shoes."

"Fuck," Connor said. He had met Brooke just a couple of weeks ago, and she had occupied his thoughts ever since. He had never encountered a woman like her before. They hadn't had sex yet, and it wasn't because she refused. It was him. As he glanced at his future sister-in-law, he couldn't resist imagining what it would be like to see Brooke round with his child.

"Connor, Connor, Connor!" Scarlett yelled, waving her hand towards him.

"What?"

"What are you thinking about?" She asked.

"Ahh, well," Connor said, his cheeks turned pink.

"Come over here and sit beside me," Scarlett said, patting a place beside her on the bed.

He came over and sat down, keeping his head down.

She placed her hand on his knee and smiled at him. "Now, tell me what is going on in that brain of yours that has you looking so serious."

"Brooke," he answered.

"I figured. Are you two having issues?" Scarlett asked.

"No, the complete opposite. Everything is perfect, though I am worried that she will hate me when she finds out that I have been keeping the family secret from her."

"So, you are serious about her?" Scarlett asked, hoping that was the case. Brooke was like a sister to her and as she got to know Connor better, she knew he would treat Brooke like a jewel.

"It's too soon," he said as he looked up.

"Can I ask you a question?"

"Haven't you already been doing that?"

Scarlett raised her eyebrow at him and gave him a stern look.

He held his hands up in surrender. "Damn, you already have your upset mother's face."

"Really?" Scarlett said happily.

Connor chuckled. "Yes. If I were your child, I would know I was in trouble."

"Alright. My question is this. Do you think you could walk away right now and know that some other man will someday hold her in his arms?" Scarlett asked.

Connor thought for a moment. How would he feel if he walked into a restaurant and saw his beautiful Brooke in the arms of another man? Could he stand by and watch as she looked lovingly into that man's eyes? Would he be able to walk away and let her go? Gripping his hair and wondering why this was so painful to think about. In the past, he had always been after one-night stands, never wanting or needing anything more.

Needed. That was it. He needed Brooke to make his life complete.

"No," he said, reaching over and pulling Scarlett into his massive arms. "I am so fucking happy that my brother knocked you up."

Scarlett giggled over what Connor had said. Yeah, she had been knocked up, though there was no doubt that she and Noah would be together even without being pregnant.

"Get your hands off my woman," Noah joked, walking into the bedroom with two boxes. "Go get your own woman and leave mine alone."

Connor bent down, kissed Scarlett on the head, and then let her go. "You know what, brother? I am going to do just that."

Connor walked out of the room with a spring in his step and a determined look on his face.

Noah came over to Scarlett with a bewildered look on his face. "What was that all about?"

"I think Brooke might be the one for Connor," Scarlett disclosed with a grin.

"Wow, just, wow," Noah stammered. "I just never thought he would be one to settle down."

Scarlett wrapped her arms around his neck and pulled him down. "When a smart man finds the right woman, he doesn't let her go."

"I must be one brilliant motherfucker, 'cause I am never letting you go," he said. He captured her mouth in a passionate, all-consuming kiss, which left them both breathless.

"As much as I need you right now, your mother will be here in a few minutes with Eve to go over wedding plans," Scarlett murmured, her body on fire after that kiss.

"Hmm, I bet my pussy is wet and needy." Noah ran his hand down inside her yoga pants. As he suspected, her panties were soaking wet and her clit was swollen.

"Noah, we can't," Scarlett moaned as she spread her legs, giving him better access.

He withdrew his hand from her pants, grabbed her hand, and pulled her towards the bathroom, closing and locking the door. "Baby, this is going to be quick and dirty." With one quick motion, her yoga pants and underwear were pooled to her feet. "Bend over and hold on to the counter."

Scarlett kicked her pants off, spread her legs, and gripped the counter. Behind her, she heard the sound of Noah's pants landing on the floor and scraping across the tile as he kicked them out of the way. Then she felt his thick cock brush against her wet lips. "Fuck, baby."

"You are so wet for me," he said as he thrust his cock deep inside her. This was heaven for him. With each thrust, he could feel her walls flutter with its impending orgasm.

God, she was a wanton mess. Every time they had sex, Noah could make her come multiple times. God, was his cock like a magical wand that caused orgasms? Damn, she was one lucky bitch and she will be damned if any other hussy could ever enjoy this pleasure. He owned her and she owned him.

Noah reached around, taking her clit between her fingers. He pinched her swollen numb and in a husky voice, he commanded. "Come for me."

"FUCK!" Scarlett screamed as her orgasm ripped through her with wave after wave of pleasure.

Four thrusts later, he was spilling his seed deep inside of her. He placed his forehead on her spine and gasped for air. "It gets fucking better every time."

"I know," Scarlett answered with a breathless sigh.

Noah slipped his semi-hard dick from her and turned her so he could see her eyes. He got lost in a sea of Irish green every time he looked into them. Over the years, he had visited his family's home in Ireland. His great-grandfather returned to Ireland and purchased a grand home for his family. The house sat on 500 acres of rolling green countryside. Scarlett's eyes reminded him of the countryside in spring. He couldn't wait to take her and their boys there.

As his heart pounded beneath her, Scarlett took pleasure in knowing that she was the cause of his excitement. Over the years, she had to sit and listen to Brooke and Eve's sexual encounters. Even though they sounded hot, none compared to what she felt when she was with Noah.

"We better clean up before we get yelled at again by Máthair," Noah said with a wink.

Scarlett's lit up in mischievousness. "I'm Máthair favorite. She wouldn't yell at me."

Noah couldn't help but laugh. He knew she was right. He took a step back when he did. The sight of their mixed fluids running down her thighs made him tremble with desire. "Damn, that is so fucking sexy," he declared as his cock again hardened with desire.

As Scarlett glanced downward, her eyes fixated on his cock, and her mouth began to water. "Hmm."

"Noah, Scarlett, GET YOUR BUTTS OUT HERE!" Eve yelled through the door.

"Fuck," they both growled together.

"Later?" Scarlett asked, a smile flickered on her lips.

"Definitely!" Noah answered, placing a chase kiss on her lips.

They quickly cleaned up and walked out of the bathroom hand in hand. When they arrived in the living room, they found Eve and Emee sitting on the couch with stacks of books and fabric samples on the table.

"We are on a tight deadline," Emee said, looking at Noah. "There is no time for self-gratification. There is a wedding and an apartment remodel that needs to be planned and time is ticking away quickly."

"Sorry, Máthair," Noah said.

"Sure you are," Emee said, narrowing her eyes.

"Sorry, Máthair," Scarlett said, as her head lowered.

Emee stood and wrapped her arms around Scarlett, pulling her close. "Oh, sweetheart. I know who is to blame." She looked over Scarlett's shoulder at her son. He was so much like his father.

"Have a seat, Scarlett. I have the sketches down for your dress," Eve said in a singsong voice.

Scarlett clapped her hands. "Let me see."

Just as she was about to open her portfolio, Eve noticed Noah was still lingering in the room. "You need to leave," she said, pointing her finger at him.

"It is my apartment."

"And Scarlett's. You can't see the dress until the wedding day. So go hang out with Finn or go do some work or something," Eve said.

"Fine, but I will be back in an hour. We have a doctor's appointment this afternoon." He placed a kiss on top of Scarlett's head. "I love you."

"I love you," she whispered, her eyes loving looking into his.

Eve revealed her designed gown to Emee and Scarlett after Noah left to attend to his business. It was a simple satin form hugging design. The simplicity of it made it extremely elegant.

"Oh, I love it," Scarlett said, imagining herself in the dress.

"Eve, it is lovely, though it is an Irish tradition for the bride to wear lace that has been handed down through the generations," Emee said.

"Emee, I don't have any lace. Noah told me I was, in fact, Irish. However, I have nothing from my family." She would have loved having something from her grandparents. Throughout her upbringing, she had only seen a few pictures of them. One had been in a box in the attic. She was about seven years old when she slipped up the stairs and explored the items stored there. Her attention was drawn to a trunk next to the only window. Pushing the latch, it popped open and she lifted the lid. Inside the trunk, she uncovered a collection of photographs in tarnished silver frames. They featured a couple looking at each other with love in their eyes. The man bore a striking resemblance to her father. Upon removing the frame, she found a box. She removed it from the trunk and opened the lid to expose a unique fabric with swirls and flowers. She wanted to take it out and play with it. However, she heard her mother calling her name. She quickly covered the box, returned it to the trunk, and shut the lid. She hadn't remembered that day until this moment.

"I took nothing with me when I left for school. Though I just remembered a trunk in the attic at my parent's house. I think it belonged to my grandparents and my grandmother's lace was in a box in the trunk," Scarlett said. "There is no way I can go back there. Weston would never let me go back into the house."

"Eve, dear, would you mind getting us some drinks? Scarlett needs to stay hydrated," Emee asked.

"Of course," Eve said, quickly getting up and entering the kitchen.

Emee made sure that Eve was out of hearing and leaned toward Scarlett. "We Kellys have a way of getting something we want. Just leave it to me to retrieve the box."

"You would do that for me?" Scarlett asked.

Emee took Scarlett's hand and squeezed it. "You are family and we do anything for family."

Eve returned with a tray of drinks, and the conversation resumed about the wedding.

"I was thinking about a lace cape instead of a veil. With the wedding happening in a catholic church, I know it is frowned upon to have your shoulders bare. This way, the dress can be as it is, just with the lace cape," Eve said.

"Eve, you are a genius," Emee praised, picking up a box beside her and opening the lid. Inside was a large piece of lace. The intricate, elegant design was stunning. "This lace has been passed down from each bride in our family. Each Irish family has their own design, and when the woman becomes engaged, her family's design is melded with the groom's family."

"So this is your family and Liam's?" Scarlett asked, fingering the delicate lace.

"Yes. We have three pieces, one for each of our sons, waiting for them to find their brides," Emee answered.

"This is going to be perfect for the cape," Eve gushed, her mind racing with how it would look.

"I need to get it cleaned before giving it to you. Would it be too late if I get it to you by Monday?" Emee asked, wanting to give time to get Scarlett's family lace before handing it over.

"No, that would be fine. I need to sew the gown, allowing for belly growth," Eve giggled, closing the portfolio. "Now to the church decor."

One hour on the dot, Noah strolled back into the apartment with Finn beside him. They had been going over the tapes again of the night their father had been shot, hoping to see something they had missed. However, they still couldn't get a good look at the face of the shooter.

"Is it safe for me to come in?" Noah called out.

"Yes, asshole," Eve answered.

"Can't you do anything with your girlfriend?" Noah questioned Finn, bumping him with his shoulder.

"Are you joking? I am afraid of her," Finn answered as he shivered.

"Just wait until I tell Connor."

"What? Haven't you heard? He is just as afraid of Brooke," Finn said, his top lip turned up.

"Are you telling me that you are afraid of a little woman?"

"Noah!" Scarlett yelled. "We don't have time for you to goof off with Finn. I have a doctor's appointment to get to," Scarlett said as she tapped her foot on the floor.

"Of course, my love," Noah said as he jumped, rushing over to offer her his arm.

Finn just laughed to himself. The Skipper was afraid of no man, but his soon-to-be wife was a different story.

Surrounded by guards, Noah and Scarlett arrived at Dr. O'Neill's office. Noah ordered Luke to wait outside the door with Cora as Thomas and Claire entered the office. Unlike most doctor's offices, Scarlett was brought back quickly. The first stop was the scales, where she discovered she had gained two pounds in the last two weeks. Next, she was given a cup and asked for a urine sample. They were finally escorted to the exam room. Five minutes later, Dr. O'Neill appeared with an enormous smile on her face.

"Scarlett, Noah, how wonderful to see you," Dr. O'Neill said. "How are you feeling?"

"I am feeling great. No dizziness or lightheadedness," Scarlett answered.

"Great. Let me look at your blood pressure," she said, placing the cuff around Scarlett's arm. As the electronic cuff began its cycle, Scarlett and Noah anxiously watched the screen, hoping for good news. As the machine beeped, everyone broke out with a huge smile. "120/75, perfect, just perfect."

"See baby, I knew you would be okay," Noah said, kissing Scarlett's lips lightly.

"Dr. O'Neill, does this mean I can return to work?" Scarlett asked.

"Scarlett, you don't need to work," Noah said.

"I might not need to work, but I want to," she retorted. It wasn't about the money. It was the feeling of accomplishment.

"You can start returning to the office, but for only a few hours a day. You are carrying twins and are at high risk. As your pregnancy progresses into the later months, it will become difficult to maintain balance."

"Oh." She loved her job at the museum, though she loved her children more and wouldn't do anything to compromise their health. "I guess I will just have to go in and clear out my office."

Noah wrapped his arm around her, hoping the action would comfort her. "I am sure the museum would allow you to work a few hours a day."

"Maybe. It is not fair for them or the patrons not to have someone who can give them a hundred percent." She wiped away a stray tear and smiled a small smile.

"Well, let's look at your little boys," Dr. O'Neill said, rolling over the 4D ultrasound machine.

"Is that a different machine?" Scarlett asked, wiping the tears from her eyes.

"Yes. This is a 4D machine, which will give us a more realistic picture of the little ones. Noah, help Scarlett lay back and pull up her shirt."

A clear image of one of the boys suddenly appeared on the screen as Dr. O'Neill rubbed the wand over Scarlett's belly.

"Oh my, God. He looks like you," Scarlett cried, grasping Noah's hand.

Noah's throat tightened, and he could not utter a single word. The tough mafia boss couldn't help but shed tears at the sight of his beloved son.

CHAPTER SEVENTEEN

With new pictures of their bundles of joy in hand, Noah and Scarlett made their way back to the apartment. Both were quiet as they were driven through the busy, congested city streets. Luke was in the front seat with Rory while the other guards rode in the SUVs in front of them or behind them. They were not only protecting their leader but the future leader as well.

Noah's hands shook as he tried to steady himself from the overwhelming sight of his sons' faces. The ultrasound picture on Scarlett's desk was the only glimpse he had of their unborn children. Despite its poor quality, the photo left him feeling awestruck. The 4D ultrasound was incredibly realistic, making it feel like his sons were right there before him. If there had been any doubt that they were his, which there wasn't, the boys' image was identical to his own. They were Kelly boys, and he couldn't wait to see if they had green eyes. The image of his children with their mother's auburn hair filled his mind with warmth.

Scarlett was wrestling with the fact she was leaving a job that she loved. When she was about to graduate, she had prayed for an opportunity to work in a museum, even if it was just as a tour guide. Then Robbie surprised her with the job as a curator. She couldn't believe she was getting paid to do what she loved every day. She was initially uncertain about whether she could perform the duties, but as she gained experience, she became more at ease in the position. Even the responsibility of acquiring money from wealthy donors. She gazed down at the ultrasound picture, tracing her finger over the tiny cheeks of her unborn children. No job was worth putting her babies' health in jeopardy.

"Scarlett, are you okay?" Noah asked, placing his hand on her leg.

"Yeah. I am sorry I was short with you in the doctor's office."

"It's fine. I understand that your whole life is changing. I only wish I could make it easier," he said.

She placed her hands on her belly. "It is changing, but for the better. Our sons are the most important thing in my life and I will do nothing to put them in danger."

Noah leaned over and placed a soft kiss on her lips. "You are going to be a fantastic mother."

"And you are going to be an awesome father."

S carlett was at the museum two days later, packing up all her possessions from her office. She called her boss and let her know that she couldn't come back to work due to her pregnancy's high risk. Despite her disappointment, Ms. Page understood the reason why she wasn't coming back.

Noah planned on joining her, but he received a call to address an issue on the docks. He had been fortunate for the past few weeks. He didn't have to leave Scarlett and got the majority of his work done from home. However, there had been increased attacks on their shipments, and he needed to show those assholes that the Kellys were not to be messed with. Although he couldn't attend, he was confident Scarlett's security detail would ensure her safety.

Scarlett had to shake her head. She arrived to pack up her office but was forbidden to pick up anything. In the office, Mark and Cora were being directed on which items belonged to Scarlett. Each item was wrapped carefully before being placed in the sturdy boxes they brought. She was granted permission to go through her desk and identify her possessions for packing.

The first thing she noticed when sitting at her desk was the small silver frame containing the first ultrasound picture of twins. Next to the frame, she saw a piece of paper with her name on it, neatly folded in half. She immediately recognized the handwriting as Noah's, noting the elegant cursive loops and flourishes. She was in awe of the powerful man's graceful writing style. The moment she opened the paper, the words seemed to jump off the page and into her mind.

I never meant to put you through pain. I promise to never do it again.
Noah.

Tears streamed down her face, and her heart swelled with emotion. He had written it the night they first saw each other again. God, she loved him so much.

"Miss Murphy, are you okay?" Cora asked, concerned that she was crying.

Scarlett wiped her tears, clutching the note to her heart and smiled. "Yes, I am fine." This was not the end. It was the beginning of her life with a man who would always fight for their love and family.

Later that night, when all the boxes were stored away until a place was made for them, Scarlett lay in Noah's arms. She had told him she had found his note. He affirmed it with not only his words but with every touch, kiss, and caress.

"Scarlett, you can't stay in the apartment while it is being painted," Emee said.

"But I could stay in one room until they get another one done." Scarlett hoped she could change Emee's mind on the issue.

"It doesn't work that way, Sweetie. The fumes from the paint will drift throughout the entire apartment, and we can't just open windows this time of the year. You would freeze to death before it was safe to stay," Emee said with a tone that she would not be backing down. "The wedding is only four days away and it would make it convenient for you to be at the mansion so we can finalize all the plans."

"And I need to tie up some loose ends before we leave for our honeymoon," Noah said as he walked into the room.

The situation at the docks had worsened. Two of his men were killed and he lost three gun shipments. Scarlett was unaware of the issue, and he made a point of showering and changing before returning home each night. The mansion is a more secure location than her old apartment. He raised the level of security around his parents after the shooting. The mansion was better protected than the White House.

"Fine," Scarlett said.

Emee came over and placed her arm around Scarlett. "Sweetie, when you return from your honeymoon, the apartment will be all done except for the nursery. You and Noah must still decide on several things before it can be finished."

"I know. It is just so much."

The past few weeks had been filled with one decision after

another. Who thought it was a good idea to have a wedding in thirty days? Oh yeah, hers. But it wasn't just the wedding. There were countless decisions to be made during the apartment overhaul. She asked Noah his opinion on things and he would state that her happiness was all that mattered to him.

"The wedding is going to be lovely and your Gaelic vows are perfect," Emee said.

"I've been practicing every chance I get. Thank you for breaking it down into pronunciation. That helped the most." She had been listening to the recording of her vows repeatedly. There was only going to be Noah's close family, Brooke, Eve, Robbie, and Garrett, at the ceremony, yet she wanted to say them perfectly to Noah.

"Alright, let's get you two packed up," Emee said. They reached Kelly Mansion two hours later, with all the necessary things for Scarlett and Noah until their honeymoon.

"Where are we staying?" Noah asked, with a suitcase in both hands and one over his shoulder.

"In your old room," Emee said as she tried her best not to show any emotion.

She kept quiet about the fact that she had renovated his former bedroom and bathroom. Scarlett didn't need to stay in a horny teenager's bedroom with posters of half-naked women taped on the walls and porn magazines hidden under his bed.

Emee climbed the stairs to the east wing, where the boys had their childhood bedrooms. She smiled as she recalled the many times she caught them sliding down the banisters or riding her good silver serving trays down the stairs. She let them know they would eventually have kids and then understand her frustration with the trays that were dented and scarred. Noah was a natural leader from a young age, and his brothers would always follow him, even in dangerous situations. But Noah was always the one to take responsibility and punishment for his brothers, even though they were all part of it. It was always clear that he would make a great family leader in the future.

"Emee, this place is huge," Scarlett said, looking around at the vast space.

"It is now, but with three young boys all within one year of each other, it didn't seem so large," Emee answered.

Then a thought came to her. She wondered whether Noah and Scarlett would be interested in taking over the mansion as she and Liam moved to the penthouse. She would have to see what Liam thought of the idea. The laughter of children needed to echo through this house again. When they reached Noah's room, Emee opened the door and stepped back, allowing them to walk in.

As Scarlett walked into the room, she let out a gasp. Noah's room was so beautifully decorated that she was stunned to know he had grown up there.

"What the hell?" Noah said, looking around the room as he placed their suitcases on the floor. "Where is all my stuff?"

"Do you really want the mother of your children to see all the posters of half-naked women you had decorating the walls? And the pornographic magazines under the mattress?" Emee asked, her mouth turning up in a smirk.

"But they were…" he began before he was cut off.

"They were what?" Scarlett asked, placing her hand on her hips.

Stepping over Scarlett, Noah wrapped his arms around her and placed a sweet kiss on her lips. "Nowhere near as sexy as you, A Chumann."

"My sweetheart?" Scarlett asked. She was spending hours learning the difficult language. But A Chumann was one of the words Noah used all the time.

Noah stepped over and wrapped his arms around her. "Very good, A Chumann."

They took in the room. It was decorated in dark eggplant and steel gray. The bed was a large four-poster canopy with a steel gray bedspread and eggplant sheets. Steel gray had been painted on three walls, while one was painted the deep eggplant color.

Two oversized gray chairs sat in front of the eggplant wall. The room had a fireplace and on the mantel were silver picture frames.

Scarlett walked over to the mantle, picked up one frame, and gasped as she turned towards Emee. "How did you find this?"

"Scarlett, dear, we are criminals."

"But how did you?" Scarlett asked, looking at the other pictures. They were pictures of her grandparents. The same ones she had seen in her parent's attic all those years ago.

"I sent a team in and stole the chest you spoke about," Noah answered.

Emee had told him about the chest and how much it meant to Scarlett. He dispatched the team to her home, directing them to carry out their task without attracting attention. While the Murphys were at church, they slipped in and took the chest, leaving no trace behind.

Scarlett's fingers lingered on the frame for a moment before she rushed over to Noah, her heart beating rapidly. "I am the luckiest woman on this planet. Thank you for doing this for me."

"I plan on giving you the world," he said before capturing her mouth in an all-consuming kiss that left them both breathless and needing more.

"Dinner will be ready in about two hours," Emee said as she closed the door behind her.

She knew that look, and if Scarlett hadn't already been pregnant, she would be in a little while. She left the young couple to christen the room and headed out to find her love, eager to release her own pent-up sexual energy. His paralysis may have rendered him immobile, but Liam still had complete control over his impressive member.

Noah wasted no time after Emee left and immediately stripped both of them. They explored each other's bodies on every surface in the room. They finally ended up in the bed, collapsing into sleep with contented smiles on their faces.

The next day, Emee organized a spa day for herself, Scarlett,

Brooke, and Eve to take a break from the chaos. With memories of a previous enjoyable visit, Oasis Day Spa was the obvious choice for a return trip. Noah commanded that Scarlett and Emee's guards be stationed at the day spa.

The women were ushered out of the limo and through the spa's front door. The moment Emee entered, she saw the woman she had been hoping to avoid. Damn, she couldn't shoot the bitch here.

"Emee, darling," Carmen said in her thick Spanish accent.

"Hello, Carmen," Emee said in a voice with no feelings. Then, she looked over at her daughters, giving them a nod.

"And who are you with?" Carmen asked, looking at the three young women behind her.

"These are my good friends, Brooke Martin, and Eve Landon. And my soon-to-be daughter-in-law, Scarlett Murphy," Emee answered, reaching out and taking Scarlett's hand.

"And which of your sons is the intended?"

"Noah. He is very lucky to have found someone like Scarlett."

"Noah?" Marta asked in a high-pitched voice, which sounded like nails on a chalkboard.

Carmen turned, shaking her head at Marta, then turned back to Emee. "What a shame. We hoped we could join the families when Marta and Noah got together."

"Oh, Carmen, darling, Noah has to marry someone with Irish blood."

"And this little thing is Irish?" Carmen asked as her lip turned up in an evil sneer.

Emee beamed, and her Irish accent became more pronounced. "Why yes, she is. Now, if you'll excuse us, we have to get pampered before the big day."

"We haven't gotten an invitation."

"That is because only close family is invited," Emee said, leaning close to Carmen. "And you are not now, nor will you ever be family."

Emee straightened back up and turned, leaving Carmen standing in the lobby looking like she swallowed a lemon.

Gianna and Scott positioned themselves on either side of the door leading to the spa suites as Emee and the girls made their way through. Carmen eyed the guard, then walked outside. Marta crumpled into her arms as soon as they were out of the building, her sobs echoing in the quiet street.

"Mama, why is that girl marrying my Noah?" Marta sobbed.

Carmen wrapped her arm around Marta. "Oh, baby. Just because they are getting married doesn't mean they will stay married."

CHAPTER EIGHTEEN

Scarlett stood in front of the mirror and looked at the finished product. As she stared at her reflection, she couldn't believe the person staring back at her was herself. Eve's dress was a flawless masterpiece that hugged her curves perfectly. Unlike most wedding gowns for expectant mothers, which were like large circus tents, Eve's design was sleek and form-fitting. The dress was made of white satin, with a plunging neckline and a fishtail silhouette. It hugged her belly, showing off her every curve. She loved the dress but adored the full-length lace cape, made from the lace of Emee's family and her grandmother. Once the laces were joined, they formed a single, continuous line that seemed to have no beginning or end.

Scarlett opened the box and shook her head. Brooke and Eve had gotten her a pair of Christian Louboutin "Kate" blue ombre crystal-covered suede pumps with a 4" stiletto heel. "There is no way I won't fall and break my neck if I wear these."

"Scarlett, Scarlett, Scarlett, these are Louboutin and they are made to be an extension on your feet," Eve said as she helped Scarlett put them on.

With caution, Scarlett stood up slowly, waiting to see if she would fall, then took her first step. Damn, Eve was right. Those shoes were the most comfortable thing she had ever put on. "Oh, Eve, they feel wonderful."

Eve gave her a wicked smile. "Haven't you learned by now that when it comes to fashion, I am God?"

Emee stepped forward and presented Scarlett with a red velvet box. "Noah's gift to you."

Scarlett lifted the lid to find a diamond necklace with a large sapphire stone in the center. It was stunning and, of course, expensive. She took the necklace out of the box and felt the weight of all the stones. "Will you help me put it on?" she asked Emee, her eyes full of unshed tears.

Emee draped the necklace around Scarlett's delicate neck and closed the clasp. When she stepped back around to the front, she gasped. The necklace hung perfectly down her neck and into the dress's plunging neckline. It was like it was made for the dress. "God, he is so much like his father when picking out jewelry."

Scarlett ran her finger over the hard, cold blue stone. It was the most beautiful necklace she had ever seen in her whole life, and it was hers. How had she gotten so lucky to have a man like Noah in her life?

"Now, for a few more things to make sure we start this marriage right," Emee said as she held out a sixpence coin. "Brooke, will you place this in her left shoe?"

"I would love to." Brooke bent over and slipped the coin in the left shoe.

"Now, let's go over the list. Your gown is new. The lace is old. The shoes are blue. This is your something borrowed," Emee said. She handed Scarlett a delicate handkerchief with a Celtic knot, a thistle flower, and a horseshoe embroidered on the soft material. Along the edge was lace which was different from the Kelly lace. "It was my great-grandmother's."

"Oh, Emee. It is so lovely and I promise to take care of it," Scarlett cried, tears rolling down her face.

"Now, now. You are ruining your makeup and we need to

leave for the church in a few minutes," Emee said, reaching up with a tissue and patting away the tears.

Eve rushed over, touching up Scarlett's makeup. After covering any signs of tears, she prepared to put on the long, white, heavy cape with a hood. It was the second weekend in November and the weather had already turned cold. According to the meteorologist, New York City was expected to be hit by a massive nor'easter on Wednesday, with at least a foot of snow. The city may be blanketed with freezing rain and ice before the arrival of snow.

After ensuring Scarlett was bundled up, Brooke, Eve, and Emee put on heavy coats over their dresses. Scarlett and Noah had chosen not to have a maid of honor or best man at their wedding. They decided to have the whole family witness their vows.

Noah had stayed at the apartment the night before with his brothers, as they gifted him with a so-called bachelor party, scant strippers or whores. Scarlett took a firm stance on that issue when Connor brought it up. No other woman would be naked in front of her soon-to-be husband. Of course, Noah agreed, stating that Scarlett's sexy body was his every fantasy and desire.

Scarlett and Emee's security detail waited for the ladies to arrive in the mansion's foyer. Instead of two officers per lady, there were now four. Upon hearing about Emee's encounter with Carmen and Marta at the spa, Liam and Noah ensured nothing happened while heading to the church.

Thomas approached them when they were walking outside to get into the waiting limo. "Hey, Mark. I can take over from here," he said. This was his last opportunity to take Scarlett before she married Noah. Eleazar had paid him a lot of money to do this, and once he did, he would be given a high-ranking posi-tion in the organization. Eleazar had promised his daughter Camila would marry him, making him a part of the family.

Mark found it odd that Thomas was here. He was on The Skipper detail and should have been at the church where he was at this moment. "We have our orders, Thomas, and shouldn't you be at the church?"

"Yeah, but the Warlord has it covered."

Mark stepped closer to Thomas. He didn't know why he was here but would not step away from his duty until commanded to do so. "Look, Thomas, I will not leave my post, no matter what you say. We don't need your help, so step the fuck back."

"Fine," Thomas said, turning on his heels and storming off. Damn, Eleazar was going to be pissed. He needed to develop a new plan because there was no way he would fail.

Mark and other team members got the ladies in the limo and on their way to the church. They were vigilant, not wanting to disappoint their Skipper. Forty minutes later, they pulled up to the front of St. Patrick's Cathedral.

Throughout the entire ride to the church, Scarlett remained completely silent. She couldn't stop thinking about whether she had the qualities necessary to be a good wife to Noah. He was anything but a typical husband. As the leader of a massive crime family, he had power and influence beyond measure. She had spent the last month getting to know an abundance of people who were all part of the same family. Noah knew every person by name, and could also recall details about their families. He had kept his promise to be around the house, except for the times when he had to leave to handle an emergency. When he returned, he went straight to the bathroom and showered. She checked on him and was hit with the strong metallic smell of blood as she saw the red water pour off his toned body in the shower. At first, she thought he had been injured, rushing towards him to see the extent of the damage, only to find that it was someone else's blood. She refused to ask who. Instead, she would collect his suit, placing it in the special container so it could be destroyed.

She felt a sudden touch on her hand, bringing her back to reality. As she glanced down, she was drawn to the exquisite diamond and emerald Claddagh ring on Emee's finger. She had been corrected that the Kelly men had a knack for picking out the most stunning jewelry pieces. Emee squeezed her hand slightly, letting her know everything would be alright.

"Liam and I are very blessed to have someone as brave, courageous, and loving as you to marry our son," she said, her voice full of conviction.

"I don't know about the brave or courageous part. But I do love your son with all my heart and soul," Scarlett said, staring into Emee's emerald-green eyes.

"Honey, to love a Kelly man, you must be brave and courageous."

Scarlett giggled, feeling lighter than she had all day. Leaning forward, she placed a kiss on Emee's cheek. "Thank you. You don't know how much I needed to hear that."

"Well, in about an hour, I am finally getting my wish."

"Oh, and what is that?" Scarlett asked, curious about what Emee could wish for that she didn't have already.

"A daughter," Emee answered, her face full of love for the young woman beside her.

Tears ran down Scarlett's face once more. Brooke and Eve exchanged a knowing glance, silently agreeing that Emee Kelly would make the perfect mother for their dear friend. Eve reached into her purse and pulled out a tissue, handing it to Scarlett, who quickly dabbed at her eyes.

"Did I make a mess of my makeup again?" Scarlett asked, looking over at Eve.

"No. You are perfect."

As the car came to a halt, Scarlett's eyes were drawn to the grand entrance of St. Patrick's Cathedral. She was amazed that Cardinal O'Malley had agreed to marry them without hesitation.

"Why did Cardinal O'Malley agree to marry us?"

Emee shrugged her shoulders and stated. "He loves his new house." It wasn't just a house. It was a vast, stately home with six bedrooms, seven bathrooms, a swimming pool, and a large media room. Emee didn't know why the media room was the selling point. When Cardinal O'Malley heard that, his eyes lit up like a child on Christmas morning, and he agreed to marry Noah and Scarlett on whatever day they wanted.

Scarlett gasped. "You paid off a priest."

With a shrug of her shoulder, she answered matter-of-factly. "Yes."

Scarlett couldn't believe that a Cardinal could be bribed. "Oh, well," she thought. She went to open the door, but Emee stopped her.

"We have to wait until they determine it is safe for us to get out," Emee said, knowing that the girls didn't understand. Even though there was no apparent danger to Scarlett, Noah didn't want to leave anything to chance.

Brooke and Eve knew the Kellys were a powerful family, but the amount of security was disarming. When they questioned Connor and Finn, they told them not to worry about it.

Mark and the other security detail surveyed the area, and just as they were about to declare an all-clear, Cora came across the earpiece. "Baru."

"Fuck," Mark growled, looking towards where Cora was positioned. Sure enough, he spotted Marta Ortiz walking towards the church steps, wearing a white see-through gown. Mark rushed over and blocked Marta's path.

"Get out of my way," Marta said. She couldn't be late for her wedding. Her mother had tried to make her wait until the fat bitch had been taken care of, but she couldn't disappoint Noah. She was aware of his love for her and realized he was only looking at the fat cow because she claimed to be having his baby. However, she knew Noah would never cheat on her. That is why she had to come to the church today to stop the sham of a wedding.

Mark seized her arm and started pulling her towards the side of the church. She never stopped screaming like a banshee. When they were at the side of the church, he gave her to Cora and Clarie. Claire and Cora worked together to restrain Marta by tapping her mouth and holding her arms behind her back. "Take her two blocks from home and drop her off," Mark commanded.

"Will, do," Claire answered, even though she had hoped that she could shut the bitch up for good. Marta was getting on her last nerve and it took all the power she had left not to pull her gun and blow her fucking brains out.

After Claire and Cora had Marta in the car, he headed back around the church and towards the limo. Opening the door to the back, he offered his hand to Scarlett. "I am sorry for the delay. Wouldn't want to spoil your day with an unsightly piece of trash," Mark said, his mouth turning up into a small, mischievous smile.

"Thank you," Scarlett chuckled as she witnessed the "piece of trash" being hauled away.

Once everyone was out of the car, they walked up the steps and into the church's entrance, where they were met by Robbie, dressed in a tailored black tuxedo.

"Robbie, what are you doing out here?" Scarlett asked, shocked to see the man who she considered her father standing in front of her.

He leaned close to her ear and whispered. "Well, I heard my daughter was getting married today to some gangster. I am here to make sure that he doesn't run off."

He straightened and looked her in the eyes. His expression was one of love. "Aria, dear, I would be honored if you would allow me to give you away today."

"Oh, Robbie, of course." Tears once again began pouring down her cheeks.

Eve stepped forward with a tissue and began blotting away the tears. "After this, no more tears until Noah gets to see you," she commanded with a smile. Removing Scarlett's outer cape, she made sure that the lace cape was draped perfectly in the back so that it would flow up the aisle.

Once Scarlett was again tear-free and perfect, Eve, Brooke,

and Emee gave her a light kiss on the cheek, then went into the chapel to take their seats. Robbie offered his arm to her and Scarlett placed her arm on his. When the Uilleann pipes played, the doors opened, and they proceeded down the aisle.

Noah's heart was racing as the door opened and he caught sight of Scarlett. He had missed her so much last night, and the sight of her caused him to crave the urge to touch, hold, and kiss her. She was a vision in white, and her gown hugged her every curve, showing off their sons. He looked closer and saw the sapphire pendant nestled between her ample breasts and Eve had given him the perfect dimension since it lay where he wanted it to. When they finally arrived at the altar, Robbie kissed her cheek and put her hand in his. Robbie might not be her blood father, but he loved her as much as he loved his own daughter.

Scarlett had not been prepared to see Noah dressed in a traditional Irish eight-yard tartan, five-button waistcoat, Victorian shirt, ruche tie, kilt socks, and kilt flashes that matched his tartan. She had seen him in suits and tuxedos, but nothing prepared her to see him dressed this way. He was sexy as fuck, and she wanted to know what he was wearing under that tartan. Damn, she was horny.

Cardinal O'Malley began the service and soon, the time had come that Scarlett had been preparing for weeks. The ceremony was done in complete Gaelic. For those in attendance who didn't know Gaelic, a special program was printed.

"I, Noah Anthony Kelly, now take you, Scarlett Aria Murphy, to be my wife. In the presence of God and before these witnesses, I promise to be a loving, faithful, and loyal husband to you for as long as we both shall live."

Scarlett took a deep, cleansing breath and began. "I, Scarlett Aria Murphy, now take you, Noah Anthony Kelly, to be my husband. In the presence of God and before these witnesses, I promise to be a loving, faithful, and loyal wife to you for as long as we both shall live."

Noah couldn't help but smile. She had said her vows in perfect Gaelic. Hell, her diction and pronunciation were that of someone who had been speaking Gaelic all their life. He would have to teach her more Gaelic that she could use while they made love.

Cardinal O'Malley then instructed them to exchange their rings. Eve handed Scarlett the beautiful milgrain gold Celtic Knot Wedding band she had selected for Noah. Noah took Scarlett's gold Celtic Knot Wedding band from Connor and placed it on his beloved wife's finger. It was fortuitous that they had both selected the same band for each other. The symbolism is not lost on either one of them, as the Celtic Knot symbolizes eternal love.

Once their vows were said, Cardinal O'Malley finally said the words Noah and Scarlett had been waiting to hear.

"I pronounce you man and wife," he said. "You may kiss your bride."

Noah wrapped his arm around Scarlett, leaned down, and sealed their vows with a kiss of promise, love, and fidelity.

CHAPTER NINETEEN

"COME FOR ME, NOW!" Noah demanded, thrusting deep inside Scarlett one last time, releasing stream after stream of hot cum into her tight wet pussy.

"YES, YES, YES!" Scarlett screamed, falling over the edge as the powerful orgasm rocked through her. She let out a contented sigh as she collapsed onto Noah's chest, the warmth of his body lulling her to sleep.

Noah held her against his chest, trying to regain some strength from his own powerful orgasm. For the last three days, they had been going non-stop like this. They were in bed constantly, only leaving to grab a quick bite or use the restroom. They would rest in between sessions, but it was Scarlett who would always wake up first and begin the next round. As they left the church, she attacked him in the back of the limo, dropping to her knees and pushing up his tartan, leaving him shocked and breathless.

"I fucking knew you were commando under this," she said, licking her lips.

Before he could answer her, she wrapped her mouth around his cock, sucking and licking. He would never forget the sight before him and just when he thought it couldn't get any better, she relaxed her throat and took him entirely in her mouth. "Fuck, baby, I am about to come." He lost himself in her emerald green eyes and came with a shuddering release. With a satisfied hum, his wife licked her lips clean after swallowing everything.

Little did he know, she would crave him non-stop for the next three days. He noticed her breathing had slowed, and looking at her face, he saw she had fallen asleep. He moved her off him as carefully as he could and ensured she was lying comfortably. He couldn't help but groan as he slid out of her slick heat. Fuck, he was sore. His cock was throbbing with pain from the excessive use it had endured, a sensation he had never felt before in his life.

"Hmm, Noah," Scarlett moaned in her sleep.

As much as he loved hearing her moan his name, he couldn't focus on that right now. The thought of finding relief was the only thing on his mind. He carefully slipped out of bed, taking care not to disturb her as she slept soundly. He took a step and winced in pain, gritting his teeth. Damn, it fucking hurt. As he painfully went to the bathroom, he gingerly handled his cock and released his bladder.

"Holy fucking shit," he groaned under his breath. His cock was so raw that it hurt to piss.

After finishing, he returned to the bedroom and slipped into a pair of roomy sleep pants made of soft material. He picked up his phone, his eyes flickering back to Scarlett once more before he walked away. He bit his lip to hold back a chuckle. She was lying on her side, with her mouth open and drool dripping alongside her lips. Her hair was a mass of tangles and knots, resembling a bird's nest. Despite everything, she was still the most beautiful woman he had ever met. Stepping out of the room, he closed the door and went to the kitchen to get something to drink. He passed the window and heard the howling wind and the sound of sleet pelting against the windows. As he approached, he saw the forecasters had underestimated the strength of the storm. Fuck, it was going to be a bad one.

He checked the clock and realized it was already five. Damn, they had been at it for over four hours. It was easy to understand why his cock was sore. He grabbed a water bottle and chugged it down when his phone rang. When he saw it was Finn, he knew something was terribly wrong. Gunshots echoed in the background as soon as he answered the call.

"Finn," Noah said, hoping that he was okay.

"Skipper, we have a major problem. We are under attack at the south end and it is snowing so fucking bad the visibility is almost nil," Finn rushed out as he continued to take aim and fire.

"Is Conner there?" Noah asked, as his heart raced. Some fuckers were trying to kill his family.

"Yeah. However, we are out-manned and outgunned. Whoever they are, the bastards are heavily armed."

"Fuck. I will get there as soon as possible with reinforcements," Noah said.

"That sounds...," Finn began, then the phone went dead.

"Finn, Finn. Are you there?" Noah yelled, his voice increasing with each word. When he heard nothing, he called back and the number just rang.

Noah's heart sank as he heard the automated message telling him the circuits were busy and to try again later. Fuck that shit. He rushed to the table and picked up the house phone, quickly dialing the security office. "Yes, Skipper," Thomas answered.

"We have a situation. Call up the rest of my detail and pull three from Scarlett's detail. Have them readied to leave in ten minutes," Noah said, his voice not leaving any doubt that he was in charge.

"Will do."

Thomas couldn't help but smile. He made the calls, but instead of three of Scarlett's detail, he pulled four. His plan was working and Mother Nature was helping.

In the bedroom, Noah found Scarlett peacefully asleep and gently nudged her to wake her up. He would take her to his parent's house and then go to the docks. Though in this weather, it would take forever and his brothers might not have that long. As he looked down at her, he knew he had to make the tough choice for the sake of their family. She was to be protected above all others, which included his brothers. He sat beside her and swiped the hair that had fallen over her eyes.

Scarlett opened her eyes and smiled up at her husband. She had been dreaming about him holding his sons. He was sitting in the overside rocker in the nursery and humming "Rock a bye baby" to them. The dream was so perfect and she couldn't wait until it came real. Her throat became tight as she held back the tears threatening to form in her eyes. "Hey."

"Hey. I hated waking you, but we have a situation and I need to get you to the mansion."

Scarlett sat up, grabbing the sheet to keep it from falling. The look in his eyes and the tone of her voice told her something was very wrong. "What is wrong?"

"We have a serious problem down at the docks."

"It's bad, isn't it?" She asked, grasping his hand and squeezing it.

"Yes. So, please get up and get dressed. We need to leave ASAP. And bundle up; it is snowing outside."

Scarlett jumped from the bed and looked out the window. It wasn't just snowing. It was a blizzard. Turning back to Noah, she said. "It will take forever to get to the mansion and you to get back to the docks. Why don't I stay here?"

He gritted his teeth and growled. "No. I don't want you to be alone."

"Stop growling. I have been alone before." She placed her hands on her hips.

"That was before you were pregnant and my wife."

Scarlett could tell by his expression that he would not budge. "How about if I go down and stay with Eve and Brooke?"

Noah was about to say no, yet this wasn't a bad idea. Three of her guards would be on duty and Garrett was just down the hall if needed. "Alright, but you must stay there until I get back."

Scarlett walked over and reached up and gave him a quick kiss. "I promise."

Fifteen minutes later, they walked into the girls' apartment, where they were met by two excited women.

"GIRLS' NIGHT!" Brooke exclaimed, clapping her hands.

"We stocked up before the storm, so we have plenty of snacks and there is a series on Netflix that we have wanted to start," Eve advised.

"Well, I am leaving," Noah said before pulling Scarlett into a tight hug. They were not going to tell Eve and Brooke about the situation at the dock until Noah knew more. There was no use in everyone being worried.

"You come back to me," Scarlett whispered into his chest.

"I will. I fucking love you so much, baby," Noah said, hating the fact that he had to leave her, but he had a responsibility to the family.

With tears streaming down her face, she said. "I love you too."

He placed a kiss on her temple and walked towards the door. "Lock this behind me and turn on the alarm."

"Aye, aye, Captain," Scarlett giggled, giving him a salute.

"It's Skipper, Mrs. Kelly," Noah said in a hushed tone before giving her a wink and walking out the door.

Once he got outside, he saw that Cora, Claire, and Scott were on duty in the hall. One was standing by the door while the other two were stationed near the elevator and stairs' entrance. "We are on high alert, so make sure you stay on your toes."

"We will, Skipper," Cora answered.

Noah got into the elevator and before he pushed the button, he took one last look at the door that had his heart behind it. He took a deep breath, pushed the ground button, and mentally prepared himself for the battle. When he arrived at the garage, the SUVs were ready to go and running. He jumped into the back and they headed out into the storm and towards the dock.

Scarlett, Brooke, and Eve had just finished their facials and were currently watching the Netflix series.

"Damn, this is good," Eve said with a mouth full of ice cream.

"Yeah," Brooke said, as her thoughts went to Conner and the things the man could do with his tongue, which made her squirm.

Eve's phone rang suddenly. She picked up the phone and saw the number of her boutique building manager. "Good evening, Alistair."

"Miss Landon, I hate to be the bearer of bad news. Your shop is on fire," he said.

Eve jumped to her feet. "OH MY GOD!" she screamed. "Is the fire department there?"

"Yes, but it looks awful."

"I'll be right there," Eve said and disconnected the call before Alistair could say anymore. "My shop is on fire."

"Holy Hell," Brooke said.

"I've got to go," Eve said, running towards her bedroom to get dressed.

"We're coming too," Scarlett said as she tried to get up. Her pregnant belly makes it extremely hard to get up.

"Oh no, you are not. Noah would have our heads. You can't go out in this weather," Brooke said, shaking her head.

"But Eve shouldn't go out there alone." Eve needed support. The shop was her pride and joy. Hell, if it were happening to her, she would love to have someone to lean on.

Brooke thought for a quick moment. "Scarlett, your guard is

stationed outside. So why don't you stay here and I will go with Eve? We will call you once we find out what is happening and how bad things are outside."

"Damn it. I am pregnant, not an invalid."

"We know, sweetie, but you are carrying some very special cargo," Brooke said, placing her hand on her stomach.

"Fine, but help me up. I don't want to be sucked on this couch all night."

Brooke chuckled and helped Scarlett to her feet.

Ten minutes later, Eve and Brooke were bundled up and heading out the door. As they rushed out, they were lost in their thoughts about the situation and didn't pay any attention to the hallway.

Scarlett locked the door behind her friends and turned on the alarm. Still upset about being unable to go, she decided to bake a pan of her famous brownies. Eve and Brooke loved them. She knew where all the cooking utensils and baking pans were kept. So she quickly mixed up the gooey batch and waited for the oven to preheat. Her thoughts were constantly on the fire and Noah. Damn, it was a stressful night, but she had to remain calm. She closed her eyes and took several deep cleansing breaths and as if they knew she needed assurance, the boys gave her several kicks.

"Oh, boys, that was strong. Mommy promises to do everything possible to keep you safe and healthy. I love you so much and so does your daddy."

The lights went out in the apartment suddenly. It took a moment for Scarlett's eyes to get accustomed to the darkness. She turned to the switch behind her and flipped it, yet nothing happened.

Well, damn, she thought. She didn't know if it was just their building or the entire city. She needed to get to her phone and try to contact Eve or Brooke. Rubbing her hand over the kitchen island, she didn't find it. It was then she remembered she had left it in the living room. She guided herself with her hand on the island's edge and slowly towards the living room. As she took small steps, she tried to remember where each piece of the furniture was placed.

Just as she turned to step into the living room, someone grabbed her from behind and placed a cloth over her mouth. At first, she was shocked but quickly remembered the self-defense moves Noah had taught her. She clawed at the arm. Her fingernails dug into the assailant's skin. She had to get away, yet she felt herself fall into a dark sleep.

Thomas couldn't help but chuckle when Scarlett finally succumbed to the ether. The bitch put up a good fight and his arm was killing him. Other than that, his plan had gone off without a hitch.

Eleazar's men were attacking the south docks with an all-out assault. Thomas knew Noah would go to help his brothers when they were under such a massive attack. When Noah gave the order to pull guards from Scarlett's detail, Thomas knew that mistake would be Noah's downfall. It was easy for him to pull Scott at the last moment from the detail and hide until the convoy of vehicles took off for the docks.

He took out his phone and called the cell phone attached to the bomb in the dress shop. He took the elevator to the floor five levels below where the Scarlett was located. After climbing the last five floors and reaching the stairwell, he used his phone to cut off power to the floor. Noah was unaware that his father was once a highly sought-after computer genius who had passed his knowledge on to his son. There was no computer task he couldn't perform, including inserting a program to turn off the power with a simple command.

Thomas opened the door and slipped into the hallway when

the lights went out. He came up behind Claire and injected her with a lethal dose of a drug in the neck. Her body went limp and he quietly moved her lifeless body out of sight. Eleazar had provided him with a lethal injection of liquid cocaine, which was one hundred percent pure. The toughest part was coming up next. He stepped out and called out to Cora.

"Cora, it's Thomas," he said.

"Thomas, what is going on with the lights?"

"I don't know. I was just up at the Skipper's apartment and everything went black. It must be because of the storm. Is Scarlett secure?" He asked, stepping closer to Cora, hoping she would notice that Claire was gone.

"Do you know if the security system is on a battery back?" Cora asked. She wouldn't leave her post until Mark sent someone to relieve her.

"It is. Has she come out?"

"No."

"Good," he said. He turned quickly and grasped Cora around the neck, plunging the needle in.

"Thomas," Cora cried out before her body slipped under the drug.

With her lifeless body on the ground, he used the key Scarlett had handed him weeks ago to unlock the door. By using the polymer clay, he created an impression of the key while she provided him with the alarm code.

After deactivating the alarm, Thomas slipped on his night-vision goggles and searched for the bitch who had been preventing him from getting his money. His eyes searched the living room, and not seeing her, he headed towards the kitchen. He heard her before he saw her. The sound of her shuffling feet on the hardwood floor grew louder as she approached him. He stepped back and leaned against the wall, pulled out the cloth, and waited. As soon as she was in the correct position, he grabbed her and covered her mouth with a cloth. She fought like a wildcat, but he was stronger.

Once she was out, he placed her on the couch and made the call. "I've got her."

"Good. Take her to the hangar and place her on the jet. When you are on board, you can tie her up," Eleazer said with a sinister grin. His beloved daughter would marry her dream man, making him the most powerful person on the East Coast. He would wait and when the time was right, he would take control of the Kelly family. "I'll be there as soon as I can."

Eleazer made the next call to the man who would make sure the bitch never returned to New York.

"Weston, we got her. She will be on her way to you as soon as the weather breaks."

"Great, and did you find out the question I asked?" Weston asked as his heart raced.

"Yes. They are boys," Eleazar answered.

"Good, very good," Weston said, his lips turning up in an evil grin. He was finally getting the sons he rightfully deserved.

CHAPTER TWENTY

"Thirty-three days, thirty-three days. DAMN IT, THIRTY-THREE FUCKING DAYS," Noah yelled, slamming his hand down on his desk.

He went over to the window and looked out over the city. His men searched the entire city but found no evidence of his beloved. They monitored police scanners for any news on young pregnant women being discovered. Up until now, there had been nothing. Garrett scoured all the hospitals in the city and even checked the morgues. Thankfully, he didn't see her there. Noah received offers of assistance from other families. The catalyst for rival families joining forces was her, which was unbelievable. The moment she was taken became clear as he remembered that frightful night.

He reached the dock and found it worse than expected. His men were trapped and facing the enemy's use of military-grade weaponry. The sound of a fifty-caliber semi-automatic rifle reverberated through the air, bouncing off the metal containers. As they neared the fight, Rory slowed the SUV to a stop, and Noah leaped out with his weapon at the ready. He instinctively sought protection behind the nearest container and scanned the area, searching for his brothers amidst the chaos. He inserted the communication device into his ear and remained alert for incoming chatter.

"Yee-haw, the fucking cavalry has arrived," Connor said.

"Location?" Noah asked.

"Southside east corner," Connor answered.

They had been pinned down for over an hour, the sound of gunfire ringing in their ears. Whoever was shooting at them had enough firepower to take down an army, and they were unleashing it all on them.

"Anyone hurt?" Noah questioned.

"Don't know," Finn piped in. "We have been pinned down since the very beginning."

Out of nowhere, an enormous explosion echoed through the air. The blast wave was so powerful that it sent everyone tumbling to the ground, gasping for air. When they could breathe normally again, they sat up and shook their heads to regain their bearings. The blast left them with a persistent ringing in their ears.

Noah's hearing returned, and the eerie silence immediately struck him. He peered around the container and saw no one else around other than his men. "What the fuck?"

"Skipper, what is it?" Finn asked.

"They are gone," Noah answered, stepping out and towards where the enemy had been just a few minutes before. "Why would they just leave? They had us at a disadvantage, even with the extra support."

Finn and Connor, along with many others, arrived at the spot where Noah was standing. The enemy's sudden departure left everyone equally puzzled. They fanned out gradually to find evidence of their attacker. All that was discovered were the weapons and empty shells. There were no bodies, blood, or indi-cation of who had orchestrated the ambush.

"Connor, what do you make of this?" Noah said, motioning to the equipment left behind.

"It makes no sense whatsoever." Never had he seen anything

like this before. They had the upper hand and it had been only a matter of time when they would have taken them all out.

As he was checking out the weapons which had been left behind, his phone rang. He took it and saw it was his sweet Brooke. "Hey, honey."

"Connor, is Finn around?" Brooke asked. "Eve has been trying to get him."

"Yeah, hold on. Finn, Eve wants to talk to you," Connor said, holding out his cell for him.

Finn took the phone. "Eve."

"Finn," Eve cried. "My shop is destroyed."

"What do you mean?" he asked.

"I got a call from Alistair stating that my shop was on fire. Brooke and I came to see how bad it was. When we got there, the entire shop was engulfed in flames," she said, as her voice cracked. All her hard work was gone.

"You went to the shop alone?"

"Yeah. Scarlett wanted to come, but we wouldn't let her."

"Scarlett is alone?" Finn asked, turning to see Noah's expression.

Noah's heart stopped when he heard the words. He had left her and for some reason, he knew something was horribly wrong. He took out his phone. He called Scarlett's cell, but she didn't answer. He hung up and tried to call Cora, but her cell phone rang without an answer.

"WE NEED TO GET BACK TO THE APARTMENT NOW!!!" Noah yelled, taking off and running towards the SUVs. He struggled to maintain his balance as his feet slipped in the snow. Nothing was going to stand in his way of getting to her. He reached the vehicle, opened the driver's side door, leaped in, and drove away, leaving everyone behind. Time was of the essence, and he needed to make his way through the city.

Finn and Connor took off after Noah and just as they neared the vehicles, they saw the taillights speed off.

"Fuck," Rory said, coming up beside Finn.

"Rory, if you are here, then who is driving the Skipper?" Finn asked, confused by what was happening.

"No one. The Skipper is driving and he is alone," Rory answered, kicking himself for not getting to the SUVs fast enough. His job was to drive and protect The Skipper and he had let him down. He had let the family down.

"FUCK!" Finn growled. "Let's get rolling."

Noah's mind wouldn't stop the deluge of horrible scenarios flashing through his mind as he raced through the city. Her safety was compromised because he ordered her detail cut. It was his fault. He had brought her into this dangerous life and didn't know if he would survive if something happened to her or their children. He parked in the parking deck, got out of the car, and sprinted towards the elevators but abruptly halted. Scott was lying on the floor. Noah reached down and discovered he had no pulse.

"NOOO," Noah yelled, standing up and pushing the elevator button. He could hear the blood pumping in his ears as his heart raced. After what seemed like a lifetime, the elevator finally arrived and he was on his way to the floor where his love was supposed to be. He hadn't realized he was holding his breath as the number ticked by one by one until the elevator stopped and he gasped a lung full of air. The door opened and with his gun drawn, he stepped out.

He glanced towards where the guard assigned to Scarlett was meant to be. The guard who was supposed to be at the stairs entrance was gone and the guard at the apartment door was lying on the ground. Upon reaching the guard, he discovered it was none other than Cora, who, like Scott, was dead. When he looked up, he noticed that the door to the apartment was open and felt a wave of dread engulf him. He pushed the door open more with his foot and looked around. He couldn't see or hear anything, so he turned on hallway lights. With each step, the reality of what happened weighed down on his shoulders. When he walked into the living room, he saw an overturned side chair and a broken lamp on the floor.

"Scarlett!" Noah yelled, hoping this was all a mistake and she was okay. Yet, she did not answer. He approached closer and felt something beneath his foot. He reached down and discovered that it was her cellphone.

She was obsessive about having her phone with her at all times. All of a sudden, a noise in the hall caught his attention. He quickly aimed his gun at the doorway, discovering it was his brothers.

"Noah, did you find her?" Finn asked though he knew from the bodies that they found that there was a slim chance of that.

"No. But I will and when I find out who did this, their blood will flow like a fucking river."

His determination to find her strengthened as he looked out at the city again. No one messed with Noah Kelly and lived.

Emee was heading to Noah's office with some food for him. She knew he had been tirelessly searching for Scarlett since she was kidnapped. Yesterday, she noticed how pale he was and his suit hung off his much smaller frame. She guessed that he had lost at least twenty-five pounds.

She hoped getting his favorite meal would make him eat. As she walked into their favorite restaurant, the owner greeted her.

"Mrs. E, what a pleasure it is to see you," Patrick said as he took her hand and kissed it on the back.

"Patrick, it is a pleasure. I wondered if I might impose on you to fix up one of your special steak dinners to go. My son is in a bit of a crisis and refuses to leave his office to eat."

Patrick motioned to a booth near the middle of the restaurant. "Not an imposition for you. Please have a seat and I will send over a cup of tea and your favorite cookies while you wait."

Emee took off her coat and sat on the bench facing the entrance. She had always been taught to be mindful of her surroundings. Never sit with your back to the door and know where all other exits are. Her guards were keeping watch outside the building, but ever since Scarlett was kidnapped, she has been extra cautious of any potential risks. The booths had high backs, allowing patrons privacy as they ate. The server arrived with a pot of tea and a plate of cookies. Emee thanked the server before pouring herself a cup of tea and picking up a cookie. She heard the voices of the guests sitting behind her.

"How much longer must I wait?" A woman said. The voice was very familiar to Emee.

"A few more weeks. The bitch will be taken care of once she gives birth to the babies," another woman answered in hushed tones. Yet it was her accent that Emee recognized immediately as Carmen Ortiz and Marta. Could they be the ones behind Scarlett's kidnapping? As much as she wanted to get up and demand them to tell her where Scarlett was, she needed to use her head and get as much information as possible.

"I still can't believe that Daddy is allowing the bitch to have those babies," Marta huffed.

"Your father is not deciding on that. The man who is holding her has his reasons for wanting the babies. As soon as the babies are born, she will be killed and they will place her body where it can be found. After a few weeks of mourning, you can make your move on the grief-stricken Noah. You have stopped taking your birth control?"

"Yes," Marta said.

"Good. If luck is on our side, one good fuck will get you pregnant and he will be trapped to marry you," Carmen said.

"I don't like waiting. He is mine," Marta said. "And a girl has needs."

"Well, do what I do. Fuck one of your guards. Hell, the guy who took her works for Noah. Fuck him for a thank you. He is a hot piece of ass," Carmen said. She knew Eleazar fucked around, though he would be mad as hell if he knew she did. However, he was never around and she had needs.

"He is hunky. I'll have to call him."

At that moment, Emee saw Patrick walking towards her carrying a brown-handled bag. She quickly got up, grabbed her coat, made sure Carmen or Marta didn't see her and intercepted Patrick. She glanced over her shoulder and sighed in relief when they remained in their booth. "Thank you. How much do I owe?" she asked quietly.

"Nothing, Mrs. E.," Patrick said. "I hope this will help your son through his crisis. He is a fine boy and I understand he recently was married."

"He was and she is the light of his life," Emee said with a smile. "Thank you."

She took the bag and quickly left the restaurant. Her guards opened the back door of the limo and she climbed in. "Tony, get me to The Skipper as fast as possible."

"Of course, Mrs. Kelly," he answered, placing the vehicle in drive and speeding through the city.

The city flew past the car windows, revealing Christmas decorations and brightly colored lights for the holiday that was only five days away. The family didn't feel like celebrating the holidays this year. They would do it when Scarlett had been returned to them. Ten minutes later, they were pulling up outside Noah's office building. One of her guards opened the door, and she grabbed the bag carrying Noah's lunch. She didn't stop to say hello to security, going straight to the private elevator. She headed to the floor where Noah's office was. It was the same one that his father had used before turning over the family business to him.

Getting off the elevator, she rushed to Noah's office door. She opened the door and saw him standing in front of the windows with his shoulders slumped over.

Lost in his thoughts, he didn't hear his mother walk into the room.

"Noah," Emee said, her heart heavy for the pain that her son was having to endure.

"Máthair."

"I have some information and food," Emee said, placing the bag on his desk.

"I'm not hungry. What information do you have?" He asked, his heart racing over the possibility that his Scarlett would be found.

"Listen here. You must eat to keep your strength up to make these fuckers pay for taking Scarlett," Emee commanded.

Noah came over and Emee started unpacking the containers from the bag. He was reluctant to confess, but the aroma was delectable. He sat down and cut into the steak. Once the piece of meat was on his tongue, he took no time to finish. Emee told him what she had overheard at the restaurant.

The knowledge that the Ortiz family had arranged this filled him with fury. Despite his urge to rush over and demand answers, he knew he needed to approach the situation rationally.

"Noah, I know it is difficult, but can you recall the commands you gave that night and who you told them to?" Emee asked.

"I got a call from Finn that he was under attack at the docks. In the background, I could hear the massive amount of gunfire. I knew I needed to get to him fast with as many men as possible. The cellphone towers were not operational, so I called the command center on the house phone. Thomas answered the phone."

He shook his head as he remembered the next part, which

caused him to slam his fists hard on the desk. "It was my fucking fault for pulling men off her security detail."

"Noah, calm down. Now tell me what you said to Thomas."

"I told him to pull three men from her detail," Noah said. Then he talked about the gunfight and how the people disappeared after the bomb went off. Then he returned and found Scott, Claire, and Cora dead and Scarlett gone.

Emee thought for a moment. "Something didn't add up right. If there were two guards died on the floor, why was Scott's body found in the garage? All of the men and women on Scarlett's detail were highly trained. This means that the person who did the killing was someone they knew. The person who did the killing knew just how many guards would be guarding Scarlett."

Noah listened to his mother as she began to talk about that day. When she got to the point about where and how Scarlett's guards died, a lightbulb went off. Why, he hadn't thought of it before, but there was only one person who knew the amount of guards. "Thomas," he said, his voice cold as ice.

"I believe you are right."

Then he remembered the day after Scarlett's kidnapping, Thomas was wearing a bandage on his arm. Finn had asked what happened and he said a bullet on the docks grazed him.

Noah took out his phone and dialed Garrett, putting it on speaker so his mother could hear the conversation.

"Noah, did you find her?" Garrett asked, concern evident in his voice.

"No, but can you tell me if you treated Thomas for a gunshot wound after the gunfight?" Noah asked.

"It was a gunshot wound. He told me he was sparing with one of the female guards and they scratched him. It was a deep gash. I was so busy with all the other family members I didn't give a second thought. But now that I do, the gashing couldn't have been made from the front. He would have to be behind the person to get the way they were."

"FUCK!!" Noah yelled.

"Is he behind this?" Garrett asked, his temper rising.

"Yes and he will suffer before I allow him to die," Noah said through gritted teeth.

"But are you certain? Because the family will want solid proof," Garrett said.

"Oh, I will. Mother overheard a conversation today between two rival family members and they indicated it was someone in our family who took Scarlett. I'll call you as soon as I have concrete information."

"Just let me know and I will be available at a moment's notice," Garrett said.

Noah hung up from the call. "If I know Marta, she will call him soon for a booty call. We will have his phone tapped by then and will catch them both. Thomas will tell me where Scarlett is, and I will hold Marta as leverage against Eleazar." For the first time in thirty-three days, he could take a full breath. He had a plan, and he would get Scarlett back.

Scarlett rolled over on the small bed in her father's church's cold, damp basement. It had been thirty-three days since she had been kidnapped and flown to Castle Rock.

She found her hands and feet bound when she awakened after her attack. She could tell she was on a plane by looking around. She struggled with all her might to break free from the ropes, but they were too tight. It didn't take long before she heard footsteps approaching the closed door. When it was opened, she recognized the man as Eleazar Ortiz.

"Ms. Murphy, so glad you are awake."

"It is Mrs. Kelly," Scarlett said, her eyes burning with fury.

"Ah, yes. Noah married you. Well, I can't have that. My sweet Marta wants Noah and I want control of New York."

"Are you going to kill me?" Scarlett asked, wanting to be able to wrap her hands around her belly to protect her unborn children.

"No. Someone else wants that pleasure."

"But I am pregnant."

"Oh, don't worry about your babies. You are going to be allowed to give birth to them. The man has wanted sons, yet his wife gave him a girl. I personally don't mind daughters. Men always think with their dicks and not their brains," Eleazar said. "Since the snow has stopped, it is time for you to begin your journey."

"Where and who are you sending me to?"

"Castle Rock, Washington, where you will have a family reunion with your father," Eleazar said as he turned and walked away from her.

Scarlett's nightmare was just beginning. As she looked at her belly, she was confident that Noah would find them. She needed to stay strong and protect their sons.

CHAPTER TWENTY-ONE

Noah had been on pins and needles, waiting for Finn to notify him that Thomas had received a call from Marta. The fucker thought he had gotten away with killing his fellow family members and kidnapping Scarlett. Yet when Noah started digging into Thomas, the fake walls that he had built crumbled down. Finn discovered the virus he implanted in the security system to turn off the lights on the floor, allowing him to enter the apartment unnoticed.

Connor bribed the fire investigator to change the report on the cause of the fire at Eve's boutique to an accident. As expected, it was a bomb that triggered the explosion and fire. It was now being ruled as a gas leak. Noah was paying for the shop replacement from the family funds. He didn't want a noisy insurance company prying into his affairs.

Finn and Connor had also been working on the connection between the ambush at the docks and the Ortiz family. The weapons left behind had been stripped of their serial numbers and fingerprints. But they didn't stop searching. It's clear from the conversation Emee overheard they were involved. Yet, they required solid proof to substantiate it. Noah needed evidence of the family's misconduct before taking out their leader. He didn't need to get into a pissing match with other families.

Even with all the new information, Noah still did not know where Scarlett was. He prayed she was still alive and hadn't given birth yet. Carmen's comments were she would be kept alive until the babies were born. Thank God. Time was running out as her pregnancy drew near. He was so upset that he was missing this precious time with her. Fuck, he had missed all the firsts of the pregnancy because of his stupidity of not leaving his number. Now, he was once again missing out because of who he was.

"Noah," Finn said as he and Connor rushed into the office. "We have them."

"Thomas?" Noah asked.

"Yes, and Eleazar," Connor said, his eyes full of excitement.

"How?"

"The asshole thought he was smart by removing all the serial numbers and fingerprints, yet he shipped the weaponry in a container. He forgot to remove the container number from the side," Connor explained. "We have him."

For the first time since Scarlett was taken, Noah smiled. "Fucking great. Now when is that fucking snake Thomas meeting up with Marta?"

"In an hour, at the Waldorf," Finn answered.

"Alright. Get the extraction team together and collect the assholes, both of them. Take them to the warehouse. Separate them and put Thomas on the table. He will tell me where Scarlett is and I will make him suffer for his deception."

"What are you thinking about doing to him?" Finn asked.

Noah placed his hands on his desk, leaned forward, and with eyes ablaze, growled. "I am going to take back my family's crest."

Finn gasped and turned to Connor to see that his expression was the same as his. Everyone in the family had a tattoo of the Kelly family crest on them. Emee even had a small one, even though she didn't have to. Finn and Connor had heard of taking the family crest back, yet they had never witnessed it being done. Only five people in the organization throughout the generations had done anything to warrant removing the family crest from their bodies. The tales of how it was performed would cause nightmares.

"Skipper, what tools do you need to accomplish this?" Finn asked.

"Flaying knives as sharp as you can make them. I want him to suffer as much as Scarlett is suffering.". He would remove all of Thomas's fucking skin after he told him where Scarlett was being held. "Also, have lots of adrenaline available. The fucker is going to be awake for all of it."

Marta arrived first at the suite at the Waldorf. She couldn't wait to work off some sexual frustration out on Thomas. He wasn't Noah, but he was still a decent option. She slipped off her Versace one-shoulder Baroque-print twill midi dress, leaving her in a La Perla black lace bra and matching thong. As she looked at herself in the mirror, she was pleased with how fucking sexy she looked.

"Damn, I look good," Marta said out loud. As she was checking out her breast implants, there was a knock on the door. She ran her fingers through her hair, fluffing it up, then grabbed her see-through coverup and headed to the door. She opened the door to find Thomas standing there, dressed in black dress pants and a white button-down shirt.

"Hmm, you looking fucking tasty," Thomas said, then stepped into the room, pushing the door shut with his foot. In one swift motion, he had Marta picked up and headed toward the bedroom. He would love to spend all day and night with her, but he couldn't.

The asshole Warlord was on his ass about covering the docks tonight. He was supposed to be on the Skipper's private security detail, yet he was staying at the office once again. After Scarlett's kidnapping, he had been questioned if he had seen anything. He spoke with conviction, lying through his teeth, explaining that he was on the dock during the kidnapping and saw nothing. There had been so many men on the docks and the snowstorm made it impossible to know if someone had been there or not.

Marta ran her long, red, manicured nails down the front of his shirt. "Thomas, you have on too many clothes."

Thomas threw Marta onto the bed. Without breaking eye contact with Marta, he removed his shirt and threw it on a nearby chair before unbuttoning his pants. Just as he was going to unzip his pants, he felt a gun pressed against his temple.

Marta was so engrossed in Thomas' undressing that she failed to observe the four men enter the room. At the sight of the gun aimed at Thomas's head, she immediately opened her mouth to scream. However, one man pointed his gun towards her.

"Don't even think about it, bitch," the man snarled, his eyes blank of all emotions.

Thomas had not moved his head, though he recognized the man who called out to Marta. It was one of his family members, Peter.

"Peter?" Thomas asked, yet he didn't hear the answer. He only felt the impact of the butt of the gun knocking him into darkness.

Marta's mind was racing, trying to find an escape route from this predicament. She thought Thomas knew at least one of these guys, but why were they knocking him out and tying him up? She decided to make use of her father's investment and slowly glided her finger toward her core, believing it was the best course of action.

"Do you guys want to have a little fun?" Marta said, licking her lips. She had never had a man refuse her.

Peter, Ben, Sam, and Randall didn't change the deadly expression they were wearing. This was what they were trained for and why they were known as The Reapers. Without saying a word, Sam pulled a rope from his bag and moved toward the bed.

"Oh, aren't you a big guy?" Marta said, her eyes fixed on his crotch.

Sam grasped her leg, flipped her over, and tied them together. Once he was finished, he did the same for her arms.

"Oh, you like it kinky," she egged on, even though she was frightened.

Ben stepped forward and stabbed a syringe into her thigh, pushing the propofol into her system. She screamed at the invasion, but she was out in seconds.

Once Thomas was tied up and both were ready to be transported out of the hotel, Randall made a call.

"Skipper, it is done," Randall said with a smirk.

"You know what to do," Noah advised.

"Yes."

Each of Noah's steps exuded confidence and authority as he walked into the warehouse. At this moment, he was just The Skipper, the leader of the Kelly family. It was crucial for him to display no vulnerability while entering the room to extract information from the traitor. There will be no mercy, only pain. His new orders would be carried out once he discovered the location of his beloved Scarlett.

When he opened the interrogation room's door, he realized his father and brothers were already there. Upon entering the room, Noah's eyes fell on Thomas, who was completely naked, handcuffed by his hands and feet to the steel table. He moved closer to the table. Thomas turned his head and looked at him.

"Noah, there has been a huge mistake."

Noah removed his coat and held it out without taking his eyes off him. Finn stepped forward, took it, and hung it over the chair next to Liam's wheelchair. Noah unwrapped his tie and once again held it out. Each movement was precise and deliberate. His face was void of all emotions. He unbuttoned his shirt several buttons so that his crest tattoo could be seen.

Noah looked at Thomas and ran his hand over the tattoo. "I wear this with pride, knowing those who also have it will always watch my back. It is a permanent reminder that whoever has one is part of the Kelly family."

"I have one," Thomas said, not knowing what was happening. There was no way he had found out about him kidnapping the bitch.

The mask of unfeeling fell and in its place was rage. "And that is the problem. Only family members can have one and you, Thomas, are no longer family."

"What do you mean?"

Noah leaned closer to his face, wrapping his hand around Thomas's windpipe, cutting off the air. "Did you really think we wouldn't figure out who took Scarlett?"

"Not..me," Thomas choked out.

Noah increased the pressure before releasing. Thomas began coughing and gasping for air once he did. He extended his hand towards Finn. Finn lifted the towel from the nearby table and selected a fillet knife, placing it onto Noah's open hand.

Noah wrapped his hand around the knife's handle and brought it close to his face to examine the sharpness of the blade. "Do you know what kind of knife this is?"

Thomas shook his head.

"It is a flaying knife," Noah said as his lips curled up. "The beauty of this knife is that it can cut very thin layers of skin. I will use this to remove my family's crest from your traitorous fucking body. Then you will tell me where my Scarlett is, or I will remove every inch of skin until you do."

"I didn't betray the family," Thomas cried.

"Oh, but you did. We have all the evidence we need to put you in bed with the Ortiz family. And because of your disloyalty, several of the men and women of the family, your brothers and sisters, are dead," Noah snarled. God, he wanted to cut the fucker's heart out, yet he needed to make him pay and find out where Scarlett was being held.

He used the knife to slide along the tattoo's edge. The ink skin cut away from Thomas's body. Thomas screamed at the top of his lungs and they reverberated through the room. He trashed and wiggled, trying to get away.

"Chief, Warlord, hold him down."

They came over and held Thomas down. Noah began again, flaying off the tattoo. Thomas yelled and cried the entire time. As the last piece of the ink lifted off his body, Noah picked it up.

"This was given to you as a clear indication that you were a loyal and trusted part of the family," Noah said. He turned to see his father had rolled beside him with a metal bowl. With a swift motion, he dropped the skin into the bowl and poured alcohol over the bloody flesh, the liquid seeping into every crevice. With a flick of his wrist, he lit a match and threw it into the metal bowl, causing a burst of flames. As the fire jumped to life, the room filled with the acrid stench of burning flesh.

Noah looked back at Thomas, who looked like he would pass out from the pain. "Give him a shot of adrenaline."

Finn picked up one of the many syringes and pushed the adrenaline into Thomas's leg. A few moments later, Thomas awoke screaming at the top of his lungs and trying again to get out of the cuffs, but Finn and Connor had a tight hold on him.

"Now that you are no longer part of this family, I can now inflict real pain." An evil chuckle rumbled out of Noah's mouth as he held up the bloody knife.

"NO, NO, please stop," Thomas said, as tears ran down his face.

"Where is Scarlett?" Noah asked, his voice cold and without emotion.

"I don't know," Thomas answered. He knew if he told the truth, he would die. He needed time to figure out how to get out of this situation.

"Yes, you do," Noah said. He slid the knife under the skin at his neck, slipping it from one side to the other, only cutting the first layer of skin. Even though it wasn't a deep cut, it still bled profusely. "TELL ME WHERE!"

"I don't," Thomas began, but Noah grasped hold of the skin before he could finish and ripped it down his chest. The prior pain was nothing compared to this. He couldn't breathe and he couldn't think. The world was becoming fuzzy. Darkness draped over him, pushing the pain away.

"Give him another dose," Noah barked. "Make it a double."

Noah knew Thomas was close to giving up the information, but he had to keep him awake.

They pushed in the next dose and Thomas awoke screaming and bellowing in extreme pain. He just wanted to die.

"Please, I beg you, stop."

"I will stop only when I know where Scarlett is being held and by whom," Noah said through gritted teeth.

Thomas knew he would never get out alive, and he had two options. The first would be not to tell Noah the location of Scarlett and die a slow, painful death. The second would be to tell Noah everything he knew and pray for a quick death. Either way, he would not get out of here alive. Fuck, why had he listened to Eleazar?. Pulling from what little energy he had left, he opened his eyes and looked up at Noah. "Castle Rock."

"What?" Noah asked, unsure of what he had heard.

"Castle Rock. She is with her father in Castle Rock," Thomas choked out.

Noah's heart dropped. Scarlett was with her monster of a father. There's no telling what he had put her through already.

"Do you know where her father is keeping her?" Noah asked. He needed to know everything Thomas knew.

"Eleazar told me that her father was keeping her close to God," Thomas answered.

"So Eleazar was behind her kidnapping?"

"Yes. He is kicking himself for not allying with the families before he tried to take out Liam."

"ELEAZAR IS THE MOTHERFUCKER WHO PUT THE HIT OUT ON ME!" Liam yelled. He finally knew who put him in the wheelchair.

"Yes," Thomas answered. "Noah, please let me die."

"I should make you suffer as long as my Scarlett has been held captive," Noah began, then took the knife and cut the carotid artery. The dark red blood flowed out and down on the floor. "But I need to save her. Enjoy your time with the devil."

Noah's gaze shifted to his brothers as he set down the knife. "Get the team together. We are going to Castle Rock."

CHAPTER TWENTY-TWO

Noah left the interrogation room, wishing he could bring Thomas back to life to make him suffer more for what he did to Scarlett. He couldn't believe that Scarlett was in the hands of her crazy, fanatic father.

When Noah tried to find Scarlett after the incredible night that turned his life around, he was given a thorough account of Weston Allen Murphy. Fuck, he was in the mafia and nothing really affected him. Yet reading what Weston had done made Noah shiver. Weston's sick and twisted views on women were medieval and barbaric in nature.

"Noah, are you alright, son?" Liam asked as he wheeled himself out of the room.

When he looked at his father, he noticed his brothers as well. He had to visualize her being fine and make his way to Castle Rock. "Connor, call the team and prepare them to leave in two hours. Ensure the guys who broke into the Murphy home to get Scarlett's grandmother's things are part of the team."

"Will do." Connor walked away, pulled out his phone, and began barking out orders.

"Finn, you will be in charge until I get back," Noah said in a cold, no-nonsense tone, turning toward his father. "You will get your revenge. I want Eleazar and Carmen picked up and brought here."

"Yes, Skipper," Finn said.

"Hold them until I get back and keep them separate. Dad, do you feel up to making Eleazar pay?"

Liam looked up at his son. He had been working hard with his physical therapy, hoping to get out of this fucking wheelchair. Locking the wheels, he pulled his feet from the footplates, placing them on the floor. He grasped the arms of the chair. He pushed with all his might until he stood on his own two feet. This was the first time his sons had seen him stand on his own since the shooting. By some miracle, he had regained some feeling in his feet and legs over the last few months. At first, it started as a strange tingling sensation in his feet, and then it traveled up his legs.

"Dad," Finn gasped, shocked that his father was standing. He never thought it would be possible.

"Bring me the fucker," Liam growled, his face full of determination.

Noah couldn't help but smile. His father was the strongest, most deadly man he knew and he couldn't wait to see what he had in mind to make Eleazar pay. "Alright. I will leave the two of you in charge, then."

Connor walked back over. "Skipper, wheels up in seventy-five minutes. The team is gearing up and will load the necessary equipment within the hour. I called Garrett and he is coming. He is also bringing Dr. O'Neill in case Scarlett needs her doctor."

Noah had not thought of that, yet it was a brilliant idea. He had no clue what kind of conditions Scarlett had been exposed to. Damn, he couldn't think about her needing her doctor. He knew Garrett would be ready for all scenarios. "Finn, when you pick up Eleazar and Carmen, do it as quietly as possible. There is no need to alert his family if we can help it."

"What about his daughters?" Connor asked.

"Fuck, I forgot about Camila and Gabriela. Pick them up also and bring them here. Just keep them away from the others. I'll make the decision about them when I get back."

"Sure thing, Skipper," Finn said.

"Skipper, you need to get cleaned up. The cleaning crew will be here soon to take out the trash," Connor said. "I left your clothes in the bath. Your vest and guns are being taken to the plane."

Noah nodded and took off to the bathroom. He removed his bloody clothes and shoes, placing them in a special container. The cleaning crew would take care of destroying them. He stepped into the specially designed shower system and let the hot water wash away all of Thomas's blood. It was hard for Noah to accept that one of his family members was responsible for the kidnapping of Scarlett and the murder of his other family members. How did he not see it? He shook his head and finished his shower. He toweled off and when dry threw it into the container with his suit. He locked the shower door and initiated sterilization. The walls and floors were drenched in bleach. This would eliminate any possible evidence of blood or other fluids that could be used against him or his family by the police. The cleaning crew would use a black light to check for any remaining evidence after completing the sterilization cycle.

He quickly dressed in a black suit, white tailored shirt, blood-red tie, and Italian leather loafers. He could have worn combat fatigues, yet he believed his suit portrayed him as the dangerous son of a bitch he was. Weston Murphy would know what happened when you messed with Noah Kelly and his family. He placed his gun in its holster and departed the room. Connor was on the phone, planning transportation from Tacoma airport to Castle Rock. How fucking small was this town? No damn wonder his love escaped it as soon as she could and never looked back.

"Where are Dad and Finn?" Noah asked.

"They have gone back to the office to plan the Ortiz family extractions," Connor answered.

"Good. Let's get to the plane," Noah said. He was getting eager to get on their way. "How long is the flight?"

"Almost five and a half hours," Connor answered. "I have our SUVs waiting for us at the hangar in Tacoma. We will have another hour from there to Castle Rock."

"Fuck. Isn't there any way we can get there quicker?"

"Sorry, Skipper, but no."

"Alright, then we should arrive in Castle Rock right after sunset, which is good. We will work on the strike plan on the plane."

Seven hours later, they landed in Tacoma with what they hoped was a fail-proof plan. Garrett and Dr. O'Neill had their plan ready to deploy if needed. They weren't happy with the limited medical center in Castle Rock, so a helicopter was on standby if Scarlett's babies were in distress. It would only take them forty minutes to get to Seattle and a level-one health center. Scarlett was at thirty-four weeks and was at risk with multiples to go into labor any day now. The babies would be smaller, depending on the conditions she had to endure for the last thirty-four days.

When their private jet landed, the team unloaded the equipment and placed it in the SUVs. Everyone put on their communication devices and checked that they were working correctly.

Connor made Noah put on a bulletproof vest. He grumbled about it but did it anyway. He needed to take whatever precautions to come out of this alive so that he could take care of Scarlett. With Rory behind the wheel, Noah climbed into the SUV with Connor, Jon, and Alec. Jon had been at the tent meeting when Noah was looking for Scarlett. The remaining guards climbed in two of the other SUVs. The fourth SUV was for Garrett, Dr. O'Neill, Luke, and Randell.

Noah felt anxious as they rushed toward Castle Rock, unsure of what he would discover. Scarlett was the strongest person he knew, and he had to be positive that she was okay. He took a deep breath and immersed himself in the Murphy house and church floor plans.

"Five minutes out," Connor called out. They went to the house first and used FLIR thermal cameras to see how many people were there and their locations within the house.

They parked across the street from the white two-story house and saw no cars in the driveway, and the only light was the one on the porch. The team surveyed the area and exited the vehicle. They inched closer to the house, using the FLIR to search each room, but found nothing. They discovered the house had a root cellar during their visit to retrieve Scarlett's grandmother's chest. The only entrance was through the door on the house's west side. Since it lacked a lock, they silently opened the door and descended the concrete steps. Once again, the FLIR was used to scan the area, but no heat signature was detected.

"No one is here, Skipper," Mark called over the mic.

"Alright, let's get to the church."

For some inexplicable reason, Noah knew she was there. The team returned to their vehicle and headed towards Weston Murphy's church. It was on a dirt road off Highway 101. There were no other buildings or houses within a five-mile radius. Twenty minutes later, they were slowly driving up the muddy road with the lights off, hoping for the element of surprise.

It was exactly like the pictures the team had taken when they were out here. The one-story church looked run down and needed a good paint job. The sanctuary lights were on and in the far back left corner of the building, a small dim light was also on.

Randal exited the vehicle and went to the building's left side with the FLIR while Jared checked the front.

"I have two heat signatures in the chapel area," Randal whispered into his microphone.

"I have one in the back room, and I believe it is Mrs. Kelly," Jared said. The person he saw was lying down and he could see that they had a large protruding stomach, like someone who was pregnant.

Noah's heart raced. "Randall, you and your team monitor those in the chapel area. Connor, Rory, you are with me. Garrett, Dr. O'Neill, you stay put for now."

With guns ready, they slipped out of the vehicle. They proceeded to the side of the church where Jon was stationed. As they neared the door, Noah nodded towards Connor, who quickly picked the lock. He took a small bottle out of his pants pocket, squirted oil on the hinges, and pushed the door open. A faint glow of light coming from beneath the door to the left illuminated the dark and narrow hallway.

Noah put his ear to the door and heard soft moaning. He couldn't tell if it was Scarlett. "Pick it."

Connor once again did quick work on the lock and oiling the hinges. He turned the knob and pushed open the door. He gave the room a quick glance before Noah was allowed to enter. It was a small room that was no bigger than seven feet by seven feet, with no windows or any other doors. A swift glance at the bed revealed a figure with red hair concealing their face.

Unable to handle it any longer, Noah shoved Connor aside. He entered the confined space, where he saw a body resting on a tiny bed, wrapped in a thin blanket that could not provide any warmth. The room was freezing cold. He walked over to the bed, knelt down, and brushed the hair back. He couldn't help but sigh of relief as he saw the face of his heart, his soul, his reason for living, his Scarlett.

"Scarlett, my love," he whispered, lightly stroking her face.

Her eyes fluttered open and she gasped. "I must be dreaming again."

Noah leaned down and placed a feather-light kiss on her dry, cracked lips. "You are not dreaming. Fuck baby, it is me."

"Noah," she cried, reaching out and putting her arms around his neck. "I knew you would find me. I just knew it, no matter what Weston said."

"Did he hurt you?" Noah asked, even though he was scared to hear what she might disclose.

"Weston has lost his mind. He thinks I am carrying his sons and that God himself impregnated me," Scarlett said. When she arrived in Castle Rock, her father proclaimed a miracle had happened.

"Fuck," Noah said. He knew Weston was a little out there, but this put him on a whole different plane of crazy.

"Ahh," Scarlett groaned, grasping her belly.

"Scarlett, what is it?" Noah asked.

"I think I am in labor."

"Shit. Alright, let's get you out of here. Garrett and Dr. O'Neill are outside and they will take care of you."

"But what about Weston and Frances?"

"Was Frances part of this?" Noah asked, hoping that at least one of her parents had been concerned about her well-being.

"Yes. She assisted him with my imprisonment and even convinced him to cut my food supply, stating that the babies didn't need that much to grow."

"How long have you been in pain?"

"About two hours."

"Dr. O'Neill," Noah called out through his microphone.

"Yes, Noah."

"We found Scarlett. She believes she is in labor for about two hours."

"Get her to us as soon as possible," Dr. O'Neill said. Her mind formulated a plan for what they needed to do once they found out for sure if, in fact, Scarlett was in active labor.

"Randall, is everything still secure?" Noah checked.

"Yes, Skipper."

"Baby, we are going to get you out of here. Stay as quiet as you can."

She sat up, throwing the thin blanket from her body. This was the first time he had seen how much her belly had grown since he had last seen her. He wrapped his hands around her belly and leaned down. "Hey, little guys. Daddy is here. Be good, boys, and stay there until we get momma to the hospital."

Tears flowed down Scarlett's cheeks as she watched Noah talk to their sons. There was no doubt of his love for her and their baby boys. The swift kicks came as their little guys gave their response to their father. Noah looked up and smiled at her.

Noah lifted her into his arms. He pulled her to his chest and headed towards the door. "We will have you safe in just a few seconds."

Connor was waiting for them and couldn't be happier for his brother and sister. "Ready to move?"

"Yes," Noah answered.

They headed out of the room and quickly made their way outside. Randall said the two people in the chapel were still there and no one else was around. They headed to the SUV, where Garrett and Dr. O'Neill were waiting. The door opened and Noah carefully sat her on the leather seat.

"Baby, I won't be long," he said, then looked up at the two doctors. "If you need to go, then you know what to do."

"I'm not leaving without you," Scarlett cried, trying to leave the vehicle.

"Scarlett, we will only go if the babies are in distress and need medical assistance," Garrett said, hoping he would calm her down.

"I promise I will be right behind you if you have to go."

Scarlett did like it all. Noah had just found her and now he was leaving her again. However, she needed to think about what was best for the babies. "Hurry and come back to me."

"Always, my love," he vowed, then closed the door. He turned towards his men, unbuttoned his jacket and walked towards the church's steps. It was time for Weston Murphy to meet The Devil.

With his team following closely, Noah opened the door and walked inside. They were here only if he needed help.

Weston looked up when he heard the door open and saw a

man he had never seen before walking down the aisle towards him. "May I help you? Are you here to find Jesus?"

"No, I'm the devil. Come to claim one of my minions," Noah said with a smirk. "My name is Noah Kelly."

"I am not sure what you mean," Weston said.

"I have come to make you pay for taking my wife and unborn sons from me."

"I don't have your wife."

"Well, not anymore, you don't," Noah smiled.

Weston looked back towards the door that led to the back of the church where Scarlett was being held. "Go, check on her," he commanded to Frances.

She jumped to her feet and ran towards the door. But Mark stopped her. He grasped her arm and twisted it behind her back, causing her to cry out in pain.

"Let her go," Weston growled.

"Not going to happen," Noah said, closing the distance between them and landing a right hook to the side of Weston's face without hesitation. His head whipped around and two teeth flew out of his mouth. Not waiting for him to recover, Noah began delivering punch after punch to Weston's face and body. When he fell to the floor, Noah started kicking and relishing in the sound of the ribs breaking.

Weston tried to catch a breath, yet every time he sucked in a breath, he cried out in pain. He sat up and tried to get to his feet.

Noah smiled as he looked down at the bloody, broken man. He took off his blood-red tie and wrapped it around his bloody hands. Stepping behind Weston, he placed the tie around his neck and pulled.

"You will suffer for every moment you stole from Scarlett and me. This was supposed to be a special time and you ruined it. I wanted to watch my sons grow in my wife's belly," Noah snarled, pulling the tie tighter before releasing it to allow Weston to breathe. He knew it would hurt like the devil when Weston took a deep breath.

Weston coughed and tried to breathe in between the pain. "They are my sons, not yours."

"Oh, you are wrong about that, you asshole. Those are my and Scarlett's little boys, and you will never get close to them again." He looked towards his brother and men. "Help me send him to hell."

Connor and Randall reached down and picked Weston up, dragging him up the two steps and behind the podium. They wondered what Noah's plan was but knew it would fit the crime.

As soon as Noah had walked into the church, he had spotted exactly where Weston Murphy's last breath would be. The man preached that he was a man of God, but in reality, he was nothing pure evil. "Strap him to the cross," he said.

His men didn't even flinch at the command. Quickly taking plastic zip ties, they tied his hands and legs to the wooden cross.

"What are you doing to my husband?" Frances screamed. She had already been secured with zip ties and was being watched by Mark.

"Sending him to his maker," Noah answered. His voice was that of ice. There was no hint of warmth or feeling. He looked at Mark, nodding his head once. Without hesitation, Mark pulled his knife from its sleeve and slit her throat. A look of shock spread across her face for a split second before her lifeless body slumped to the floor with a pool of blood around her.

Weston had watched the entire scene from his vantage point strapped to the cross. Frances may have been his wife, yet she had let him down by not giving him the sons that he needed. She was dead and that was okay with him. He looked away from Frances and saw Noah step closer to him. What was he going to do now? Maybe he could talk his way out of whatever he was planning.

"As much as I would love to stay here and make you suffer before I end your sorry excuse of a life. I have been away from my wife too long to waste any more time on the likes of you,"

Noah said. With a tilt of his head toward Connor, he reached into his jacket and handed him a trencher knife. Noah slipped his fingers through the grip holder and stabbed Weston's midsection with one fluid motion. The blade laid him open. His guts and internal organs tumbled out and down onto the floor. Noah heard Weston gasp at the first contact and made a grunting sound.

"God, help me," Weston said, his voice weak and shaky before his heart gave out.

"Sorry, Weston, God is not listening today." Noah stepped back and watched the blood flow like a river from his body. He returned the knife to Connor, picked up the white linen tablecloth, and wiped the blood off his hands. He turned to Connor. "Burn it to the ground."

Connor nodded, and the team rushed out to get the gasoline cans to dowse the building. Noah followed them out and was happy that the SUV holding Scarlett and her doctors was still there. Walking over to it, he opened the door and climbed in. "Are we okay here?"

"Yes, but it looks like we'll need that helicopter after all," Dr. O'Neill advised with a smile. "Your boys seem to want to be born before the night is over."

"Is it over?" Scarlett asked, just finishing a strong contraction. She had been worried about Noah ever since he walked into the church, though she knew he could take care of himself. She had seen him walk out of the church. His suit jacket was torn at the shoulder, his tie was missing, and blood was on his shirt and hands.

"Yes. You will never have to worry about them again," Noah declared, kissing her lips.

CHAPTER TWENTY-THREE

"You are doing great," Noah said as he watched the screen. "You are coming down from the peak. Breathe through your nose, then out through your mouth. Release the tension in your toes, now your feet, now your legs. Now, continue up your body, releasing until you reach your head. Good, now one deep sigh, and it is over."

"Damn, that one hurt," Scarlett said, gasping for air.

"You are doing so well," Garrett said with a smile, patting Scarlett's hand on the other side of the bed. He had just returned to the birthing suite after arranging with the head of pediatrics to be the one to take over the care of the babies once they were born. At first, Dr. Poo wouldn't even consider taking on the case, instructing that several highly qualified interns would be happy to help. However, money always had a way of changing people's minds. The hospital welcomed them with open arms after Noah funded the new Scarlett Kelly Neonatal Wing.

"Thanks. We only got two classes in before I was taken," Scarlett said as Noah wiped her forehead with a cool rag.

"Well, you are a natural."

Scarlett turned towards Noah. "I wish Brooke and Eve could be here, as well as our parents."

Noah placed a kiss on her forehead. "I know, sweetheart, yet I promise the next time, everyone will be here cheering you on."

"Next time?" Scarlett asked.

"Yeah. I hope to have a house full of children looking like my lovely wife."

"Hmm. I don't know about that because I wanted to cut your dick off just a few minutes ago," Scarlett giggled.

"Ah...really?" Noah stuttered as his cock tried to hide.

"No, baby. But let's get these little guys out first. Okay?"

"Okay."

The relief he felt was immense when they found her in time. Once Weston and Frances were killed, they made a quick escape to a waiting helicopter and headed towards Seattle.

After they took off, he could assess the damage done to Scarlett. Her appearance was something she was very particular about. She frequently took at least two showers a day. Her hair was always neat and tamed. Only during their intimate moments did he see it disheveled, spread out wildly on their pillows. But now, it was a tangled mess in oily clumps to her head, and her skin appeared unwashed for days if not weeks. She had on a threadbare dress that fell just below her knees. The only area where she put on weight was her stomach. Everywhere else, she was skin and bones. Her eyes were sunken in and she looked sickly. Dr. O'Neill and Garrett started an IV and a vitamin bag before boarding the helicopter. Her arms and knees were covered in bruises. When asked by Noah how she acquired them, she explained Frances would grab her arms while escorting her to the bathroom. Or when she would have a weekly bath in a shallow metal tub with cold water. Her knees were bruised because she had to spend at least six hours a day on her knees praying. She admitted that she only had one prayer for him to find her.

Once they arrived at Virginia Mason Hospital in Seattle, she was rushed to the birthing suite and Dr. O'Neill did a full exam with a complete blood workup. A 4D sonogram was done and they were able to see their sons. Even though Scarlett was under-weight, it looked like the boys were doing great. Dr. O'Neill believed that any food Scarlett had eaten had gone straight to the babies.

Conner and the rest of the team arrived and were in the waiting room. They kept the rest of the family up to date with text messages. Finn told Noah that Eleazar and Carmen were taken with no problems, yet Gabriela and Camila were nowhere to be found. Finn was trying to get the information out of Eleazar, careful not to let it go too far so Liam could attain justice. What surprised Noah was that his sweet, loving mother was doing the same thing to Carmen.

He knew that his mother had killed two men in the past, yet that was self-defensive when they had broken into their house. However, he would have never imagined that she could do something like this. When Noah asked why, Finn informed him that Máthair wanted to make the bitch pay for hurting her baby girl.

"Baby, I know you are tired, but we need you to push. You are so close," Noah said. He knew she was running out of energy, though it would be safer for her if she could deliver naturally in her current condition. While she was resting between contractions, Garrett and Dr. O'Neill informed him of this. The last resort would be a cesarean.

"I can't," Scarlett cried, leaning her head towards him.

"You can. Our son is so close. Just a few more big pushes and he will be here."

"He is right, Scarlett. I see his head, just one or two more pushes, and he will be out," Dr. O'Neill said.

Scarlett was so tired. She didn't think she could push anymore.

"Damn, he is in distress!" Dr. O'Neill yelled as the fetal moni-tor's alarm blared.

"Do we do the cesarean?" Garrett asked.

"No time," Dr. O'Neill replied. "Scarlett, you need to push NOW!"

She didn't know where it came from, yet hearing that her baby was in distress, she pulled every ounce of strength she had left and pushed.

Dr. O'Neill couldn't help but smile when the baby's head emerged. "Don't push, don't push. I need to turn him a little so the shoulders will come out."

"I have to push," Scarlett cried. The need was too much for her to stop.

"Breathe, baby," Noah said, then panted, hoping she would mimic his breathing. When she did, he continued breathing with her and would until it was okay to push again.

"Alright, Scarlett, one more push and he will be out," Dr. O'Neil said.

Scarlett stopped panting and bore down. She felt her son as he slipped from her body and she cried in relief. Suddenly, the room was filled with their son's cries.

"He is perfect, Scarlett," Dr. O'Neill proclaimed. "Noah, would you like to cut the cord?"

Noah was torn. He didn't want to leave Scarlett's side, even for the short time it would take to cut the cord, yet he wanted to do it so badly.

"Go, Daddy. I will be right here when you are done."

He placed a quick kiss on her lips. He jumped up and headed toward where Dr. O'Neill was standing, holding their son. Garrett places a pair of scissors in his hands and points to where he is supposed to cut. Once he did, Dr. O'Neill walked around and put the baby on Scarlett's chest.

"Say hello to your son," Dr. O'Neill whispered.

Scarlett placed her hand on her son's back and looked down at the precious little miracle. "Hello, Liam. I'm your Máthair."

Noah had returned to Scarlett's side and couldn't take his eyes off his son. Other than his mother, he was the most beautiful sight he had ever seen. Placing his hand on top of Scarlett's, he leaned down and kissed her head. "Fuck, baby, he is perfect."

"Noah, you will have to watch that mouth of yours," Scarlett giggled.

"Mr. and Mrs. Kelly, I need to take him to check him out," Dr. Poo said.

Scarlett hated giving him up, though she knew it was the best for him. She removed her hand and watched as Dr. Poo gently picked up Liam from her chest. As he was being checked out, the urge to push again began. "FUCK!"

Dr. O'Neill turned to see the expression on Scarlett's face and then up to the monitor. "OH SHIT!"

"I think we all will have to watch our mouths around the children," Noah joked.

Dr. O'Neill got into position and was shocked to see that the second baby's head was already crowning. "Scarlett, give me a big push. Liam's brother is in a hurry to get here."

Scarlett tucked her chin to her chest and pushed. Moments later, the room was once again filled with crying. Noah rushed forward once again and cut the cord. The little baby was laid on Scarlett's chest, just like his brother.

Laying her hand on his back, she looked loving down on her second baby. "Hi, Robbie, I'm your Máthair and this guy is your Athair."

Noah was so emotional he didn't think he could even speak. He was a father of twin boys, no identical twin boys. Garrett took little Robbie to check out while Dr. O'Neill finished with the necessary things after the birth. She was happy that Scarlett had not bled excessively and that the afterbirth was intact. They needed to worry about getting the weight back on Scarlett.

"Do we have full names for these perfect little boys?" Dr. Poo asked.

"Liam Patrick Kelly and Robert Anthony Kelly," Scarlett answered, her face full of excitement over the names. She and

Noah only knew them and couldn't wait until they told their family.

Dr. Poo and Garrett brought the boys back over to Scarlett and Noah. "They are perfect. Liam weighs five pounds ten ounces and is nineteen inches long. Robert weighs five pounds eight ounces and is nineteen inches long. They are identical twins, and I have placed an ink mark for now on Liam's big toe. Over time, you will tell them apart, though it will be difficult right now. We have taken their footprints, so if you get them messed up, we can determine who is who," Dr. Poo advised.

Noah climbed on the bed beside Scarlett. While she held Robbie, he held Liam. "Baby, thank you for giving me this wonderful gift," he choked out.

"No, thank you."

Three days later, they were on the jet and returning home. Scarlett was doing much better and was given supplements to help her weight gain. She had been extremely disappointed that she could not nurse their sons. After breaking down, Noah assured her she would still give him a house full of babies so she would have lots of time to nurse. She wondered how lucky she was to find a man who could quickly lift her spirits.

Liam and Emee were beyond happy to see the pictures and videos of their grandchildren. They couldn't wait to get their hands on the precious bundles of joy. Liam called Noah and told him that neither Eleazar nor Carmen had given up Gabriela's or Camila's whereabouts. Noah was told Finn was still looking for them and wouldn't stop until they were found.

"I can't wait to get home," Scarlett said, looking down at the large basket that held Liam and Robbie.

"Me either. However, I need to take care of one more piece of business when we get there, and then we can begin our life together as a family."

Scarlett didn't necessarily know what he would do, but she knew it had to do with Eleazar Ortiz. She didn't want to know what, just that their children were safe. "I understand."

"Eve, Brooke, and a contingent of guards will stay with you at the mansion."

"The mansion? I thought we were going back to the apartment," Scarlett asked. They planned to exchange their apartment with Liam and Emee for the mansion. Yet, they didn't get to plan it any further since she had been kidnapped.

"While you were taken, Emee arranged for the move. She wanted you to come back to our new home. All the stuff is at the mansion and the nursery is completed to your vision."

"I don't know what to say."

"Are you happy? Because if you are not, we can move back to the apartment, or hell, I'll buy you a house or fucking build one of your dreams."

Scarlett climbed onto Noah's lap, placing her hands on either side of his face. "I am so happy and can't wait to live in the mansion with you and our children. Still, there is no way in the world I am filling the mansion with babies," she laughed.

Noah wrapped his arms around her and pulled her into a long, passionate kiss of love and need. He knew they couldn't do anything for six weeks, though that didn't stop his cock from getting hard. Finally pulling back, he rested his forehead against hers. "Fuck, it is going to be a long six weeks."

"I know," Scarlett sighed.

Hours later, they landed back in New York and Noah took Scarlett and the babies to the mansion. After settling them with Brooke and Eve, Noah, Liam, and Emee headed towards the warehouse. Noah was still shocked that his mother declared she was caring for Carmen and Marta. When he tried to pull his position on her, she gave him a look that made even him quake in his shoes. Fuck, his mother was one scary woman. She demanded to be brought to the warehouse. He shut up and supported her. His father had told him he hadn't told his mother about being able to stand, wanting it to be a surprise.

Pulling up to the warehouse, Conner and Finn met them. Noah stepped out of the car and pulled down the curtain on his emotions. He was Noah Kelly, the Skipper of the Kelly crime family, and he was one mean son of a bitch. The door opened and he walked in with his family following behind him. Eleazar, Carmen, and Marta were tied to poles in the main area.

In the middle of the room was a large industrial-grade meat grinder. It was used to grind whole hogs simultaneously without slowing down. Emee stepped forward-looking the epitome of a mafia wife. She walked over to where Carmen was tied up. She stopped in front of her and gave her a look of pure disgust.

"Emee, help me, please," Carmen said. They had pinned her up in a cage for the last four days, only giving her one meal a day and a pot in the corner to do her business in.

"Carmen, why the hell would I do that? I am sick and tired of years of listening to how great you and your daughters are," Emee spat.

"But Emee, Marta would be a much better wife for Noah than that little nobody bitch he had been forced to marry," Carmen said. She had been told that the little slut had been taken care of and was giving Noah time to grieve before Marta made her move.

"Had? I don't know where you are getting your information. But our loving and caring Scarlett is at home taking care of our glorious grandsons," Emee said with a large smile.

"That can't be," Carmen snapped.

"It is very true. Carmen, you like to think of yourself as Kobe beef. However, you are nothing more than ground chuck," Emee said, turning towards the grinder and flipping the switch. She nodded to Noah, who tilted his head to his men. They untied Carmen and Marta, carried their kicking, screaming bodies up the steps, and threw them into the grinder without a second thought. Their screams echoed through the building. Then, there was nothing but silence. Emee Kelly had just killed two people and didn't even get a hair out of place or a wrinkle in her expensive dress.

Eleazar was stunned, silent. He could not believe that Emee had killed his wife and daughter. How had he been so stupid to be captured so easily? He knew he had to turn the tide and show just how badass he was indeed and put baby Kelly in his place. "Are you too much of a pussy that you have your mother doing your job?"

Noah stepped in front of Eleazar and stared into his black eyes. "I would have loved to grind your entire family into a pile of chopped beef, yet I would never deny my mother the pleasure she requested and deserved."

"Is she going to do your job where I am concerned as well?" Eleazar growled, then looked over to Liam in the wheelchair and smiled. "Or is the cripple going to do it for you?"

Noah looked back at his father, who gave him a smirk. Turning back to Eleazar, he gave him the same smirk. "I don't think you should have said that, fucker."

Noah stepped back and waved his hand from his father to Eleazar. "I give you permission to take your vengeance against the man who put the hit on you. Do with him as you will."

Eleazar couldn't help but laugh. He had turned the once-feared Liam Kelly into a cripple. Hell, he bet he couldn't even get his dick up to pleasure Emee. Looking over to Emee, he surveyed her body from her full lips, ample breasts, thin waist, and round hips. "Hmm, Emee, now that was one pussy he would love to sink into," he thought as he licked his lips.

Eleazar hadn't heard Liam as he moved closer to him and locked the wheels of his chair. He placed his feet on the floor and pulled himself up. Liam Kelly was standing tall and strong on his own two feet. Liam heard Emee gasp, yet he had not taken his sights off Eleazar and the lecherous way he looked at his wife. Taking two steps, he was now in front of Eleazar. He reached for the brass knuckles from his pocket and slipped them on. Without hesitation, he threw a power punch to the right side of Eleazar's face, causing his head to whip around. "Take your fucking eyes off my wife, you fucking asshole."

Eleazar wanted to rub his aching jaw, but his hands were tied behind his back. His mouth was filled with blood, so he spat it toward Liam. "How the fuck are you standing? I had you shot in the back. YOU SHOULD BE DEAD, MOTHERFUCKER!"

"Easy. Your fucking attempt to kill me failed and now I am walking, so you lose again," Liam chuckled darkly.

"The other families will kill you if you harm me. Fuck, when I am let loose, I will play the grieving widower and they will come to my aid," Eleazar said.

"That is where you are wrong. You just admitted to having put a hit on a family head. By doing so, you have forfeited any help that the other families would have given," Liam advised, pointing up to the camera on a pole facing Eleazar. "Furthermore, you had the wife, no correction, the pregnant wife of a family head kidnapped. Noah has spoken to the other families and as we speak, they are eliminating every one of your family members."

"You can't do that," Eleazar growled, fighting against his restraints.

Liam leaned closer and whispered. "Yes, I can."

He stepped back and looked over to where the guards were standing. "Bring over the table, strip him down, and secure him face down."

A long steel table was wheeled over with wrist and ankle cuffs. Conner and Mark untied Eleazar and removed his filthy clothes with a knife. They dragged him, fighting and kicking across the concrete floor to the table. Conner picked him up and slammed him hard into it while Mark and another guard secured his hands and feet.

While Eleazar was being secured, Emee stepped over to

Liam. She couldn't believe he was standing and walking. She cupped the side of his face. "How is this happening?" she asked, her voice cracking with emotion.

"I noticed that feeling returned a few weeks ago," Liam answered, then moved close to her ear. Running his tongue around the shell and taking her earlobe into his mouth, giving it a suck. "When I finish here, I plan on taking you home and making love to you all fucking night long."

Emee's eyes grew large and she panted. "Oh, my."

"Why don't you go ahead and leave? Have your guards take you to the apartment and take a nice, long, hot shower. Be waiting for me in our bed, naked and wet."

Emee kissed him and walked out of the warehouse, happy and excited.

Liam closed his eyes and willed the massive hard-on he had to come down. Fuck, he needed to finish this dirty business so that he could get home to his wife. With each step he took towards the table, he breathed deeply, feeling his nerves settle. He felt the strain in his legs but pushed himself to keep going. With the knife in hand, he stepped forward, positioning himself in front of Eleazar to show him what he had found. "As much as I would love to stay here all night and bring you to the brink of death over and over again, I am afraid that will not be the case. I have an extremely beautiful and seductive wife who is hot and wet for me in our bed."

"Emee needs a real man," Eleazar sneered. "I bet your dick hasn't been hard since I had you shot. Fuck, I bet you probably have a pencil dick."

The sound of Liam's hearty laughter filled the air. He placed the knife on the table and unzipped his pants, revealing his erect member. He was long, thick, and hard, just what his lovely wife loved buried deep in her hot pussy. "Does this look like a pencil dick, fucker?"

Eleazar was surprised by what he saw. The powerful Liam Kelly was back and at that moment, he knew he was screwed.

Pleading would not work, nor was begging for mercy. Insults were probably adding to the upcoming pain.

Liam placed his cock back in his pants and picked up the knife. "I have always liked the saying, an eye for an eye. However, today, I think it should be a spine for a spine."

Liam took the knife and sliced down both sides of Eleazar's backbone, causing him to scream in agony. After finishing, he took the jigsaw and separated each rib from the spine. Eleazar passed out from the pain and Liam ordered an adrenaline dose to revive him during this stage. Liam leaned over to his face as soon as he regained consciousness. "No one messes with my family and lives."

Liam took the jigsaw and cut the C1 vertebrae. As the life faded away in Eleazar's eyes, Liam reached down and pulled the spine from his back. With a grin, he threw it onto the ground. "A spine for a spine."

Noah had stood back and watched his father in all his glory. He was in awe of him. He only hoped that he would be half the man his father was and that he could protect the family with every bit of passion he had demonstrated.

"I am done," Liam said as he motioned for his chair. He was still not back a hundred percent, though there was no doubt he could burn that fucking chair soon.

Finn helped his father into the chair and commanded the clean-up crew to handle all the evidence. The crew came in and began caring for the blood, bones, ground flesh, and Eleazar's body.

"Just throw it in the grinder," Noah advised.

"Yes, Skipper."

As the crew cleaned, Noah helped his father into the bath area. "Do you need help?"

"No, I have got this," Liam answered. "Thanks for letting me take care of Eleazar."

Noah placed his hand on his father's shoulder. "It was your right and I am so fucking proud to be your son."

"You are a great Skipper, son. The family is lucky to have you," Liam said, his eyes a little misty with tears. He had hoped that he raised his sons correctly to be the next family leaders and now he could see they were.

Noah arrived home and went looking for his lovely wife. As soon as he hit the second floor, he heard her sweet voice singing in the nursery. He opened the door wider and saw his wife sitting in the rocking chair. The boys snuggled up to her. As he stood and listened to her sing, he was overwhelmed with love for this woman.

"Rock-a-bye baby in the treetop. When the wind blows, the cradle will rock. When the bough breaks, the cradle will fall. And down will come, baby," Scarlett sang, then stopped. "No, Liam and Robbie, that is not right," Scarlett cooed, looking down at her two precious little boys. She began to sing once again. "Rock-a-bye baby in the treetop. When the wind blows, the cradle will rock. When the bough breaks, the cradle will fall. Your daddy will catch you, cradle and all."

They had been so close to a broken lullaby, but the power of their love helped them overcome the dangers that came their way.

EPILOGUE

"Daddy, you can't catch us," Liam and Robbie yelled as their little five-year-old legs carried them across the backyard, with Noah running after them. Scarlett couldn't help but smile. Her life started out as a living hell, but it only took one night to change it for the better. On that night, Noah gave her the beginning of a beautiful future. They still had their ups and downs, but she wouldn't trade one day of it.

She didn't ask what happened to the Ortizs. Noah said they would never cause problems again and that was all she needed to know.

Eight weeks after Liam and Robbie were born, Emee threw a massive reception at the Central Ballroom to celebrate Scarlett and Noah's wedding. Families from all over the country came to see the new leader of the Kelly Family and his wife. Emee prepared Scarlett for the event to ensure there would be no doubt in anyone's mind that she was the backbone of their home.

"I'm not the backbone," Scarlett said as they discussed the reception.

"But you are. Your husband is the backbone of the Family.

You are the backbone of your home. When they enter their home after a trying day, you are there to give them a shoulder to lean on. You are there to allow them to show their vulnerability. You are there to celebrate their victories and their losses. When the unthinkable happens, you will be by his side as he tells the loved ones their husband or wife won't be coming home. You will stand beside him at the funeral and be there for the loved ones left behind," Emee said.

Scarlett never thought of it that way. She would be there for Noah and The Family no matter what.

Emee showed her how to carry herself when she was out in public and how to handle a gun. Scarlett gasped when she opened the box and found a small pearl-handed handgun.

"As you know, I carry one with me at all times. You never know when you may have to use it. Now, let's go down to the gun range and teach you how to use it.

"Gun range?" Scarlett asked. Where was the gun range?

"Oh, my dear, I guess Noah hasn't given you the grand tour of the mansion," Emee said with a smile.

Scarlett couldn't believe how big the basement was and what it held. Not only a gun range but a weaponry filled with every gun imaginable. But there was also a safe room that would be used if the mansion's security was breached. She and their children would be taken there and remain until it was safe. She didn't like the thought of being in there without Noah. However, she knew his place was beside his men and women caring for the assholes who tried to harm them.

The reception went off without a hitch. Noah received much praise for finding the perfect partner. By the time they got home, they clawed at each other's clothes and spent the rest of the night making love.

Their lives seemed to calm down, but life always threw a curve ball when you least expected it. Four weeks later, Scarlett felt off. She was out to lunch with Emee while the nanny stayed home with Liam and Robbie. They were discussing the boy's christening when, all of a sudden, Scarlett felt faint. Emee immediately called Garrett. He rushed to the restaurant and evaluated Scarlett's symptoms.

As he listened to Scarlett, he felt like he was reliving the past. "Scarlett, dear, when was your last period?"

Scarlett opened her mouth to answer but closed it. She couldn't remember having one after the birth of the twins. "It is impossible."

"Have you and Noah had sex?" Garrett asked with a smirk.

"DAMN HIM AND HIS MAGIC SPERM!" she yelled.

Eight months later, a product of Noah's "magic sperm," Declan and Brian Kelly were born. Irish twins. So, in less than a year, she was the mother of four boys.

Noah walked around like a proud peacock, showing everyone pictures of his boys. Scarlett tried to breastfeed Declan and Brian, but she didn't produce enough milk for both of them. She was upset, feeling she wasn't a good enough mother. To overcompensate, she threw herself into doing everything for all four boys. She did every feeding, diaper change, and bath, no matter what time of day or night.

Noah was busy with the takeover of docks in Boston and was often away from home. He didn't know her downfall until it was almost too late.

She was only getting two or three hours of sleep a night. During the day, she was always doing something for the boys. Most days, she forgot even to eat or didn't have time to go downstairs to get something. Scarlett instructed the cooks not to make meals unless Mr. Kelly was coming home. One night, she had finished putting Brian down and turned to start a load of laundry when the world went black.

Noah arrived home after having a celebratory drink with Finn and Connor. The Boston dock was now under the Kelly Family's control.

"How is everything going?" He asked Joshua, one of Scarlett's guards.

"Ms. Kelly hasn't left the property and all is quiet on the security."

Noah walked in and looked around for Scarlett. She was probably up in the nursery. She was such a wonderful mother. He felt bad about getting her pregnant so soon after Liam and Robbie were born. But the blessing of Declan and Brian, his Irish twins, was something else.

He walked toward the nursery and heard the boys crying. He rushed into the nursery and the sight before him caused his heart to stop. Scarlett was lying on the floor unconscious. The boys were all crying, sensing something was wrong with their mother.

Noah dropped to his knees and gently rolled her over. "Holy Hell, when did she get so thin?" he said out loud. He laid his hand on her chest and sighed with relief when he felt it rise and fall.

He pulled out his phone and dialed Garrett.

"Noah?" He asked, concern in his voice. Noah didn't call unless there was an emergency.

"GET TO THE MANSION AS SOON AS POSSIBLE!" Noah yelled.

Garrett heard the boys screaming and crying in the background. "What is going on? Is one of the boys sick or injured?"

"No, it's Scarlett. She is unconscious in the nursery. She is so thin," Noah said as he looked at her. She was nothing but skin and bones. How did this happen?

"I'm on the way. Make sure you stay with her and if she stops breathing, call 911," Garrett said as he ran from his apartment. When he got in the elevator, he called Liam.

"Garrett, how are you?"

"Liam, we have a situation at Noah and Scarlett's home."

"What is wrong?" Liam asked, rushing through the apartment to find Emee.

"Scarlett is unconscious in the nursery, and Noah says she is extremely thin. Have you or Emee noticed anything strange with her?"

"Emee and I just got back from Ireland. We have been gone for a month."

"Shit," Garrett growled.

"We will be right behind you," Liam said.

Garrett arrived carrying his med pack. He ran up the stairs and found Noah on the floor beside Scarlett. Damn, he wasn't joking about her being thin. She was worse than they found her after her crazy father kidnapped her.

He dropped to his knees and began checking her vitals. He didn't like her blood pressure or her breathing.

"Noah, I need one of the O2 tanks from the safe room," Garrett said. Noah looked up at him, all color draining from his face.

"Please, save her," he said, stroking her hair.

"Noah, the O2."

"Yeah," he said as he texted one of the guards.

Five minutes later, the O2 tank was in the room and Garrett was hooking Scarlett up. He was about to start an IV when Liam and Emee rushed in.

"OH, GOD!" Emee cried, falling on her knees beside Noah. "What is wrong with our little girl?" She couldn't believe what she was seeing.

"I'm unsure, but we must get her to a hospital. I need to run a battery of tests," Garrett said. "I've called for an ambulance and it should be here at any moment."

Liam knew he couldn't do anything for Scarlett, so he went to the cribs and tried calming his grandsons. "Hey, little guys, why are you so upset?"

Liam and Robbie were standing up, holding onto the railing, crying. Declan and Brian were too young to stand but kicking their chubby legs and screaming just as loud. "Emee, could you help me here?"

Emee looked up at Liam and finally heard her grandson's

cries. She was up on her feet and over the cribs, soothing the little ones. She couldn't do anything to help Scarlett, but she could help with the boys.

The ambulance arrived. Scarlett was placed on the stretcher and wheeled out of the room with Garrett and Noah behind them.

"Noah, you won't be able to ride with her," Garrett said, waiting for him to blow.

"WHY THE FUCK NOT? I'M HER HUSBAND!"

"Noah, listen. Rory is right there with your car. Follow us to the hospital and I promise I will get you in the room with her as soon as I can."

Noah grabbed Garrett's arm, his face marred with worry. "I can't live without her."

Garrett places his hand over Noah's. "You won't. Now we have to go."

Noah watches as Garrett climbs in the back of the rig and it takes off down the drive with the sirens blaring.

"Come on, Noah, let's get you to the hospital," Rory said.

Noah waited all alone in a room similar to the one his mother waited in when his father was shot. Well, he wasn't all alone, his and Scarlett's guards were outside the door. After what felt like an eternity, Garrett finally walked in. He jumped to his feet.

"How is she?" Noah asked.

Garrett motioned to him to sit and he sat across from him. "She is awake but very weak. I need to ask where the boy's nannies are?"

Noah paused and tried to remember who was hired to be the nannies, but he was coming up blank. He remembered a conversation with Scarlett about how his mother had nannies, but it didn't mean she could do as much as she wanted to. Nannies were to take the load off her. Ainee was hired after Liam and Robbie were hired as the day nanny, while Brandy was the night nanny.

While she was pregnant with Declan and Brian, they had

talked about hiring another day and night nanny. After they were born, the Boston takeover became crazy. He was going back and forth, a show of force to the O'Sullivans who didn't want to give up the docks. Fuck, he couldn't remember the last time he had seen Ainee or Brandy.

"Garrett, I don't know," Noah said running his hand threw his hair.

"She has been doing it all since Declan and Brian was born," Garrett advised. He couldn't believe it when Scarlett told him. How could The Skipper's wife not have nannies to help out? Hell, there were four babies under one.

"I didn't know."

"Well, she has and has been doing a phenomenal job. They are healthy and happy, but at what cost? She only sleeps two, maybe three hours a night and because she is taking care of their every need, she doesn't have time to eat on a normal schedule, if at all," Garrett said, hoping he was stressing why she was here.

"What do I need to do to get her healthy?" Noah asked.

"I'm not going to sugarcoat this. She has a long road ahead. Not only does she need to get rest, but healthy meals. I want to start her with five small meals daily, and I don't want her to be on her feet for more than fifteen minutes an hour. I don't know how she was even strong enough to lift those boys, but she can't do that until she gains fat and muscle weight."

Noah bowed his head and allowed the feeling that he had let her down to wash over him. She was always taking care of others and never asked for help.

"Noah, you need to make sure she follows these guidelines because if she doesn't, she could damage her organs or, worse, die," Garrett said, hoping he stressed the dire situation.

Noah couldn't lose her. He knew she would fight him about the guidelines, but he wouldn't leave her side until she was healthy. When they first got back together, he worked from home and would do it again until she was healthy. Finn and Conner would have to step up.

He was able to take Scarlett home three days later. She did try to fight the guidelines. However, he put his foot down. Ainee and Brandy were back, along with Jennifer and Aubrey. Emee and Liam moved in and assisted with both the boys and Scarlett.

Six months later, Scarlett regained her healthy weight and slept eight hours a night. It took her weeks to come to terms with how sick she was and how she could have died. Noah never left her side until she was healthy. Even when he began leaving, he always checked in with her several times a day. Communication between the two of them was even better than it had ever been.

Scarlett learned she didn't have to do everything for the boys to be a good mother. The extra hands allowed her to smother the little ones with all the love she never received from her mother and father.

On Declan and Brian's third birthday, she learned she was again pregnant. Thankfully, it was only one this time and it was a little girl. Aisling Eimear Kelly was born on a hot July evening with auburn hair and clear green eyes. From the moment she wrapped her tiny hand around Noah's finger, she had him.

"Daddy, wait for us," Declan and Brian yelled out as they tried to catch up to their daddy and brothers.

Scarlett held Aisling, rocking her back and forth as she watched her boys chase after their father. Noah fixed her Broken Lullaby, and she couldn't wait to see what the future held.

The End

ABOUT THE AUTHOR

Amber Joi Scott or the Wicked Writing Wench, born and raised in the South with a snarky attitude and kiss-my-ass mentality. Also, being born in the month of August, she embraces her Leo sign, letting her inner lion roar through her writing.

She lives in the beautiful Shenandoah Valley with her big, burly husband and their many animals. Raising her children to be polite, hard-working young adults is and will always be her biggest accomplishment. When deciding on her pen name, she dedicated all her writing to her children by using parts of their names as her pen name.

She doesn't plan to stop writing anytime soon and hopes that people fall in love with her characters as much as she has.

BOUND SERIES

Bound to the Family

Bound Together

Bound and Dangerous

Bound and United

In a Heartbeat

Trust and Obey

Heart of the Mafia

Wishing Upon a Snowflake

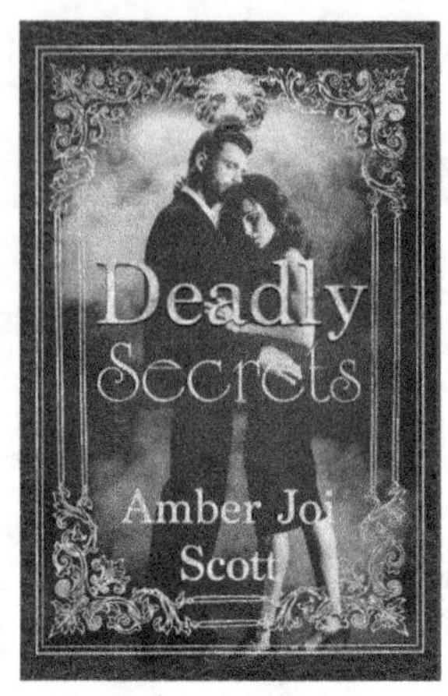

Deadly Secrets

JOIN THE SCOTTIE SQUAD

Be the first to hear about new projects, ARC opportunities, and many other fun activities.

https://www.facebook.com/groups/132293344050028
Facebook.com and search for The Scottie Squad